PORTALS OF
AMERTHINE

K.D.M ZAJAC

Halo
PUBLISHING
INTERNATIONAL

ISBN: 978-1-63765-106-3
LCCN: 2021916517

Halo Publishing International, LLC
8000 W Interstate 10, Suite 600
San Antonio, Texas 78230
www.halopublishing.com

Printed and bound in the United States of America

Thank you, to the health care workers, my family and friends, and those who believed in me.

A special thank you to my cover artist Brooke Bittel, my photographer Josh Quint, and my editor Alexander Wagner.

Contents

PRELUDE

The continent of Amerthine had a temperate climate, possibly much like where you are sitting now. But this story takes place long ago in a different land. In this world, the North had a longer wet season compared to the South. The beautiful continent wasn't particularly large; the populated areas were relatively small, being denser in the cities. The continent was filled with hills and mountains that separated people. Proper communication, medicine, and cleanliness habits were not known yet, resulting in lower human populations.

The humans of Amerthine were now beginning to attain a lifestyle that was sustainable for survival, but their population was still much smaller than one would expect. Communication was getting to the point where the villages had different methods of speaking, and people seemed to be working with one another to establish a prosperous land.

Magic was known throughout the land, allowing certain people to manipulate the world with the elements. These magic users were born special and were able to tap into their surroundings and harness the power of nature.

Some humans found themselves imbued with the ability to change their bodies to match the forms of animals—attaining the vocal patterns of various creatures and being able to rival the efficient flight of the swiftest bird. These shifters were along the same bloodlines as the magic users, but they could not use magic to control the elements. Such magical beings were rare but becoming more well-known.

Time had allowed humanity to gain knowledge of each other's existence, and with this knowledge eventually came conflict. Amerthine became split in two. The top portion of the continent contained wetlands and rivers, and it was known for an abundance of magic users. The South, divided from the North by a large riverbed and forest, was filled with people of a more primitive mind-set who forced their will through brawn. Magic was a studied practice, and many Southerners did not have the concentration nor the patience for such a skill. The humans from the North and South had opposing views from first perception; the North saw the South as uneducated and ignorant, while the South viewed the North as imposing and controlling.

These views were reflected in how they ruled over their lands. The Southern villagers were much more interested in notoriety, using their people, and working them until exhausted in awful conditions, in order to receive gold or attain profits. The Northern villagers were obsessed with efficiency and, in turn, sacrificed strength—always believing in mind over matter.

Both civilizations had a way to work in Amerthine. In the South, people did deplorable things for power—overworking and torturing for profit. People's lives were threatened for the sake of prosperity. In the North, however, leadership was known to manipulate in order to attain power, deceiving those who believed in them.

The land had been threatened by portals that were un-locked in order to provide more resources, and humankind did not know the toll that the portals would have on them. The respective leadership of each civilization decided their own way of handling these portals, which had been opened by wizards. The village leaders, using their own magic or ways to manipulate the portals, had promised profits. Greed dominated the land since people could rely on the worth of coin and abundance to work for them in the exchange for goods or services.

Amerthine was in turmoil due to the portals. Both civilizations believed themselves to be more capable of leading and handling the crisis in a better way. Northerners had been trying willfully to close specific portals. These portals were known to unleash terrible atrocities upon the land, allowing entry to horrific creatures, such as demons, ghouls, and even trolls. The villages were able to hold back these evils, but in doing so, they shortened the flow of their supplies from the portals, the resources that were bought and sold. They wanted the portals to remain open so that they would be able to profit from them, and the opposing villages of the North and the South desired to get an upper hand over each other with the supplies. Competition is what kept the humans' blood boiling.

The Southern philosophy was to use their workers in order to extract resources and contain any monsters that might escape from the portals. The South thrived on keeping the portals open, tossing anyone they had on hand at the portals in order to sustain profits and gain supplies. They had lost many lives in doing so, but this approach allowed them to profit off of the portals, and this had been the way the Southern Empire worked. Coin was the name of the South's game, and the coin held weight, which allowed them to sustain the structure of their civilization. If they truly ran low on supply, they could just buy their way out of it. They also bought their way out through their military might; they attempted to remove any perceived shortcomings by always appearing to be strong.

The North had tried with all its might to shut the portals, to end their existence. In doing so, they had lost many heroes, but had closed many portals, as well. Only a few portals were still open in the North since the people were adamant about closing them. But this action caused their villages and cities to become stretched extraordinarily thin on supplies, and they now lacked valuable minerals, magic, and resources. The North had the support of the people, so even with thin numbers, they were able to sustain a life enhanced by magic and focused on arts and learning.

Even with the looming threat of the portals, war between the empires of the North and South was imminent.

The initial focus before the main story begins will be on the magic users of this world who created the portal issue.

Enter two very strange wizards.

Lightning struck, bringing the sound of rumbling, thunderous booms. A crazed wizard was standing in front of a large table in a laboratory filled with books, beakers, and vials. Steam billowed from one of the concoctions on the table. On the far side of the room was a bench made of thick cherrywood, upon which the clean-cut wizard was sitting and musing over his notes.

"You're doing it again," a middle-aged wizard said from the bench. He wore flowing robes and a large, wide-brimmed, conical hat. His face was smooth and symmetrical, presenting a calm and collected demeanor. His long hair was in a neat ponytail, bound in simple golden ties. He stroked his long brown beard, which had been elegantly braided.

"You think I am doing it wrong?" another middle-aged man said. This one had a crazed look on his face, although he was very similar in appearance to the first man. He, too, had a long beard, but it was not braided and was very much disheveled. This wizard did not have a neat ponytail or hat, just a wild mop of hair on top of his head. Even with these stark differences in appearance, the eye could tell that they were twins.

"I truly believe this will finally work. Imagine…an endless supply of resources." The crazed-looking wizard was poring over his own notes. "Endless this time." He was rubbing a crystal in his hands as notes were being tossed around as if a breeze were making them move—the air in the room was dead, however.

The well-kept wizard stood up from the bench. "This will cause an issue," he said as he approached the table with the flying notes. "This could easily cause a war, Fizz."

"I agree with Kerr," a third man said. This man looked drastically different from the two wizards. He was noticeably muscular, with a chiseled jaw and crop-cut hair. He had a sword strapped to his belt, along with a striking fur coat that draped over his leather jerkin and loose-fitting pants.

"The wars will start anyway, Guymuir. This will make us rich!" Fizzrik exclaimed, his beard shaking in excitement.

A concerned look materialized upon the other twin's face. "At what cost? The portals will need to close eventually."

"The temporary kind won't be worth nearly as much—if anything. I can mass-produce actual ones that last. We will be wanted everywhere." The excitement behind Fizzrik's beard couldn't be mistaken.

Kerr began to twirl his smooth beard in his fingers. "You will break everything. The magic council, in that last meeting, warned us to not do something like this."

Fizzrik had a sour look on his face. "Always telling me negative things. When have we ever listened to the council anyway? Who even is the council?" His face suddenly turned pleasant as he continued, "Look at the bright side, brother! Gold, power. We will finally be respected."

Fizzrik waved his hands in a fluttering motion. "Patentibi," he whispered as he reached his arm into what looked like a sleeve, a pocket that had opened in midair. He then grabbed a fistful of similar-looking dark crystals from the air pocket, each honed to look like a different shape, from spheres to cubes. "We just need to combine these!" A few crystals spilled out as he made hand motions to spin the invisible sleeve.

"You need to stop going to that mountain. Get rid of those, too," Kerr demanded in a serious tone.

"Don't be such a Kerr," Fizzrik said with an oil-like slickness.

Kerr blinked his eyes rapidly. "Fine, let's talk to the elders, see who is in the market. We had better see some fair coin." Kerr still had a grimace on his face.

"That was almost too easy. Are you growing soft on me?" Fizzrik asked menacingly. The brothers were staring at each other.

"This is up to you two to figure out. I want no part of this, honestly," Guymuir said upon seeing the twins' heated exchange. "I go where you go."

Upon meeting with the human leaders, the wizards and humans agreed to terms. The wizards would receive gold in exchange for the portals remaining open so that humans could get resources from them. The leaders were made aware of what would come with their wealth of supply, that an abundance of dangers from other planes of existence would emerge from those portals to the unknown.

The humans wished to take the risk after Fizzrik showed them examples of the riches they might receive; he opened a temporary portal for them to walk through a mine Fizzrik created with his mind, a maze inside of a massive mountain. They were delighted with the results. Much like other magics, the portals were feared by many, but most humans wanted the finer things in life, especially those with the easiest forms of access. Greed made people strive for what would come easiest to them.

Fizzrik's ambitions were to always be in the pursuit of gold, fame, and, finally, immortality. When he first came across the crystals, the intentions of the wizard did not change; however, he had grown an attachment to them—the crystals allowed him to pour his deepest, darkest fears and secrets into them, providing his addled brain with a much-needed relief that fueled his already dark attachment. The allure of the crystals pushed him to keep conjuring more of them. Those crystals were clearly not ordinary pretty gemstones.

Kerr, on the other hand, had a baby on the way and his family to care about. People of the land were afraid of wizards, so although the brothers would try to sell simple potions and charms, many peasants had turned them away out of fear, and coin was difficult to come by. The option Fizzrik had offered seemed like the only feasible one at the time—a way for Kerr to sustain his family.

Time passed. The use of the portals continued, and they had become increasingly important to the livelihoods of the people in Amerthine.

———————————◆———————————

Kerr raced downstairs. "Guymuir, we gotta go."

The large man was sitting on a cushioned chair. His thumb rested on the pommel of a bright, shiny sword that leaned against the arm of the chair. He ran a massive, calloused hand in quick brushstrokes through his dusty-brown hair. His face had the hint of a grin as his hand moved from his hair down to rub his green eyes. He stood from the chair, his build putting him a foot taller than Kerr.

"What did he do now?" Guymuir said in an exasperated tone.

"I think this time he went too far. I think he has found one that is too big. Humans won't be able to hold this one back, whatever comes from it. His mind is a nightmare."

Kerr swiftly kissed his pregnant wife good-bye. He then pressed his hand on her belly and said, "I will be back."

"You do know we are fine without him, right?" she called to her husband. "Please don't go."

"I know. He is my brother, and I am afraid I am in too deep this time. One more for the road." He gave her another peck and made sure to grab his bag and staff before dashing out the door.

Kerr and Guymuir raced from the residence. Kerr paused and looked back at his humble, ramshackle hovel, which currently was boarded and looked abandoned.

Guymuir had Kerr's horse's reins in his hands. "How much time do we have?"

"At this point, I fear I do not know. The reports stated an overwhelming number of trolls were in the area. His obsession with their regenerative powers has clouded his judgment," Kerr shouted as their horses galloped.

"You know as well as I do…the crystals!" Guymuir shouted back. Their pace slowed as the sands became softer.

Kerr quietly contemplated as his horse eventually came to a stop. "It was my fault for not taking them seriously from the beginning. The way he came across them was strange to begin with," he said.

"Do not fault yourself; it was his mind, his decision." Guymuir attempted to say comforting words, but his voice lacked sincerity.

"Guymuir, this can't have been my fault." Kerr was struggling to hear the man's tone of voice.

"You did agree to this initially, so you are partly to blame. You have to figure out a way to deal with them. They have been created by man; therefore, they should be able to be destroyed by man, as well."

"Give me your sword. I think I know of a way. Magic is the only way to break them." Kerr held his hand out.

Guymuir drew his sword from its sheath, dismounted, walked over to Kerr, and handed his sword over.

Kerr hovered his hands over the blade and whispered a spell, "Tantum opus."

The sword then glowed, and a strange lettering appeared on it.

"I can't stop him on my own anymore. I need you."

Guymuir stared in wonder at the now-radiant, glyphic sword. The glow died down over time. "This will be able to destroy the crystals?"

Kerr took a small crystal out of a pouch in his pocket. "Careful. I believe you to be stronger willed," he said as he placed the crystal on a nearby cactus arm. "Don't stare directly at it. It tries to draw on the evil in you."

Guymuir was still looking at Kerr. He dropped the horse's reins, and in a swift, chopping motion, he hit the crystal with his sword, cracking and eventually fully breaking it. A satisfied smile appeared on his face. "Destroyed. Kerr, I am impressed."

"I never thought it would come to this." Kerr still sounded distraught.

"I really do not remember the last time you smiled, Kerr. Better change that, kid." Guymuir was still marveling at the new glyphs that had been etched on his sword by Kerr's spell. "This is a good thing, a purpose. How many did he end up making? It hasn't been too long, has it?" Guymuir asked.

"It has been too long, and far too many from the South have requested these. Along with a few who were easily manipulated in the North. I am telling you—we have really messed up this time. We need to get riding. He is still opening them, but I believe I know where he will be soon. He will run out."

Kerr took the reins and guided his horse back to a more solid-looking path, one that had been used before.

As time went by, Fizzrik continued to go about opening more portals for the people of Amerthine, and for his own pleasure. The portal situation grew and soon got out of hand. Humans had to start creating armies to defend against what had started to escape. They had underestimated the portals. Many people were paying with their lives. But a certain wizard had an insatiable thirst for the crystals.

Humans had started a mining operation in the area near the mountain, a small village, and Fizzrik had been around just by chance on the same day that a crystal was found. From then on, Fizzrik was enticed by its magical properties, and the crystal had spoken to Fizzrik and his needs. The crystal had consumed him.

He needed more, and so Fizzrik ended up buying the small village. He set up a hasty system of working the mines that served his need for more crystals. Fizzrik's crystal-portal operation was in full swing once the locals bought into his silver-tongued marketing schemes. He had met with land-owners, lords, and even kings. Business was booming.

Fizzrik had sought fame and gold; however, he grew bored, so his next search was for immortality. He constructed a way for humans to mutate and become disgusting, warped versions of themselves. But in exchange, they were able to regenerate. He called them trolls. Their regenerative properties were a key that Fizzrik believed he needed to attain immortality.

He opened many portals after a falling-out with the villages, which occurred once the portals had become increasingly dangerous. Some portals contained his failed experiments—the trolls. They were known as laboratories in which Fizzrik did his experiments. There were different portals, too, but a few had been specialized in accordance to how Fizzrik wanted to experiment. These particular portals—Fizzrik's labs—were in unsuspecting areas and created unforeseen issues. Fizzrik didn't stop at trolls; he had made other horrific mutations to see how far humans could be pushed, see if there was a way to extend life. Many had died in his trials.

The fallout happened just the way Kerr predicted: The experiments turned evil, and then things eventually got bad, to the point where they could no longer be handled. Humans became outmatched. The wizards had to figure out a way to hold back the portal menace.

Kerr had an apologetic approach towards the human lands, while Fizzrik had a wild and menacing attitude. It ended with the brothers breaking apart. As much as Kerr wanted his family, diplomacy was not his strong suit, and Fizzrik's insanity was sinking in. Kerr, even with the brotherly bond, realized that his brother had become a menace to humanity and needed to be stopped. Kerr knew he had to end his brother.

Fizzrik had to return to the mountain from which the crystals originated so that he could replenish his stock. That was Kerr and Guymuir's next destination.

———————•———————

"You need to stop!" Kerr cried out when he finally found his brother.

Fizzrik's eyes had lightning-bolt veins of darkness surrounding them. He was a shallow husk of what he used to be, and he looked very much different from his twin brother.

They were on what was noticeably the largest mountain in the land. It was tall and completely separate from any other mountain. It just so happened to be the place where the crystals had all originally been mined.

"I knew you would be here! I knew you would run out!" Kerr continued to shout.

The mountain was buffeted by strong winds and harsh rain. Amid the sound of raindrops slapping the ground along the mountainside, two men could be heard screaming at each other. Meanwhile, another man was leaping and lunging with a sword at one of the robed figures.

With their beards flapping wildly in the wind, the two wizards were staring at each other, one menacingly and the other pleadingly.

"This is not the way, Fizz. These crystals have driven you mad!" Kerr screamed at his brother. A loud crack of thunder rumbled across the mountain, adding to the weight of Kerr's echoing, desperate pleas.

Fizzrik cackled maniacally. "Do you believe your way is like my way? Your way, the right way?"

Guymuir swung his sword with all his might and struck air where Fizzrik had been standing. It seemed as if Fizzrik were blinking in and out of existence. He seemed enhanced by some magical property and was able to deftly dodge the incoming sword swipes. The crazed wizard started to chant words, almost musical and rhythmic, his arms flailing in a dramatic way.

"Fizz, why?" Kerr asked, bracing himself.

"Nigreos eritque arcus!" With a flick of his wrist, a beam of negative light shot from Fizzrik's hand. A bright smile lit the man's face after he chanted the spell.

Using the butt of his exceptionally long, wooden staff, Kerr deflected the beam of negative light into the sky, rendering it harmless. "Why do you never listen to me?" Kerr cried. "I made a mistake. I am sorry!"

Guymuir's sword was still swinging at the wizard, but not connecting, instead striking the air between the two figures.

Kerr could not understand the next spell Fizzrik chanted, but it sounded as if it did not bode well, and it was not something he had devices to defend against. His brother's mind was lost. "Just no, brother," Kerr said, his voice sounding defeated. "You need to run, Guymuir!" he yelled to his friend.

Guymuir stopped swinging his sword and started running down the mountain.

"Run, Guy! You need to live!" Kerr called after him.

"Haec est finis!" Kerr let out a primal scream as he spun his staff in his arms and slammed the ground.

A burst of negative air sucked the surrounding space and ground from existence; the world disappeared. The things that remained were living creatures petrified into a stonelike state and dropped a significant distance to shatter on the ground.

Kerr's spell worked much quicker than anticipated. Guymuir was still running; he attempted to jump from Kerr's encroaching spell. He stumbled down the mountain, trying desperately to run from the negative air. Kerr and Guymuir discussed this scenario happening, and Guymuir had feared that this would be the conclusion.

Guymuir lost his footing while trying to quicken his pace, which made him stumble and fall. The negative energy coming for him stopped after swallowing half of his body. Guymuir was staring at his lower half as he came crashing down, sword still in his fighting hand. Guymuir slapped the ground with a fleshy thud. His labored breathing gradually slowed, but the fierce resolve on his face remained as he passed from bleeding out—a true warrior.

The mountain was missing a section, as the negative energy had eaten it, and it began to fall in on itself. Avalanches of rock and snow began to violently crash down. There was nothing to hold a giant section of rock up, so the mountain collapsed with a loud, thunderous boom. The world shook.

Two statues—the wizards—remained, one with an expression of deep concern and the other laughing into the air.

In the distance, an absurdly large and ugly head emerged from a spiraling blue portal. The head tilted up to the sky as it breathed in wafts of air. The rest of the body began to show as the hideous creature peered from the portal. It opened its jowls wide and bellowed out a primal scream.

———————•———————

Beyond the mountain, Amerthine was in turmoil. Armies had been built up and were busy combating the creatures that were pouring out of the portals. People continued utilizing the portals in different ways, too, marching workers and troops into them.

Kerr's wife had gone into labor back at their residence. The nursemother was standing by her side, working with her through the delivery.

"Keep it up now! That is a lot of blood." She started to look around, and panic struck her face. "Do we have anything clean to stifle this blood?"

Another woman close by shrugged her shoulders and pointed at a rag that was very clearly not clean. The rag looked as if it contained dried-up chemicals from its previous use, but in the panic, it had to suffice—it was dry, after all.

"Oh, help us," the nursemother said as Kerr's wife passed after pushing out a screaming baby boy.

"Any news of his father?" the nursemother asked her assistant.

"No word," she responded.

"Oh no, no, no," the nursemother said. When looking down at her patient, she noticed that blood had started to spread around the body. A stretched-out hand lay above where a G was written in blood. "Oh, this poor boy. His mother might have wanted to start his name with a G."

"Well, no one to name him now. Up to you," the assistant added.

"I am not good at this, nor am I particularly clever," said the nursemother, "but I think I got it."

1

"Dust"

"**G**reyson, wake up," a rusty voice spoke as a hand was pressed on the tent wall. "You gotta hear this lot."

Shouting could be heard from outside. Two men were sounding the alarm early with their voices.

"What is even happening?" Greyson grumbled as he stirred, rubbing his eyes with his hands. He got dust in his eyes and then pounded the sand next to his sleep mat, creating a cloud of even more dust. Dusty, everything is dusty.

Greyson's tent was located in a small, remote mining village called Haneserrath. Slightly south of the border from the northern lands, it was a town known for being in the shadow of a great, broken mountain and a feared mine. It was named after the leader, Hanes, a stubborn elder who was the chief of the village. Hanes ruled with an iron fist and had seen profits from her mine. She was known to have a hard temperament, and she had her villagers on a tight leash—she would be the one to crack the whip in the mines, and she was the one shortening the cactus crops if things were too slow for her liking.

In turn, her people were worked to exhaustion; as such, she profited from their work. The village appeared to be doing better in a prosperity sense, not an overall happiness sense. Hanes had her miners work the mines in difficult and stressful times. Her stringent and heavy-handed rule, however, had produced a disciplined guard with the best officers in the land. Haneserrath had been known for its safety, in turn, thereby making the feeling of being safe a priority above overall happiness.

As the first to speak with the twin wizards who controlled the portals, Hanes was able to lead the village to prosperity with the mines. Hanes maintained control of the village and lived to a ripe old age. Her legacy had been handed to her son, the ungrateful Karnaugh.

Karnaugh had grown up in the capital city of Odh Varol, where his father had served as a warrior for Lord Korgak. Upon the passing of his mother, because of lineage laws in the South, Karnaugh became the leader of the village, the Hogfaw of Haneserrath.

Hogfaws were Southern nobles, the wealthy side of the established caste system. In that system, the more wealth and respect from religion one had, the more one was awarded by the social elite. The Southern nobles awarded those who were more zealous in the teachings of Troutus, but, more importantly, the rich.

And luckily, Hanes was at the right place of worship, at the right time, with the right amount of wealth. When Karnaugh showed up, however, he brought his own cast of characters—his circle. He got rid of the majority of Haneserrath's good officers, leaving his own boys in charge.

There was a strange power dynamic in Haneserrath because of how Hanes had run the village with her iron fist. Others had absorbed a power issue, feeling so repressed by their former leader that they lashed out. After Karnaugh dismissed most of the decent officers, what was left behind ended up being the rougher, sloppier crowd.

There were friends of Greyson's who had been in the village since it was created. They had lived their miserable lives in the mines and had died there. Those lives hadn't reflected much, either. There was no life outside the mine, from what they knew—just Haneserrath, the desert, and the broken mountain.

Greyson had met people from outside who had been brought into the village, and he always thought there had to be more to life than the mine. His days consisted of getting in line for the trough of food, going to the mine, mining for the day, and then going to sleep. Rinse, repeat…from day to sweaty day.

Greyson's home was a small cloth tent, as were most of the other miners' living quarters. The tents, supplied for all of the miners in the village, were just large enough for a small rack able to hold a few possessions. Greyson's tent held only a small cabinet with a candle. That summed up all the space a human miner was given. If a couple were joined in Haneserrath, their tents were sewn together to make more living space. More room was more incentive to start a family. Greyson still resided in his single. He slept next to his mining pickax, his water container, and a small bucket with a flag on it—his trinkets, he called them.

Greyson was trying to pick dust from his eye, but he couldn't quite get it. He closed the compromised eye and looked around to reorient himself, giving the appearance of someone in a drunken stupor. Small beams of sunlight shone through the many edges of patches that were used to cover holes, as well as to decorate the tattered dark-green canvas of his meager tent. Greyson rolled around, still looking around the tent in a confused manner. He had placed his boots farther away than he thought.

The other miners, waking up in the surrounding tents, could be heard—the clacking of slapping rocks and idle chatter. Greyson turned in his bed rack and stuffed his feet into well-worn boots, taking a look at his reflection in a dirty piece of glass. "Found you," he muttered as he looked at his face, the good eye zooming in on the compromised other eye. He had long, straight brown hair that was desperately in need of a cut. His last haircut was from a rather blunt blade that left longer hairs and haphazard patches. Genetics were kind to him in a physical sense, so he had a handsome face with a warm smile. Built like the miner that he seemed born to be, he could fit into a crowd and was indistinguishable among the other villagers. His eyes were the color of "swamp water, if you've seen it," as he called it, but they were more on the brown side with a twinge of green. He had a scar—the size of a small finger—that curved across his face by his left eye, hitting the bridge of his nose. Other than that, he just needed a bath to make himself look like a human, not a troll.

"Got it," Greyson said.

"You don't ask anyone else! Just you and your neighbor. How convenient!" a man hollered.

"Be reasonable!" another man responded with his voice raised; he sounded a lot younger.

Greyson scratched his eyes again, relieved that the annoyance was gone. He gathered his thoughts. Well, if the camp wasn't up before, it is certainly up now. He lifted the tent's door and stood up to stretch. "Why are we getting loud out here?"

A young man with dirty-blond hair and scrawny arms was facing off with an older gentleman who had a giant frown on his face. The younger man's handsome face was red as a beet.

"And also, was it necessary to be right outside of my tent?" Greyson sighed.

The two men looked over at Greyson. "Sorry, man," they said in unison.

"What's happening, anyway? We gotta get chow soon, right?" Greyson refastened a buckle on his boot.

The young man spoke up, "Old man and his neighbor there decided to be wise, throwin' our camp's crew under the cart, so they get more chow. Now, he is trying to make excuses and shit."

"Now, before you start…" the old man started to explain, waving his hands.

Greyson stomped his boot after readjusting the buckle. "Wait a tick. What is going on with chow now?" A frown grew on his face.

"This man is trying to tell me we deserve less chow because we produced less than the other camps, so now a portion of our rations goes to them." The boy clenched his hands into fists.

"The weight is the weight, boy," the old man stated.

"So…do you expect us to produce more, being underfed there, guy?" Greyson's scrunched face with its pink hue showed he was getting more upset as he turned towards the older man.

"Listen, Greyson, the rules are the rules. We must adhere to them, or we will get punished." The old man knew he was barely getting his message across, and he looked at Greyson with pleading eyes.

Greyson's eye was twitching. "Better fix this."

"Greyson, please." The old man held his hands together in a praying gesture, his eyes glazing over.

"Do you want me to get loud? That's the best way to do it. Fuck this place, and fuck you. You will not be taking your bullshit out on everyone. Matter of fact, your own chow should be snagged. I am not dealing with some weak-ass shit when there is a job to do and other workers who have to sustain themselves. How much do you know, old man? How much time do you spend in the mines with us?" Greyson started to point an accusatory finger towards the old man's chest. "See how we are living? This is hard enough. If the others had needed it, then understandable. But the workers have the need right now," Greyson stated.

"I simply cannot do that," the older man said. He had noticeable sweat beads on his forehead.

"Go talk to the other elders, talk to Pops—I am sure we are on the same page here. Nothing changes. Now, I am glad you were arguing outside of my tent. Nice work, Garrett." Greyson nodded at the smaller man. "I am fucking pissed now. What do you need to allow us to be fed, then?"

"We need double, and if a piece can be found…" The old man looked at Greyson timidly.

Greyson gave a slight chuckle. "You do know how irrational that is. You do know that those crystal shards are very few and far between…and extraordinarily hard to spot in the dark shaft." His ears were turning red.

The old man was shifting from side to side. "Greyson, I do what I can. These are their demands."

"We will give ore and a half. We need to be fed. Anything given more, and this cannot be done." I am going to set all their shit on fire. Greyson nodded at the man.

Garrett was grinning ear to ear.

The intimidated old man huffed and nodded. He then turned to leave the miners' tent area.

"Listen, Garrett." Greyson paused, sighed deeply, and continued, "The louder you are, the sharper you will sound, and the more weight your voice will carry. So, speak with confidence," Greyson said, opening and closing his dry mouth. "I am thirsty."

Karnaugh's cactus farms and mining operation at the mountain had been set up by Hanes and established for some time. Karnaugh had made feed troughs for the miners, and, just like cattle, they were fed twice a day. They were taken to a muddy water hole once a day to collect dirty water. The impurities were boiled out, and then the water was stored in gourds that were owned by Karnaugh.

Greyson reached for the water pot left outside of his tent for the rare occurrences of rain. It had been a few days, and the pot was getting dry. He had to refill it from Karnaugh's gourds. Greyson picked up the pot and took a chug—a little dirty, as was everything, but still thirst quenching.

Karnaugh knows how to keep everyone in check and how to make sure his village does well enough that he can feel good about himself. Fuck everyone else, just so long as he "feels good." I can't stand it. He posts himself nearby and just watches us sweat, get lashed, and eat from a trough. It is so strange. He could be helping, but he sits on his fat ass because he has that flashy armor, followers, and a damn sword. Power-hungry asshole.

Greyson and Garrett headed towards the trough tent, which had benches where rows of miners were sitting and staring at each other. He and Garrett picked up stone slabs and joined a long line of miners who were eager to get to the trough in the ground,

At the head of the line, a couple of villagers were scooping and plopping gruel onto the miners' slabs. "Right, next," said the worker behind the trough. "Hurry up, next," he said without patience.

"Fuck, man, we're not huffing oil over here. We are moving," Garrett said to the worker.

◆————————●————————◆

"Troutus!" was yelled down the mine shaft, and it echoed several times.

"Oh, come on" was heard right after.

"Well then, I guess I got up at the right time, after all," Greyson said as he started to walk towards the mines. "Thanks again, Garrett. You look after yourself, now."

Garrett waved his hand at Greyson. "Whoa there, Greyson. I'd like you to meet this new guy, Martimil. He came from a ways away. What were you, a sea captain? The boys found him and his wife in the desert. He is—how do I say this?—well fed, compared to us minerfolk." He slapped the larger man's back. "But he seems to be a good man."

"Which tunnel will he be going down?" asked Greyson.

"Second left, so third rope in on the cord," Garrett quickly responded.

"All right. Say, Martimil, you need some help, pick up this cord here, and give it a few tugs. I should be able to feel it." Greyson smirked at the man.

"He calls it 'sea-blasted.' Get a load of this guy," Garrett said shining a torch up to Martimil's squinting face. Martimil was slightly taller than Greyson and had a much wider build. He was bald, but had a scraggly red beard.

"I'll show him a sea blast," a miner chuckled.

Martimil started to undo his belt buckle.

"Whoa there, friend," Garrett said.

"What? Sounded like he was curious to see a different kind of sea blast?" Martimil quipped.

The miners laughed and continued on with their day.

The tunnel was dark, and being left in darkness for prolonged amounts of time is no good for any surface-dwelling human. The miners marched down the tunnel, followed by guards who ridiculed, dehumanized, and slapped them around. Greyson was well liked by the other miners. He was humorous and attempted to play pranks on guards when they were unaware.

On the way down the mine, there was an old skeleton sticking out of the ground. It was called Mister Ragz—the protector of the mines, they said. There was nothing noticeable about Mister Ragz; he was just a skeleton leaning on an old and rusty sword. The miners would tap on his skull for good luck before entering the mine. It was only a meaningless ritual since the mines were never known to be a safe place.

Greyson tapped the skull. "I really do apologize for the mess I am about to make. Please understand, Mister Ragz, I need to get the hell out of here. You know, as well as I do, that there is more to this. Well, see you later, mate." He continued walking down the shaft.

A fellow miner lightly jogged to catch up with him. "A quick question for you. Was there a time that you were happy, Greyson?" the miner solemnly asked. "Like, really felt it? Generally wondering."

"That's a little out of the blue, but, yeah, I have been happy before. Like you feel nothing is wrong. Might not be right now, it might not be tomorrow, but eventually you'll feel it."

What felt like miles of underground shaft was only about a tenth of a mile into the mountain. The miner continued to walk beside Greyson. "How?" he asked.

They finally paused at the end of a rope line, readying to swing their picks. "Can only tell you my opinion. People make me happy—all of you, with your own humor, your own personalities, watching you grow, seeing your accomplishments. Learning." Greyson spun his pick in his hands. "I think setting yourself up for success starts with an understanding of each other, telling the overly comfortable people to get real." He started swinging and motioned for the other miner to do the same. "They forget how to sweat, but we forget what it is like to not be in this darkness."

They swung a few hard hits before taking another breather. Greyson continued speaking, "The last time I was truly happy was when I was with her."

"You know how much rock we've collected so far?" the miner asked.

They heard the cracking whip and barked orders of the approaching overseer. The terrifying sound struck the miner who had been talking, and he winced in fear as he turned to see the overseer rear back and whip Greyson.

"Ah, Troutus. Why?" Greyson rubbed where the lash had hit.

"Because!" The overseer was strutting, puffing out his chest with the beer-mug standard emblazoned on it.

Greyson watched as the heartless man kept moving down the line, receding in a flicker of candlelight. That is their answer every time we ask why.

The other miner waddled up next to Greyson. "I get why you try to escape this. No happiness here." Careful not to attract attention, he asked in a hushed voice, "That last time, what did you do again?"

"Feigned illness and was taken to the outhouses. I was able to get the keys to the gate out of the miners' camp. From there, I headed out," Greyson said calmly. "The guards are good, but are they really that good?"

"I wouldn't be able to tell you," the miner said.

Picking another rope line and following it, Greyson got to his mining spot in the tunnel, his regular spot where he had left a bucket with a dirty rag. Need something to mark your spot. He put down his water container, placing the strap near his bucket. The tunnel was dark, and he could kick or knock into the bucket so that he would be able to find the strap for his water. He twirled his pick in his hands and gave a few good hits to the ground, his strong hand on the upper shaft and the lower part covered by his other hand. He brought his arm down with all the weight he could muster for each strong-armed swing, smashing the stone to pieces with a powerful impact.

The strikes could get into one's head, the same monotonous beat over and over. With every hit Greyson made, another miner made a follow-up strike, creating reverberations down the tunnel. Greyson smirked to himself. He followed his next hit with full force and then another hit at half strength, making a pleasant rhythm that could be heard echoing farther down the mine.

"Greyson!" came a whispering shout that also echoed down the shaft.

"That you again, Garrett?" Greyson saw a dirty-blond man come running up to him. "Of course, it is you again. Hey, bud, what did I tell you about shouting my name in the shafts?"

"I apologize, Greyson." Garrett looked remorseful. "Great swings, by the way."

"Firstly, thanks. Second, what is it, Garrett? You already got me up this morning. What else ya got?" Greyson was tapping on his pick's handle.

The young man held his hand out.

"What's that?" Greyson asked.

"Well, hold out your hand. You are going to want to see this," Garrett said.

Greyson was hesitant at first. "Not messing with me, are you? It isn't a booger this time, correct?" He let out a sigh and held out his cupped hands expectantly.

Garrett dropped a small black crystal into Greyson's hands.

Greyson shifted the crystal to one hand and inspected it further. "Garrett! Are you kidding me? Just outside my tent this morning, I thought we were going to starve." He dropped his pick and clicked his heels.

"Isn't this insane? I can't believe my luck after this morning. Thought I would start the day doomed." He was staring at the crystal in Greyson's hand. "What should I do with it? I have never found one before."

There was a sound coming from down the mine shaft again; it wasn't other miners doing work. It was the crack of a whip coming their way.

"I wouldn't suggest mentioning it to this guy—Hank, I want to say. You will get it taken. Keep telling miners; the guys who wear those beer-mug seals cannot be trusted." Greyson looked seriously at Garrett. "Listen, I will give you credit for this, absolutely. We will get fed, Garrett, and more than the usual, if you would just let me hold on to it. Not that I do not trust you."

"You don't trust me, I know, and that is why I am here. Words have meaning, and I want to eat as badly as you do. Keep it." Garret's voice was serious. "I am trusting you with this, and also I think you'll be able to get it by Hank there. You seem to have stirred his hornet's nest already."

Greyson pocketed the crystal. "I cannot thank you enough, Garrett. You turned this ordinary day into something extraordinary. You need to take off. As much as I would enjoy some company, the longer you stay, the more suspect we become. Take off." He was beaming at the young man but had made the statement in a serious tone.

"What is going on down here?" The beer-mug-emblazoned guard wandered back to where Greyson was standing.

What timing. Greyson started his mining again. "Nothing to see here," Greyson answered. Garrett had already returned to where he had originally been mining.

"What were you talking about? What was all the excitement about? I know it was you. I heard your name, Greyson," the guard said as his wide body turned the corner.

Dammit, Garrett. Greyson grabbed his water pouch. "Argument outside the tent this morning, made an oops with the water container. Someone got one for me. No big deal." The words spilled effortlessly from his mouth.

"Ask me if I believe that," the guard spat at him.

Not today, not this guy today. "Who hurt you? I do not know what you want from me, then. Unless you want some of this water—we have been low, however. Would you know anything about that?" Greyson asked.

"Show me your pile," the guard said.

"It is right over there. Honestly, all you are doing is slowing me down, and you know that."

The guard walked over to Greyson's mined rubble. He kicked into the pile, knocking it over.

"That is going to be annoying to pick back up," Greyson said.

"So what if it is?" the guard sneered, kicking a few more rocks at Greyson.

"Are you done now? Can you move on?"

"Empty your pockets," the guard demanded.

Greyson dropped the crystal on the ground, hoping it would go unnoticed. It was a good thing the crystal was rather small and black as night, making it almost invisible in the dark shaft.

The guard, indeed, had not noticed. He started to pat Greyson down.

"What is the hustle today?" Greyson asked.

"None of your business," the guard retorted quickly. He got closer to the floor as he was searching down Greyson's pant leg. "Well then, what is this I see?" The guard sounded as if he was drooling in eagerness as he took a sharp breath. "I swear I can feel something around here somewhere. I know you were excited about something."

Greyson kicked his feet at where the guard was looking. "What do you see down there?" he asked after the blatant kick.

"You little, slimy peasant." The guard stood up from where he had been searching. "That was not smart, Greyson." He cracked his whip.

"Don't do this. Which one are you? Hank? Look, today is just anoth—"

The lash extended and wrapped around Greyson's leg. Greyson was pulled off his feet by the guard. As he fell, the guard was raising his arm to strike again.

A tripped Greyson grabbed on to his pick, attempting to use it to help himself get back on his feet. Luckily, because of the low light, it was considerably harder to hit someone. The guards carried around the whips mostly as an intimidation tool, enjoying the casual flick of the wrist.

The guard threw a punch in Greyson's direction, but he missed completely.

"Is there any reason for that? Let me get back to my mining," Greyson said.

The frustrated guard couldn't just let it go. As his first swing missed, he dropped his torch on the ground so that he could strike again, trying another stubborn shot from his other fist. Greyson didn't have to move; the next throw was just as bad as the first, and the guard ended up punching the wall.

"Where are you, you little punk? Where is the crystal? I felt it!" The guard got on his knees and began futilely searching the ground.

Greyson saw the glint of the crystal in the corner of his eye, a flash reflecting the light from the torch. He looked back to see the guard, still on all fours, looking around with desperation in his eyes. Greyson grabbed the crystal and the torch and started to sprint. He passed several miners on the way out, and they cheered him on, the clanging of their picks still in rhythm.

Just as Greyson saw the light of the entrance, he was welcomed by a giant scorpion tail, a long, black-scaled ligament the size of a tall man's leg. It was complete with the telson stinger barb. As he approached, the tail vanished. He continued on, thinking it must have been a figment of his imagination, perhaps a hallucination brought on by the mine fumes and the darkness.

As soon as he was washed over by the light of day, Greyson saw a tall, blond man with sharp features standing before him. The man was slender and had shiny silver armor with a beer mug emblazoned on it.

Today is really my day. Greyson's run came to an immediate halt. He held his arm out with the torch away from his body. "Sir, I am assuming you will be needing this."

"No, I don't believe I will," the man gruffly replied, giving Greyson a look of disgust. "As a matter of fact, I think why I am here just came running out to me." He looked beyond Greyson, down the mine tunnel. "And it appears as though you are alone."

Greyson looked down the tunnel as well. "It does appear that way, sir."

"I assume you know what it is I seek, then, ha-ha."

"If it isn't this torch, I am afraid I am at a loss." Greyson shrugged his shoulders.

The man shifted his gaze from the mine shaft back to Greyson. "You had better fix your tone with me."

A couple of miners pushing carts of ore were heading back out from the shaft. The tall man looked at them, and they continued pushing their carts. One of the miners asked, "Sir Crix, would you like to inspect the carts?"

Greyson shifted uneasily in his boots. "I need to get back to my tent, sir. May I be excused?" He attempted to walk around the man.

"You have not been excused, ha-ha." Crix extended his arm, halting Greyson's stride. "Empty your pockets."

Greyson made a show of slapping his pockets and held up his hands with a shrug. "There is nothing in my pockets."

"Turn them out. Do not make me search you, ha-ha," Crix said.

He went into his pockets, fished out the crystal into his hand before grabbing the cloth of his inner pant and withdrawing it as if there were nothing to be revealed.

Crix frowned. "Raise your arms and open your hands. You do know the longer you try to play little games, the more guilty you appear, ha-ha."

Greyson's hands went into the air, and he opened his fist.

The crystal dropped.

Crix's eyes widened as soon as the crystal appeared. "What was that? What dropped?" He rushed to where Greyson was standing, sputtering out chuckles and desperately reaching for the crystal that was now lying on the ground.

"Let the people be fed," Greyson said. "That was supposed to be a bargaining chip to feed us."

Crix had the crystal in both hands. He held it up to the sun and kissed it. "I hope you know that you have made my day, ha-ha." He immediately pocketed the crystal.

His body then contorted, skin peeling and bones protruding to create an armorlike shell. Snaps and cracks issued forth as his tailbone extended into a tail with a stinger, and his arms transformed into chitinous legs. Crix had turned into a giant, man-sized scorpion. He skittered away towards the inside of the camp.

Greyson had a flabbergasted expression but managed to speak. "The people need food!" Greyson shouted futilely at the fleeing scorpion.

"All bark with those guys." He rolled his eyes and grabbed his pick off the ground. Why not just give Crix the crystal shard to begin with? All of them, they are all selfish with those things. It changes some of them. They take them, and they forget us.

The miners with the carts of ore were now wheeling back towards the tunnel. The two stopped their creaking wheels next to a bewildered Greyson.

"You all right?" the closest miner to Greyson asked. The other miner had a similar look of concern.

Greyson was standing motionless with his head down, feeling defeated. "I think I just lost us our chance, boys."

"Our chance for what, Greyson?" one of the miners asked.

"Never mind, boys. I am really sorry," Greyson said solemnly. He started down the tunnel, the carts right behind him.

The one closest to Greyson asked, "Do you think we'll get some extra gruel tonight? Stomach has been absolutely growling all day." He rubbed his belly longingly as his stomach groaned.

"We had better get moving, then," Greyson said. Without another word, he spun his pick in his hands and continued onwards.

Both of the miners veered into different tunnels.

I need to run.

Greyson heard a man swearing to himself call out, "You, with the torch, who is that?"

He'll find me eventually, but at least it won't be today. I've had enough. Greyson picked up a rope and started to tug for Garrett, but the rope had begun to come towards him instead of leading to the miner—the rope had been cut. Fucking guards.

He immediately went back towards the entrance. As good of a time as any to try again for a run at it.

Greyson started at a jog, thinking of what could possibly be done to distract. The tents? No, there might be people still in them. I have to make sure the flames do not make it to people's homes.

There were casks of oil outside of the mine. The oil was supposed to protect from the sun, and also masked the rank smell of the unclean miners. Beside the oil were mounds of ore and tents containing more ore that would be shipped to the rest of Amerthine.

Those tents.

Greyson gritted his teeth as he quickened his pace, thinking up his hasty plans on the way out. More guards showed up as soon as he exited the tunnels. On seeing the guards make their approach, Greyson readjusted the torch in his hands and cocked it back before sending it as far as he could towards the tents containing the ore, which were quite a distance from the mine entrance.

The guards were stupidly staring at Greyson and watched as the flaming torch was tossed. It hurtled through the sky, end over end with the flame spinning, and then landed directly on to the hems of an ore tent, which quickly caught on fire.

The guards started to panic, but a snide laugh came from the back of the regiment. One of the guards stepped forward. This guard had a straight, rectangular mustache, carefully groomed and meticulously brushed. He looked over at the flaming tents, then back at Greyson again.

"That will be some extra work. I am going to have to warn you, bud," the straight-mustached man said.

"No, don't go soft on him. Didn't you just hear what I said about him? He is a con!" big man Hank cried at the guard. He was out of breath as he exited the mines.

"Clearly, this rebellious outburst didn't do much, Hank. The guy is a punk, but get him back in the mines. From what I hear, we are still behind in the shipments," said the straight-mustached guard. "He produces, and we need that."

Hank's face reddened and puffed. He appeared visibly upset as he stomped his feet in frustration and blew air out of his nose.

"No, not again. What escape trial number is this, Greyson?" Hank said, tapping his billy club. He had beefy hands to round out the broad shoulders and giant frame of his meaty figure, a handlebar mustache of his own complementing his intimidating appearance.

Now out in sunlight, Greyson had the full spectacle.

"Is this a weekly occurrence now? I have to come here to whup your arse?"

Greyson fidgeted with his hands. Fuck. "Well, you got me. However, has anyone spoken to you about the Lord and Savior Troutus?" Why do they always smile like that? It isn't a smile for a humorous joke. It's the smile of this guy that wants to hurt me.

Hank lifted his billy club and smacked Greyson across the face.

"Time to head back." He picked up Greyson off the ground by a clump of his hair. Greyson lay limp, reeling from the hit to his face. "All of you think you are sumfin'—I deal with idiots who wants to escape all the time. Next week, we'll be back." A dopey smile still lingered on Greyson's face as the guard shook his head roughly.

Motherfucker, he got me again. Everything hurts. Should have realized they don't give a fuck about burning tents, and I probably did more harm than good. But I need to get out somehow. How, though? Guy is right; I have tried this more than a few times. And I just do not see myself stopping until I get the hell out of here.

Greyson was by no means a small man in stature, but the guard managed to drag him. He was going to be tossed back into the worker camp again. They passed the market, where curious onlookers gawked at Greyson. The villagers could be seen from the market-tent huts and surrounding small gardens, and they knew that Greyson was always plotting to get out. He was seen as a threat to escape, and he had hoped to get thrown away forever at this point.

Every time I think something will change, and nothing ever does.

The occurrences of Greyson's escapes were so frequent that no one but the new villagers really paid him any mind—those looking for solace out in the empty desert, the ones who had been frantic for work so that they had become trapped in the monotony of the village. There wasn't really anywhere one could go in the desert, especially alone. The villagers knew this. The village was the only place of refuge for miles around, until the settlements north of the desert. Stories had been told of getting trapped or taken there. Sanctuary was found in Haneserrath, but with that sanctuary came complacency.

Greyson had his fans in the village. They admired his courage and ability to really speak his mind to the guards.

The guard gritted his teeth, mumbling as he dragged Greyson, "How many times do we have to go through this? You're not clever; you're just an idiot—not only that, but a weak idiot." The guard slapped Greyson twice in the back of the head. "You fucking idiot," the guard added for good measure. He did this several times over, expressing his joy in giving Greyson pain, one hit after another. One bloody gash and then another.

"Hey!" A woman came running over to the guard and the limp body of Greyson. "We are being attacked by trolls!" The woman was shorter in stature and wore a long shawl, which was mostly black with a hint of a scarlet hue. She ran past them, unstrapping a bow from her back as she headed towards the village walls.

Shouts could be heard at the walls, an alert that the desert trolls had come looking for food. The guard dropped Greyson. "I'll be back for you, guy. You gotta be kidding—you lucky bastard." After giving Greyson a swift kick to the ribs, he drew his sword and took off towards the walls.

Greyson immediately clutched his bruised body, wincing in pain. He brushed his face. They haven't made it too far back to the trough tent—good, that place makes me want to vomit. He rubbed where the guard had smashed his forehead with the billy club. Fucking prick.

Eventually, Greyson rolled onto his side. He could hear shouts coming from the wall. Then, a bell was rung, the sound echoing throughout the village. I really need to move.

The excited shouts had turned into horrified screams. If ever there was a time to have that mining pick…

Trolls had climbed their way above the wall and were entering the village. An absolutely massive one could be seen chewing on a guard's femur. It had lanky arms and beady black eyes attached to an ugly, warped face. This troll had not seen Greyson, as it had been busy hunting for more pesky guards firing arrows at it.

Greyson brushed off his injuries, slightly wincing again. He started to sprint, weaving through the streets of Haneserrath.

One could see a majority of the village contents from the wall. Haneserrath was a small village that scraped together just enough from the nearby mines, a bright flame from the center making the village a beacon under the mountain.

Karnaugh wants us all to die. Fucking awful. Work for this asshat until we drop. I can't stand the guards, but it's these miners I give a shit about.

Greyson was coming up on the miners' camp and making his way towards his tent. He had a grim look of determination on his face as he tried to find a pickax as quickly as possible. These trolls won't stop. Karnaugh should be alerted by now.

A troll screeched and threw a guard's boot from its mouth. It scratched its wide chest and leaped down from the wall into the village, followed by more salivating desert trolls. The trolls were angered for some reason, with white-hot looks in their eyes while they attacked the villagers and guards.

There were warped-looking trolls, ones with larger arms or smaller legs, all gargantuan in size. Their faces were similar to humans, but the skin seemed to be stretched and warped, causing them to be bloated and distorted in various ways. Most trolls were at least thirteen feet in height, but they varied drastically, being oversized, warped versions of humans, with claws and teeth, and typically an intellect not to be desired.

After noticing the screeching troll, a guard along the wall nocked three arrows and fired them off. The arrows sailed towards the desert troll, which was licking its lips and rubbing its stomach as it had just digested a meal of human flesh. Three plunks thumped as the arrows scored home on the troll's chest.

The troll looked unfazed. It started to gallop towards the guard archer. Leg after lumbering leg progressed towards the frightened guard. The troll tried to swipe, its heavily wart-caked arm barely missing its target.

"You need to add fire to your arrows!" cried the shawled woman, who had now come out from the shadows.

There were barrels of oil for the lanterns around the village to light up the night so that the mining never ends. The woman dipped an arrow in a nearby barrel. In one swift motion, she withdrew a tinderbox from her pocket and lit the arrow. She drew the flaming arrow back and then let it loose on the troll.

The arrow soared through the air, and the troll noticed the doom that was flying at it just before it struck. As soon as the arrow landed, the troll burst into flames. The troll writhed on the ground as its skin was eaten by the flames.

The woman sprang into action, grabbing more arrows that had been stored at the village's walls. She clumped the arrows together and set them ablaze. In the distance, one could see more guards desperately parrying reckless blows coming from the flailing troll that was on fire.

"FIRE ARROWS!" the shawled woman shouted.

I don't think they understand what she means. How long since the last troll attack?

A troll lifted its ham fist, a long, beaky nose and violent, sharp teeth protruding from its face. Hank thrust his sword into the troll's chest, and the troll responded by emitting a shriek. Hank was shaking, but still had his hands on the hilt of the sword as it plunged into the troll's chest between the ribs.

The troll's ugly face sneered, looking directly into the guard's eyes and causing him to freeze. It wound up its fist, giving the guard enough time to prepare for the oncoming blow. The troll smacked Hank with such force that he was launched into a nearby tent.

"You need to light them on fire!" the shawled woman shouted to the other guards.

There you go. Really pathetic that these guards do not know what to do against them.

The guards dipped their swords and arrows in oil and set their weapons ablaze. They began a counterattack, driving the trolls back and fighting the few that lumbered behind that were not scared off by the flames.

Something had clearly angered these trolls enough to attack the village. The trolls showed confidence when the last guard was dispatched; however, when they started noticing the flames, their confidence shattered immediately.

Fire. I just lit those tents on fire. "We can use the fire I created!" Greyson exclaimed, feeling proud of himself.

The shawled woman ran over to Greyson, giving him a confused stare. "The fuck are you still doing here? You idiot, run!" She slung her bow over her shoulder.

Why is everyone calling me an idiot? Greyson stood with a mining pick in his hands, blank-faced and bewildered.

2

"Strange Acquaintances"

"**I** need you to do me a favor…," said another tall, sharp man with wide shoulders and a broad chest. He was speaking to an absolutely abhorrent, warped, square-faced yellow troll in the middle of the Great Desert, under the light of a pale full moon. The troll was much bigger than the large man, at least double his size.

The troll walked in a circle, orbiting the smaller man. "What is the need?" The troll's square face showed a deep pout as it wandered over to a cactus and smashed it with a heavy fist.

"I have some friends coming, and, frankly"—the man paused and tapped his sword—"there are some people I need you to take out."

"Do you have more oil, Karnaugh?" The troll had a devious smile.

"Who do you think I am?" Karnaugh said to the troll with a lick of cockiness. He walked back over to his desert horse, a hyder.

Hyders are basically the same as a normal horse, but their legs have grown accustomed to the softness of running on the sand, their hooves more like feet. When watching a hyder run, it looks as if it is gliding through the sand.

Karnaugh's unit of soldiers that followed him everywhere were in the distance. His hyder had a small carriage attached to it, with several barrels in the back compartment. He slapped two of the barrels, making an echoing thump.

"This is what you want, correct?" Karnaugh asked.

"Open it; open it. I would like to see the contents," the troll replied.

"Not trusting of me, Til'lock?" Karnaugh repeatedly smacked the barrel tops as if they were drums.

Til'lock spit on the ground. "I trust you as you trust me," it bellowed before letting out a shrill cackle. The troll walked over to the cart. "Once again, open it."

Karnaugh popped a seal on one of the barrels in the back of his cart. "You ready for this good oil?" The inside of the barrel was filled with a thick black substance. "Go ahead; try some. I insist."

The troll cupped one hand and picked the barrel up with the other to pour. The liquid covered the surface of its palm, and Til'lock took a drink of it. The troll's face burst with excitement.

"This is everything!" the troll roared.

"Yes, yes, of course," Karnaugh said. "One more thing—do not touch travelers coming to the village. They might look good, but they are for my party."

"Whatever, human!" The troll was still on its high as it danced with its legs moving back and forth, flailing its arms.

"I shall take this back to the other trolls and discuss with them what we have discussed here."

Karnaugh watched as Til'lock hoisted the heavy, liquid-filled barrels under its great arms with ease before walking off with them as though they were not even there. "Until we meet again, Til'lock," he said as he waved to the troll.

"You still disgust me, human," the troll said. "I will be back with some friends." The barrels made swishing sounds as Til'lock lumbered off into the desert.

———•———

The miners' camp was located by Haneserrath's southern exit, which was closest to the mountain. The village was one of the Southern territories' farthest bases north for operations and closest to a water source in the desert as well. The village contained a smaller mining facility and cactus farms. Its location in the desert hills had once been near a popular mountain. The mountain was the largest in the land, so it had brought visitors. It was now a windswept crater called the Desert's Moon.

It was said that Haneserrath's mines contained dark crystals worth a hefty sum. Karnaugh kept the crystals in the shell of Desert's Moon because the place was barren. No one, except his people, went into the mines.

Karnaugh was a real thick-headed type, and his motivations lacked any awareness for the needs of others. His insatiable desire for oil had left people starving. He was often fearful of betrayal, so he surrounded himself with yes-men.

Those meatheads were in the same unit as Karnaugh when he was still in the South's army, just not nearly as ambitious or as charismatic. They were not the strongest of minds; however, for what they lacked in brain, they brought power to the table with their brawn and the wealth provided by the crystals of the South. They wore fancy silver armor emblazoned with Karnaugh's banner of the beer mug with a gaping, sharp-toothed mouth.

Karnaugh was their hero, and they knew better than to try to one-up the man who wore a unique suit of bejeweled golden armor. Being close to Karnaugh provided them with a larger purse and notoriety.

Karnaugh's Keep was actually a large and elegant tent, almost the size of everyone else's tents combined. The tent had been sewn with gold and rare furs. Of course, it needed to be on top of a hill with a commanding view of the village. The fully outfitted interior of the tent was a sight to behold. Wooden floors lined the many hallways, replete with opulent furnishings, a firepit, and an immense dining table in the magnificent central chamber. There were separate rooms in the tent that had their own doors—the only other solid door in Haneserrath that was known was the one to the giant shittery, or as some of the villagers like to call it, the hotbox.

Swords and shields lined the tent's long hallway that led to the double doors of Karnaugh's room, and besides all of the extravagant decorations within his room, there was a port that accessed an alchemy lab where the oil was made. The tent's grandeur was a beacon to whoever went to the village, as everything else there was dull like the desert sand.

Karnaugh pressed his forefinger against the pearl cap of his vial, circling it round and round and using his thumb to keep it from falling. The pearl cap was in the shape of a skull that aligned with the opening of the vial.

"All right, fine…" He moved his thumb and took a swig. He lifted his face to the sky, and his eyes turned black.

The town of Haneserrath was nothing in comparison to the city of Odh Varol, especially to Karnaugh. He wanted to go back to the attention and glamor that was in the city. The village was too new, and he didn't want to be responsible for the villagers, but duty had called him when his mother passed. Karnaugh had to adjust his sensibilities to accommodate for the small village of Haneserrath. He was used to the big city—the firepits, the arena fights, the whorehouses, and the population difference. He did not care for this village, and that had been apparent as soon as his entourage moved in.

"We need to go, my guys!" Karnaugh was feasting on a leg of meat, and pieces were flying from his mouth as he spoke.

His pack of handpicked, large goons had joined him in his tent. They surrounded him and imitated his gestures, just nodding their heads and not doing much else—laughing at his jokes and occasionally grunting.

Karnaugh fed them the oil that his alchemist made. He always had his eyes on his barrels, taking a dipstick and testing them as he passed, making sure he had not lost any substance. The oil in the barrels was priceless to him, and he believed the liquid would lead to his fortune in Haneserrath.

Karnaugh stood up from his furred chair, pointing at the door. Shouts and screams could be heard from outside his tent keep. He knew the trolls had breached the wall, as it was part of the agreement they made. But the agreement did not exclude him from being a part of the fun, and he wanted in on some of the action—or there would be no action at all.

The growth had been extraordinary in the village, and as he took another bite of meat, he wondered what his mother had been doing this whole time to make the villagers multiply and become so cocky.

Karnaugh took two more bites of the leg and then tossed the scraped bone. "Where are you, Reevus? I need the gear on me!" Karnaugh looked around, and he saw out of the corner of his eye a smaller man folding some of his clothing.

The feeble man was unarmored and wore tattered robes, looking quite diminutive compared to Karnaugh and the rest of the boys. Splotched makeup accentuated a sharp, beak-like nose, but his other facial features were much smaller.

"Reevus!" Karnaugh called in an exaggeratedly melodious tone. He pointed a finger at the small man, causing him to shake with fear. "I need to be strapped, little man," he demanded, pointing at dangling straps from his armor while bouncing his words. "Put that gear in my hands, and make it quick." Karnaugh moved towards his armoire, which was decorated with carvings of wolves.

Reevus slithered quickly in his excitement, scrambling before Karnaugh to start putting on the gear. The golden shine of the armor was blinding, and that, combined with the vine-like patterns of pearls and rare jewels, made the suit even more like a piece of art.

First, he grabbed the chest armor, a huge, heavy breastplate that he had to almost drag on the floor. However, dragging it would ruin the shine, so Reevus had to hunch, arms encompassing the suit, and hover the armor about an inch off the ground, making sure not to blemish it. Reevus hefted the breastplate up a small set of stairs, in front of which

Karnaugh was standing. Despite Reevus's steady effort, the weight of the armor caused him to almost hit a step.

With beads of sweat on his forehead, the small man was finally able to strap the chest plate on Karnaugh. With a huge sigh of relief, he went to grab the rest of the gear.

Reevus took great pride in cleaning the armor; he was obsessed with keeping things tidy and was often seen straightening out-of-place objects.

"How many are there?" Karnaugh had a large frown on his face while adjusting his bejeweled chest plate.

"Last reported, there were about two dozen or so trolls, differing in size. It appears as though the villagers have taken down a few, and some of the others are running. Our guards are doing wonderfully," Reevus replied in a high-pitched voice.

"Ooh, they thought they had us when they dropped in!" Karnaugh whooped, causing his armor to shift uncomfortably. "Do we have a contact near the walls? What's that guy's name, chubby dude with the funny mustache? Is he still alive?"

Karnaugh got his leg armor strapped on next, then bracers, and, lastly, a plumed helm—all gold, of course.

"We should be getting a shipment in soon, but make sure it doesn't come with the trolls. Hopefully, they have had enough and left."

"Last of the reports stated that he was alive, sir," Reevus replied. "They have listened to the orders."

The mining operation at Haneserrath had slowed recently. The villagers were starting to figure out efficiencies in growth, but it was a gradual process with Haneserrath's small population. That wasn't quick enough for Karnaugh. The resources were being taken from the portals instead of local sources, and the necessity for Haneserrath's mine had waned, but not altogether—not with the knowledge of its contents…and not with war looming, either.

The South wanted to take advantage of the portals. The North had had enough of the South's behavior, and so, fights had broken out along the border. The need was not the same as in the days of Hanes, but the necessity of the ores had increased with the outbreak of the dangers from the portals.

The transition to Hanes's son hadn't changed the daily operations, and most of the village didn't even know that Hanes had passed. Karnaugh hadn't formed any fortifications or protections for the village, nor interacted with the villagers at all. He hadn't even introduced himself. Only Karnaugh's enormous, ancient advisor, Forgar, had shown his face and announced their presence to the village after Hanes passed.

The villagers were accustomed to how their day-to-day had become. The village struggled to establish itself, and their current situation was to live under the rule of Karnaugh's careless leadership; however, the villagers did not care who was in charge, as long as they were fed and safe. The villagers wanted their lives to get better, but had been happy with the predictability of their daily routines and the pace at which the village was expanding. Having the mines close by, and with able people to do the job, the villagers could get the ore from the mine that was needed to sustain themselves. The village seemed as though it was growing.

The broken mountain was valuable because of its peculiar crystals that were the talk of Amerthine. People had seen how beautiful the gems were, and some said that the crystals had special properties that spoke to them. The Haneserrath miners were digging day in and day out, and those crystals made this particular former mountain worth almost the equivalent of a portal. That is what was told, as Karnaugh was keen on owning something nobody else owned.

Reevus had found a way to create a magical mixture—the oil. The alchemist was able to break down the crystal and mix it with the cactus water, making it into an oily substance. He came from Odh Varol, as well, and he had been dragged to Haneserrath so that the crystals were more readily available to make the oil for Karnaugh. All the gold was nice, but the oil and its properties were overpowering. Karnaugh needed Reevus, and for him to stay safe, for him to continue producing the oil, and to continue towards the profits that would come of it.

To Karnaugh, for the most part, they were having a good time. The oil made him feel elated and invincible, but out of his mind. Karnaugh needed to flaunt the oil, his treasure.

The village was slowing his income down, due to him having to support it and its people. Karnaugh thought that, sure, they were mining the crystals for him, but he could sacrifice the lot and just get new people from the capital to do his bidding. His friends were all from Odh Varol, and they would get high and party with Karnaugh. He missed them dearly. They were powerful figures in the capital, ones who could get him cheaper replacements for the villagers.

There was a portal a slight distance away from the village. The villagers feared the monsters that came from portals.

There were already dangers in the desert, but the portal made it extremely worse, thereby detracting anyone from running away, which was useful to Karnaugh.

The trolls communicated with Karnaugh, and they made an agreement to keep the trade routes safe in the desert in exchange for oil. It was a battle at first, but after the humans shared some oil with the trolls, they made an uneasy peace. Karnaugh would provide the oil, and the trolls were crazy for the stuff, just like his own cronies. The trolls would be allowed to pick off some of the outlying passersby in the desert. Travel through the desert to Haneserrath would be somewhat protected, but it would still be perilous. The rewards of the desired oil, however, were worth the risk—at least in Karnaugh's belief.

Karnaugh wanted to make a resort out of the crystal-oil sales. The broken mountain, controlling the village that was closest to the sea, the sale of the oil, and the thoughts of this resort and the potential greater prosperity for himself —these were all factors that provided comfort to Karnaugh and eased his mind. He would often muse about how no other village could offer what he had.

"From what we have heard, Hank has been tossed by a troll. It is unknown whether or not he is alive or if he might be in critical condition," one of Karnaugh's men said.

"Fine, fine, I guess. Let's go get some trolls, boys!" Karnaugh gave a high five to a trembling Reevus. After taking another chug of his oil, he pointed a menacing finger at Reevus and rapidly moved it back and forth. "Let's go; let's go; let's go!"

A fully armored Karnaugh went over to his crew. He hopped from one foot to the other on his way, marching with his men in a side-to-side motion. "It is time to get it, boys. They can't stop us. They don't want to, baby." He was riling them up, and it was working.

His crew started to chant Karnaugh's name. They turned to the left and headed out the door in unison. In eager excitement, one of the henchmen jumped and slapped the top of the wooden double doors in the tent.

The exit was quiet for a split second, and then Karnaugh's face poked back into the tent. "Hey, say, don't take it easy. I really want a big party to happen with more people than before. It should be a part of that caravan I was talking about." He tapped his forefingers together. "Meaning the oil, Reevus, more of that oil. That last batch you made—perfect. Do it again."

Karnaugh stared at Reevus and gave him a wicked smile. "Until we see each other again. Stay in the basement till those trolls leave. I need a number of villagers gone to be replaced by my partygoers." Karnaugh popped his vial again.

"Yes, of course, I still have quite a lot boiling in the basement," Reevus squeaked. "I really do need more ventilation down there; I do not think it is good for the ink." Reevus turned to enter his hole in the ground, which was located in a far-off corner of the tent, quite a distance away.

Karnaugh was already gone. Karnaugh's unit of boys all headed in the opposite direction from the village, along the southern trail. They grew bored, forgot their original mission, and started to hunt boar for a roast they planned for later. It was a solid plan in their minds: go find everyone meat for a feast. They were each outfitted with fine silver armor and weapons that gleamed splendidly in the desert sun.

When not concocting his oils, Reevus spent his time making polish and cleaning. Reevus enjoyed making the suits shine, and he was quite the chemist with polishes experimenting as Karnaugh did his business.

Reevus's chamber was in the back of Karnaugh's massive tent, under a small port, down a hatch in the floor. The room was filled with leaking cauldrons, and hanging from the walls were vials that contained different liquids and powders of varying hues, a few of them even glowing. Reevus was swirling the contents of a pot, adding potions and ingredients from his belt—a lizard tail here, an underwater root there. The more potions and ingredients he added to the pot, the clearer a picture of a face showed in the brew.

"Praise it be!" the face shouted. "It does, in fact, work. Hello there, young strapping Reevus. Pray, do tell me how that little town of Haneserrath is doin'. Also, how long do I have word with you?"

"Oh, my master, I mean, Great Korgak, the town has been short on supply. We are struggling to feed the people. We might not be able to make the next payment; not much time remains," Reevus whimpered.

Korgak was the current leader of the Southern Empire, a man who was full of zealous rage but used his words sweetly. He was a devout follower of the god-creature Troutus. He was also obsessed with the portals, especially the creatures that poured from them. Korgak believed he could convert them and lead the Southern Empire to victory over the Northern Empire once and for all. But, above all else, Korgak wanted to be worshipped.

"Well then, the Great Lord Troutus is upset by those words, and does he know that you need a bit of rain up there? I surely do hope that you'll be able to acquire that gold now, ya hear?" Korgak was still smiling, but there was an obvious anger behind his eyes.

"Of course, of course," Reevus sniveled, tapping his fingers together in frantic agitation. "I believe he has found a way to finally set up here a good business that will profit."

"Pray, do tell me more, little Reevus." The floating head's chin raised.

"The trolls will come at dawn. We will have eliminated the extras that are unneeded here. On their demise…" He paused and took a breath. "I apologize. Hard to breathe." He coughed. "On their demise, we have a caravan of wealthier investors who would like to try some of our product here at Haneserrath." A madcap grin crossed his face as he shook and dangled some vials in a playful manner.

"I am liking the sound of this, Reevus. You are doing me very proud." Korgak put on a soothing tone to show he was impressed.

"Thank you, sir," Reevus responded, his eyes glistening with pride.

"You don't want to disappoint the Lord, however." His face started to swirl in the pot. "Be good now, Reevus." Only a muck-like substance remained in the pot after the swirling finally stopped.

A large, older man who had been lingering in the room for the duration of Reevus's conversation came out from the shadows after the face in the pot disappeared. "I need more oil from you. The boys are getting dry again," the old, hulking figure said.

"I still have more left—not much more, however," Reevus replied. "We need it for shipments. How much is it that you need?"

"We need more of it," the hulking man stated with finality.

"The miners have got to find more of the crystal. Even a shard like this will do." Reevus held out a small crystal that was cracked. "More gold and gruel to whoever finds one," he said. "I can make a batch for you right now, but I only have this little guy to work with."

Reevus looked at one of the pots that held a bubbling concoction. He then took the small crystal shard that Crix had dropped off earlier and tossed it into the pot. "Give it a bit of time, please," he muttered, his voice becoming as quiet as a mouse.

Billowing smoke shot out from the pot as the shard hit the liquid.

◆———————•———————◆

Greyson's legs were moving as fast as they could. The only thing with which he had to defend himself and the other miners was his mining pick. Looking around for a suitable weapon to use, he approached a grisly scene where one of the guards had been eaten. A boot and sword were the only things left of the man. Greyson picked up both and ran towards an oil barrel.

That was way farther than I anticipated.

Out of breath, he dipped the boot and sword into the oil. He lit them both aflame from a nearby torch. Greyson then sprinted farther back towards the miners' tents, feeling better prepared.

A few trolls were rampaging and heading for the miners' tents. They were still near the wall and, fortunately, not yet close enough to the tents to do harm to any of the miners. The village guards had been overwhelmed by the trolls. Their numbers were now incredibly low, and with or without flaming weapons, they no longer had the help of an archer shooting fire arrows. The men were hesitant to approach the trolls since getting too close would lead to the risk of being eaten or ravaged. But more guards were equipping themselves with the necessary items to follow the archer's lead.

Greyson braced his body into a wind-up position. He exhaled sharply, took a great spiral leap to gain momentum, and then threw the flaming boot at the closest troll. The boot went hurtling through the air, a flaming cannonball in slow motion.

The troll watched in stupefied awe as the glowing projectile came towards it. The boot made a metallic slap when it smashed into the troll's face. Falling to the ground with a thud, the boot extinguished in the sand. The troll looked directly at Greyson while rubbing its flattened nose, sneering menacingly. It appeared as though the boot really hadn't done much of anything.

Now would be the time to run. Looks like I just pissed that troll right the fuck off. Hurling that flaming boot really seemed like an amazing idea. On seeing the boot fail while he was in midcharge at the troll, Greyson took a sharp turn and headed towards the mines. Anywhere but the miners' tents.

Trolls are already inside the walls, so maybe this will give people enough time to evacuate the area, and then that useless piece of shit, Karnaugh, will show up and save the day.

The trolls were continuing to slowly make their way through the village, destroying the villagers' homes and areas for gathering. Guards and miners alike appeared to be banding together to hold them back.

The troll had never felt such anger before, which was made clear by its guttural screams. At a full-on sprint, it started after the offending human who had hurled the boot. With exaggerated grunting and a bouncing stride, the troll scraped its nails along the sand as it advanced towards Greyson. Then, the troll suddenly stopped and prepared to take a tremendous leap, bending its knees and licking its foul lips in anticipation.

As he ran towards the mines, Greyson looked back just in time to see the angry troll lunging towards him. In an instant, the troll was grabbing at his legs, eagerly swiping the air with its gnarly fingers.

"Fuck!" Greyson exclaimed, spryly leaping out of the way of the troll's sinister hands. This thing is way quicker than I anticipated. I will not be able to outrun this bastard.

Greyson landed and rolled to a stop. Dusting his face off, he looked back up to see a familiar skeletal figure. "Mister Ragz, we meet again," Greyson breathed heavily. "I don't know if tapping on your head will do here, but I need that rusty sword."

He pushed aside the dusty bones and thin, tattered cloth, grabbing the sword Mister Ragz was leaning on. The sword was caked with rust and dulled by years of being half-buried in the ground, a lone relic believed to have been from a bygone day of defending the mine.

In an arc that was much like the swinging motion of his pick, Greyson hacked the sword through the troll's extended arm. The limb landed on the ground with a lifeless thump.

Well, that was a decent swing. I can do this.

The troll shrieked, its face purple with rage. It desperately attempted to nurse the wound with its other arm.

That allowed Greyson to regain his footing after the chop.

The troll's stump was immediately scabbed over, but it had been cauterized by the flaming sword, the application of fire appeared to have negated its regenerative abilities.

Clearly, that woman was correct; the fire is effective.

Luckily, the sword was still aflame. Hoping the fire would last, Greyson raised his sword and charged at the troll. This madness needs to end soon.

The troll used its remaining arm to give Greyson a good backhand.

Losing his sword and his footing, the hit launched Greyson towards the mine entrance in a deadly spiral. Greyson stood back up and looked over at the wounded troll.

The last shriek had got the attention of the others, and more trolls were approaching.

Sweat dripped from Greyson's brow as he gripped the sword tightly in his hand. He was no swordsman, and he knew that. He tapped the head of Mister Ragz one more time. "Maybe I'll see you sooner than you think, Ragz." And off to finish this troll he went, or at least he hoped that he could dispatch it.

Suddenly, the troll was shot by two flame-engulfed arrows. It started to slap the fire with its one arm, setting the rest of itself alight. Soon, it was in a fetal position, crackling in flames.

The shawled archer appeared on top of the wall.

"She is my hero!" Greyson cried out as he ran over to the foot of the wall where the shawled figure was now standing. He was panting, wiping the sweat off his forehead. "I gotta know. What is your name? You seem to be saving my day over here." He was talking to himself; she was already gone.

What the hell? Better get rolling, then. He began running in the direction that the shawled woman had run. She seems to know what she is doing, and, judging by the screams going on in the village, this has not ended. The trolls are so strong—I wonder if there is a more efficient way of killing them.

Greyson caught up with the woman in the village. He waited for her to go in after the trolls. Attacking trolls as a team worked better, as proven by the last one they took out. He thought they worked well together.

The shawled woman gave Greyson an exasperated look. "Dude, run. These trolls will wreck you. Did you see that femur toothpick? A one-armed troll was about to swallow you whole. We have no time. I need to run, and I highly suggest you run, too. I may not be there to save you next time." She ran back towards the market.

That must be where the trolls are heading—population density, plus they smell the humans and the market. The market contains the cactus-farm collections, the gruel, and the water.

Greyson dismissed what she said. "I mean…but you could be…," Greyson said sarcastically, but she was already running.

"Fuck, Greyson." He took off after her.

I don't have a game plan. It appears she might be okay on her own, but, realistically, she won't be able to fight all these motherfuckers off alone.

Greyson didn't know what he would do if he came across another troll. He needed a way to reset his sword ablaze. He clutched Mister Ragz's rusty sword apprehensively, scanning for a fire source. Greyson's movements were becoming labored; he was very exhausted. A nearby bench looked inviting to his tired eyes.

Then, a shout from a female broke Greyson's fatigued reverie, and he headed in its direction to investigate. Greyson walked past two crispy troll corpses that lay on the ground along with a slew of dead villagers.

The shawled woman was in combat with a troll. She was out of flame arrows, and it really looked as if she was at the troll's mercy.

Greyson lifted his sword above his head and boldly charged forward.

Saliva dripped from the troll's mouth. It stabbed one of its gnarled, crusty fingers into the shawled woman's leg as she was trying to squirm away.

Greyson leaped nimbly, leading with the sword, and his swing scored home, slicing right through the troll's head while it was distracted by the shawled woman. The troll's head combusted, bursting into brilliant flame upon being cleaved by Greyson's sword. As soon as that happened, the woman seemed to forget her injury. She had a completely shocked look on her face, and Greyson forgot all about the troll.

"Are you okay? Did you take on three of these things? Are you nuts?" Greyson kicked the smoldering shell of the troll away from them. "Will you be all right continuing on with that leg injury?"

They were near some of the market tents, and Greyson moved about in search of supplies. Most of the people had evacuated; some stayed behind to make an attempt at fighting off the trolls. The villagers were severely outmatched, but holding their own. He followed the shawled woman deeper into the village marketplace, where there were tools, clothing, and different knickknacks still hanging around. Greyson was able to get some water satchels and dipped a few remaining arrows in oil.

"How many more trolls do you think are left?"

"You need to chill with the questions. Shit happens. There are still a few left. Thank you for your assistance with that last one, but how did that troll's head burst like that?"

Greyson tossed a satchel of water over to the woman, and she began to bandage her wound after cleaning it.

"I have absolutely no idea, but guess whose sword this was?" Greyson paused due to his own excitement.

The woman shot him a bemused look that indicated he wouldn't be getting an answer to his question.

Greyson changed the subject. "I have no idea what your name is, by the way, nor have I seen you before—both, just horrible things. I know we have to get moving."

"My name is Allarie, and you would be correct. You haven't seen me, but I have seen you. Bravo on the escape attempts, no matter how foolish. I am still surprised they have kept you alive. That is some damn good resolve." She removed her shawl. The tan-skinned Allarie had bright-green eyes, tiny pointed ears, and braided red hair. She was an attractive human, by all means, causing Greyson to do a double take.

"Gotta be more than this, right? What's the point of just waking up and mining to look for something for someone else, rinse and repeat?" Greyson then took a mocking tone. "We'll treat you like shit." He paused and looked wide-eyed with excitement at Allarie. "I'm all set on that. I'll fight you—not really you, but you get my point." Stumbling on his words, he continued, "This is Mister Ragz's sword, the defender of the mine!" His face glowed.

They picked up the rest of the supplies that they needed. Greyson found a bag, and he filled it with some leftover food and a rope. "Let's finish this and get outta here. I haven't seen a guard in a sun turn."

"I'll help you take these trolls out, but I will not be able to leave." Allarie kneeled and started to restring her bow. She then slung the bow over her shoulder and stood up again. "Let's get going. We need to get this done. A conversation for another time. Don't get distracted." She nodded her head and strapped the bow in place, reaching back to pull the string and give it a twang.

There were villagers running on the sand paths, heading back to their tents. They were scrambling with great fear and panic, running to their places of comfort. It appeared as though this area no longer had any trolls.

Where could they have gone, then?

A few of the trolls that remained were taking human prisoners and leaping back over the wall. Other trolls not yet finished off by fire had one of the guards moving them away from the miners' tents, migrating them to an open area in the village.

There was plenty of damage along the way—ripped, thrown, crumpled living quarters. The market contents had been tossed, and many items in the village had been torn asunder. Many villagers and guards had lost their lives to these trolls, and even more villagers had been captured by the few trolls that were now escaping. Some of the fleeing villagers approached their fallen kin, tears streaming from their eyes.

Where in the fuck are Karnaugh and his crew? These trolls caused so much havoc. Why? Where did they come from? How do we prevent them from coming back? Will they come back after so many died? So many questions.

Greyson pulled the straps on his new bag and gripped Mister Ragz's sword, the rusty piece of metal that obliterated the troll. I am absolutely amped right now to destroy trolls. Greyson reveled in his newfound confidence. This sword is badass, and it looks like absolute shit. Of course, as a memento of the mines, the sword he was holding was the real gold.

Greyson headed towards a crashing noise in the distance. Making his way through a sea of dead bodies, he found another troll that was being fought off by a ragtag band of villagers. They were using pitchforks and spears to keep the troll at bay, but heavy sideswipes and lunge attacks were picking the villagers apart.

Greyson charged right in, sword in hand, confidence beaming from his face.

The troll watched the grinning lad charge with all the heroic confidence in the world. The remaining exhausted and injured villagers were truly in awe of this guy's guts.

Greyson swung right at the troll's face, and the troll responded by throwing its much larger fist at him. Greyson ate troll fist, and with the weight of the blow, he was lifted off his feet and dropped several yards away.

3

"That's a big K'naugh for me"

Allarie let loose oil-soaked flaming arrows from her bow, striking a troll with three thumps in rapid succession.

The troll furiously slapped out the flames as it rolled on the ground. It then leaped back onto its feet, turned around, and rushed towards Allarie. The troll was slobbering in anticipation; gushing rivulets of drool dripped from its gaping, eager mouth.

The troll's hide was a sickly yellow hue, a leathery surface covered with boils and scabs. A beak-like nose protruded from a nest of wild hair, having a beard but no mustache—a standard troll look. Its beady eyes were very close together and gave a singular stare of intensity akin to that of a Cyclops. It was an oversized human that looked as though it fell from the ugly tree, hitting every single branch on the way down and bouncing on a few of them twice.

Trolls have tub-like bellies, and this particular group had abdomens that were especially bulky. Unfortunately, they looked well fed, much to the dismay of the villagers—being that their friends and families were the ones who had filled the guts of these vile creatures. There were quite a few villagers missing, and zero guards in sight. The guards might have been the first who had fallen, or, perhaps, they were cowards who had fled the scene.

The troll's corpulence made its lumbering frame sway as it charged. It threw one sweeping punch, which Allarie was able to roll away from initially. But it then turned around and followed up by jackhammering its gigantic fist in a crushing downward motion, hitting Allarie's shoulder and ceasing her motion mid-roll.

Greyson gripped some gravel and stood back up. With his sword firmly in his opposing hand, he steeled his nerves before getting back to the task of slaying the troll. He had seen Allarie roll away, and this was his opportunity, now that the troll was distracted.

Greyson swiped with his rusty blade, and it sliced right through the troll's arm, severing it. The troll grabbed on to Greyson's shoulder with its remaining arm and lunged its face in for a vicious bite. Greyson extended his free hand to shove the snapping maw away.

Allarie dropped her bow and went charging in, clutching a flaming dagger in each hand. She stabbed the gnarly arm that was pinning Greyson down by his throat, then quickly spun around and kicked the troll in the face.

The troll turned to her and screamed, spitting out an unbelievable amount of saliva. Allarie tucked and leapt with her dagger leading. Now, its head turned back towards her, and Allarie did not hesitate to stab one of its monstrous eyes.

The troll screamed and pawed at its injured eye with the remaining hand. The troll's guard was down, and its attention was diverted to tending its wounds.

Greyson ended its life with an arcing swing to the neck from his sword. The sword plunged into the troll, its flesh giving away like soft butter. Rusty dirt and all, the sword went right through, ending the troll's life.

The villagers in the area were cheering for Greyson and Allarie. They had seen significant loss, and the damage caused by the trolls was severe.

A slender, tall, elderly man and a heavyset, older woman walked over. The tall man started shaking a pointed finger at the two. "Thank you for all of your help. We really appreciate it. I thought this would be the end for the rest of us. The trolls were more than we could handle. The guards appear to have vanished and left us to fend for ourselves, the bastards. You went from village clown to village hero. What part of the trough did you eat from at sunrise, there, Greyson? We could all do with some. Who do you have here with you, Greyson?"

Allarie freed her knife from the troll's eye socket. She walked over to the large tent in which the others were now congregating. With a bright, shining smile on her face, she wiped her blade on the end of her shawl and then sheathed the dagger. "Pleased to meet you. My name is Allarie. Spread that around; I would rather not introduce myself to each of these people, and I know how word travels in the mine." She sounded as though she hadn't just ripped a dagger from a troll's eye socket. She nodded her head, grinned, and started to bounce-walk to go pick her bow back up.

"She's a looker, Greyson." The old man eyed her.

"Pops, she's standing right there. Address her like a flippin' human." Greyson extended his arm as if to slap the man upside the head. But he didn't hit the old man; he just flicked his wrist and made a whooshing sound with his mouth, imitating a gust of wind. "This guy's name is Pops Havven. He is the overseer of the miners, and to be honest, I am surprised he is alive. And the lovely lady is Nurse-mother Haan." Greyson took a knee. "A pleasure, Haan."

The nursemother looked at Greyson with a smile. "Get up, you fool, and give me a hug."

Southern mothers weren't known to live through child-birth, and those who did live were forced again into the mines or cactus farms. Nursemothers bore the responsi-bility of child-rearing while work was done by others. In the South, this was believed to be the most efficient way for the population to function.

Nursemothers were highly regarded in the village of Haneserrath. They were the village elders, a group of women who raised the children while their parents worked. The vil-lage needed the parents to work, even until too tired. The villagers had little to no interaction with their own children, and the children would only occasionally be able to meet their actual parents.

Nursemother Haan was the caretaker and mother for everyone in the village. She was there to raise the kids until they were of guard or miner age, and, year after year, the children were forced to take on these roles at a younger age. She stayed with the children until they became adults and acquired a tent of their own.

Along with other orphans, Greyson was corralled and sent to many different places during his childhood. Haneserrath had a need for a larger population of workers, and so he was sent to the village. Haan was recruited by Haneserrath to help take care of the children, as the population had increased significantly due to the many orphans sent from other villages. The two had bonded, and Greyson considered Haan to be his true mother.

Pops made a slight bow of greeting, the thin cloth of his oversized white coat draping outward and dusting the sandy ground. "Same to you, kid. Have you seen any of the guards or even that coward of a man, Karnaugh? This is a question for either of you. I haven't ever seen you around," he said, turning to look back at Allarie, wary of her presence. He eyed her suspiciously. "He allowed villagers and my miners to die, and he is nowhere to be found!" The old man started getting heated and began to pace, his fragility more evident as he wobble-walked with his lanky legs.

Allarie cringed visibly at the mention of Karnaugh. She shook her head and said, "Nor did I want to be seen just yet. Well met. Timing couldn't have been better."

Greyson's brow furrowed when he noticed Allarie's reaction to Karnaugh's name. His thought process immediately changed, and he paused. He needed more. "Oh? Details on the 'Naugh?" Greyson couldn't take his eyes off her. In anticipation, he grabbed some hardtack from his bag and chowed as he lingered, waiting to hear her words.

Allarie gave him a pensive look. "Another time. He is just not on my good list." She looked physically uncomfortable talking about the man; her hand rubbed her opposite arm apprehensively. She winced in frustration. "I've been watching, and the way the trolls were handled is not acceptable. Now, I refuse to stand by." Her hand went from rubbing her arm to making a clenched fist. "That being said, nope, haven't seen the shit. Been looking for him myself."

"Fair enough," said Greyson. "I haven't paid attention to the shiny prick. I have seen a few dead guards in the streets; however, I know there's more gone than those few."

"I could talk shit on him for days," Allarie declared.

"Same," Greyson said dreamily.

Outside the tent, guards had come running over from the wall barracks. They were all wearing shiny, unblemished armor. One of the guards held the Karnaugh standard, a clean ruby red with an emblazoned golden beer mug. The standard of thick cactus weave was attached to a pole and carried in front of their formation.

"All right, you maggots!" A surprisingly small guard appeared in front of the squad. He wasn't looking at his own soldiers, but at Greyson and crew instead.

"Allarie, you aren't from around here. I suggest you flee this time. They will lose you in the city of tents in the miners' quarters. I see the fire in your eyes. Today is not the day—just look around."

There were villagers tending wounds and helping others clean the area. Karnaugh was nowhere to be seen, but it was guaranteed he would expect the same amount of minerals from the mine as yesterday, as though the troll attack had never happened.

"We have to come back another day," Greyson said as he went over to the others, helping them cover their wounds with some supplies from his bag.

Allarie glared at the guards; then, she turned to the others and said, "It was nice to meet all of you. Hopefully, soon I will see you again." She waved at Greyson.

He tossed her some of the hardtack he had been eating and then took off for the miners' quarters as she sprinted away.

"You two made quick friends," Haan said.

"Don't get crazy now, Haan. She just saved my life, is all, and I did the same for her. It's a mutual respect, okay?" Greyson then headed towards the guards, rolling his eyes. "My ma…"

●————————●————————●

The short guard abruptly stopped, spun on his heels, and started to scream at one of his men. "Half-right face. Move!" He had crew-cut hair, small eyes, an upturned nose, and the usual short, pointed ears that were typical of those who hailed from the South. Southern folk had a darker hue of skin from being under the desert sun. Their bones were thicker, which created a wider frame for many.

The guard's legs moved faster than his torso as he was maneuvering through his troops. The troops looked clean and very professional, but their equipment was not as flashy as what was worn by Karnaugh's boys.

Greyson's face went flat, and he marched over to where the guards were standing. "Where in the Troutus ass were you all during this?" Greyson had left his sword with Pops. Less threatening you look to these softies, the better. Don't let their flexing fool you. After all, they believe me to be cursed. Confidence, Greyson. Confidence.

"What, what…what? Try Sergeant Killmead. Also, try fixing how you address the guards." The sergeant took out his billy club. The speed at which he moved was like that of a shadow. His body disappeared, suddenly reappearing right in Greyson's face. "What was I doing during this?" Spittle was flying, hitting the tip of Greyson's nose. "Tell me where it says that it is any of your business? Shouldn't you be swinging a pick and hitting some rocks? Pops!" His eyes remained fixed on Greyson as he moved towards the tent Pops was sitting in.

Greyson stood bewildered. In Troutus's name, do not drop. A little bit of the sergeant's spittle glistened on his nose. Unsure if he should move or not, Greyson remained still as Killmead kept screaming orders and requests for Pops. This guy won't shut up. He contemplated wiping the offending saliva off with a sleeve. But, now, this dude is grilling the snot out of me.

Killmead's arm flew out vertically as he rotated, moving as fast as his little legs could carry him on his approach to Greyson.

Meanwhile, Greyson was still trying to keep his composure.

Killmead was staring eagle-eyed at Greyson. "Pops! Drop. Move!"

The way this dude chews air pisses me off.

Killmead walked past Greyson, his eyes never losing contact.

"What the fuck are you doing, Killmead? He is ancient—you will kill him." Panic started to strike Greyson; he did not want to see old-man Pops killed by this loathsome guard.

Killmead scratched his upturned nose. "No, just no. You do not tell me what the shit to do!" Killmead's small, pointed nose was now touching Greyson's chin. He was so close to

Greyson's face that one might assume they were quarreling lovers about to make up and kiss each other. Some of the soldiers behind Killmead could be heard snickering.

"You call me Sergeant Killmead, boy…" He rotated on his polished boots and puffed his chest. "And for that, you can drop!" Sergeant Killmead screamed into Greyson's ear.

Greyson dropped and started pushing. Don't worry; it's a means to an end.

Haan walked towards them both. "Now, Sergeant Killmead, we will need you and your soldiers' help cleaning the area. We have been severely…" Tears started to form in her eyes.

"Whatever you need, Haan." Whatever resolve Killmead had, it started to melt away as soon as Haan stepped out of the tent, children climbing all over her.

"We've lost so many miners. Where were all of you?" Haan's kind face formed into a frown. "Don't you walk away from me, Sergeant."

Sergeant Killmead sulked. "Haan, please understand. We were ordered to stay in our barracks, ma'am. Let me get the men moving."

He sprinted rapidly towards the platoon again. The snickering ended immediately. As he stood in front of the other guards, he began barking about cleaning the area and assisting those who were down. He stormed over to his guards, getting into a few of their faces to shout and giving them times to meet with him afterwards. He then dismissed them and went back into the barracks.

"Get up, Greyson. He knows better…and the right thing to do. Life is not as it should be here; he knows that. He should be doing his job instead of listening to that sad sack."

Haan stood confidently, rotating her wrist and waving for Greyson to come closer. "I might not be able to swing a sword like you anymore, but I believe I have to remind that man. I am also his mother. Along with the majority of those men."

Haan moved towards Pops and helped him up. He had taken Killmead's push-up order seriously, his string-bean arms wobbling as they strained to hold his body bridged. Pops headed over to Greyson and handed him his sword, which was wrapped in cloth. "I think they need you," Pops said wearily.

Greyson took a swig from a water satchel and then exchanged it for his sword. "Drink water, old man. It is hot out." Greyson unwrapped the old sword. He then went along with some of the guards to help with picking up the wreckage.

The trolls had hit the area hard. Claw marks tore the cloth of the villagers' tent homes, and the different objects from the market were everywhere—various wares and food-stuffs. The salvageable items were placed back where they had previously belonged.

The village of Haneserrath was not wealthy. When anyone showed up at the market and purchased something, it was the talk of the village. They were economically developing and had acquired currency through their work, but a shameful amount was earned per day.

Pops was thinking out loud. "There is a reason the guards keep him alive: He gives them hope. Greyson doesn't give up, and that inspires them to keep going, because maybe this isn't it. Their small, miserable mining lives isn't it—getting beaten the shit out of isn't it. I like to see the optimism in it; however, more than likely, they just like seeing someone else getting their ass whupped." He gave Haan a toothy grin.

The market had a large bonfire in the center that was surrounded by vendor tents. No one went near it—it was too hot—but there were barrels of boiling mush close by that had been collected from the cactus farms. Bird feathers and mud drawings decorated the tents and surfaces around the mine, giving a small splash of color to an otherwise dreary area. The pigment used in the mud paint was drawn from the flowers that blossomed on the cactus grown in the farms.

There was a separate hut farther down the road. That particular hut attracted birds. It had attracted the trolls, as well. A troll's gruesome form was hunched over beside the hut, and it appeared to have just finished munching on some body parts.

4

"A Gull in the Desert"

Allarie was running through the miners' quarters. Dodging in between tents, she got tripped up on a stake in the ground and stumbled for a moment. She paused. She had to disappear or start hanging with the miners for a bit—some way to not be noticeable enough to catch Karnaugh's attention.

She was deep in thought. *I guess it couldn't be that bad around here. Fuck, am I hangry. Nor can I leave. I just exposed myself.* Allarie remained on the ground, staring up at the sky. She took a hunk of the hardtack Greyson had given her and ate it along with some leftover edible mushrooms that she found on her way to the village of Haneserrath.

Allarie had spent quite a lot of time in brushy areas on her journey to Haneserrath, and most of that time was spent hungry. As a result, she found that she enjoyed hunting for mushrooms—under logs, in bushes, growing on giant trees, or wherever humid spots could be found in the arid South. Keeping the mushrooms dry in the sun prevented them from molding, and they could easily be kept as provisions that would last a long time. She had a small journal that charted her collections and listed her favorite mushrooms. She had become sickened and had thrown up plenty of times in her quest to find the right fungi, but, luckily, nothing had been poisonous enough to down her.

The particular mushroom she was munching on at the moment had a consistency that reminded her of chicken, a slight taste of chicken, too—a true hen of the woods. Chicken is not a food found on the road, and Allarie relished the taste and texture of this mushroom. She peeled off a few small, dark pieces, placed them on the hardtack, and took a bite.

A tall, broad man and a short, stocky human with wild hair approached Allarie, their faces covered with dust and grime. "Do you see her? What is it she is eating?" one of the miners whispered to his companion. "I am so hungry. They haven't filled the trough today."

"I can hear you, you know," Allarie called to them. "It's a mushroom, guys. I found them on my way here. They're rare this time of year. I have some left if you want to split it."

"Wait…did you say 'on your way here'?" The two came from around a nearby tent. "Martimil is my name. I ended up here after encountering a group of the guards on the road. They did save me, however." Martimil's hands made a sweeping motion across the village.

He had a long mustache and beard, a round face, and his nose was a smashed button with an abundance of freckles. Despite his childlike face, he was about a tent and a half tall.

"Here with me is Ella. And we are the Timbers. Pleased to meet you, and I am going to take you up on that offer of food. We are a bit hungry."

"Allarie. But a pleasure all the same. Did you say you are also not from around here? From the looks of you, that is apparent." Allarie rummaged through her bag for more edible mushrooms. "I have a bit more of the hen mushroom and a shelf mushroom."

"Ella, take some and eat it first, so I know if it's poisonous." Martimil made way for Ella.

Ella shoved Martimil out of the way lovingly. "Don't mind if I do. I just know the less spicy it is, the more poisonous, poisonous. I am a big fan of spice, a spicy spice, if you will. Out of the way, you big baby." She started to lick her lips. "This is awfully kind, by the way. Are these people, people rubbing off on you kindly, too?"

Allarie took out what she could spare. I could use all the friends I can make, and since these two are not from around here, there is an extremely low chance of being recognized. She interrupted Ella and Martimil, who were bantering among themselves. "I try to be pleasant, in hopes of pleasant reactions. How did the two of you end up here?"

She watched as the couple went from playfully bickering with each other to attacking the food in front of them. It really isn't that much. Hopefully, they have some water. That hardtack is fairly dry.

Ella started to choke, so Allarie handed Ella her water satchel. Martimil was also choking and reached to take the satchel from his companion. Ella pushed Martimil's hand back. "My goodness, is this dry. Oh, we come from a bit around. Not really about specifics, but we come from a little island. All right, all right."

Martimil paused to catch his breath after a coughing fit. Ella handed him the water as he was starting to turn purple. He took a long chug, finishing off what was left of the water. "We are simple fisherfolk. We had a stroke of bad luck. Our boat capsized, and we drifted aground here. Now, we are miners, somehow."

Ella started to fuss with Martimil's hair. It was a bit crazy; with his long mustache and beard, it almost appeared as if all of his hair had fused together.

"Ella and I were in the middle of wrestling a fish when the boat capsized. Was a big bitch, right, Ella?"

"Right you are, Martimil, a big bitch, bitch. Was the size of almost the boat. We were lucky that day." She cracked her fingers and proceeded to grab another mushroom, gingerly picking at it. "Anywho, here we are, now very much more alive, alive, thanks to you feeding us. Tell us, where you are from, then?" She looked at Allarie curiously.

Should have anticipated that. "An exchange of information: I tell you a little, and then you tell me a little," she offered.

"Deal, deal," Ella responded. "You do know that you, like me, me, stick out like a sore thumb around here, correct?"

"Yes, of course. However, a seagull in the desert does need some explanation. I know of folk like you, but a seagull out here?" She looked curiously at Ella.

"I do not know if you know this, but a seagull is kind of a bastard bird, bird, but they are in abundance where Marti and myself are from. Also, also a better choice than the ram here. I would be eaten, eaten," Ella replied.

Allarie looked at her in confusion, with an eyebrow raised. "What are you rambling on about?"

"Just, this is not a place for us," Martimil piped in.

"Kick off where you came from, then. This is the most I have gotten to speak to someone in weeks, it feels," Allarie said.

"Kick yourself off as well, well." Ella took a stool from outside a nearby tent and sat on it, observing Allarie.

"I am from a Southern town along the coast, probably would have been fisherfolk like you; however, with the direction of things, that was not an option. I did not capsize a boat, though, and my mission here is more one of observance." Allarie did not want to give too much away, and she paused briefly before continuing, a stern shift in her eyes as she looked at nothing in particular. "I am here because of Karnaugh."

Disgust and annoyance could be seen on the faces of the couple when Karnaugh's name was mentioned. Martimil was the first to chime in. "We are no fans of his. He is particularly absent-minded, self-absorbed, especially when it comes to the health and well-being of these poor miners. You think we are hungry? Those poor bastards have been eating from those nasty troughs for years. I couldn't believe the conditions I had to put Ella through. We used to live on a boat, my boat!" Martimil was clearly flustered, and his ears turned rosy. "We try not to eat from those troughs, and the food we do collect we cook using our flames. These people do not know of the sickness that can be shared through the troughs."

Martimil grabbed a jar from his tent. He unscrewed the lid, took a small whiff, and visibly recoiled. "Gruel." He shook his head in disdain. After dumping the contents on a rock, he snapped his fingers, then wiggled them a bit, and the gruel was on fire. He used his magic to make the flames larger. "You heat it like such for a little. It becomes edible.

You should add a pinch of salt to it." Excitement grew on his face.

"We should do that with the mushrooms. Near the flame —not in it, though—then cook this mush over where the mushrooms were. Might soak up some of the juices." Allarie went through her bag. "Tell me more of the troughs," she said.

"They are not sanitary, as people are shoveling food with their dirty hands."

Martimil scraped the burning gruel aside. He placed the mushrooms down near the flame and took a flask from his belt. "This is from the sea," he said as he poured the flask's contents into a bowl. He wiggled his hands, and water rose from out of the bowl. It swam in the air for a moment before being waved into a small bottle. The man moved his hands and did not say a word while conducting his magic.

Dry white grains were left at the bottom of the bowl, what almost looked like sand. Martimil nodded his head in approval as he held up the grains, and then he mixed them in with the mush. "This is moderately better. I wish I still had fish to eat, but there are few to be had here. They would kill me if they saw me cooking one or even just smelling one—religious people in the South." He paused.

Ella rolled her eyes and then peered at Allarie.

"That potent smell—you know, I miss it. Like, tremendously. Fish could save us. Just saying." He illustrated the wafting fish aroma with an exaggerated wave of his arms.

"Save us?" Allarie asked.

"Yeah, you know, fill our stomachs with something other than cactus mush." Martimil's face flushed with disgust.

"The amount of horror you would see on people's faces if you cooked a fish. Our souls are supposedly tied to them," Allarie said.

"As if Troutus is anywhere close to here in the desert," Martimil replied.

Ella and Allarie tried some of the modified mushroom mush, and their faces lit up.

"I haven't had something properly cooked in a long time. This is a fantastic ingredient! Get your whiffs in—we need to stamp that out before we attract attention. I wouldn't be surprised if we already have. I just do not have enough mushrooms for everyone, or we could have turned this into a good time," Allarie said with a smile.

"You're right. We can only enjoy for so long, and we need to sleep and head to the mines in the morning! Another thing—we saw you jumping around with Greyson. He's a good lad, but gets himself in trouble, trouble. Best you keep clear of him." Ella started stomping the remaining embers on the ground.

Why would Greyson do that? He is honestly a bit crazy… and an excellent distraction. How could I not want to know more about the guy? "I guess I will be a miner for a day, as well," Allarie sighed.

"You don't want to do that. You need to leave, Allarie, however you came, while these guards are distracted. I was contemplating that move, move, as well. I can feel the sea breeze still from afar. This desert, this mountain, they are not for me, me. And the South lacks a navy, which is unreal to me. I believe, with all that is happening, we could sneak out of here."

Martimil began fidgeting with his hands as he paced. "I am not into mining for another day, and the guards have severely thinned out now." He glanced over at the wall. "Don't worry about Ella; she can fly out of here."

Allarie gave him a very quizzical look and shook her head. "Come again?"

"Her seagull form, which is very useful for our boating trips. She can sense the fish. Very cool. She is one of those shape-shifting people, or what is referred to as a druid in many circles. The people from the island, if you remember. She talks to animals and caws sometimes." Martimil smirked and got a far-off look in his eyes as he started to play with his mustache. "People do look at me strangely when I am speaking with a seagull. She might be slightly out of place here. I have some talent with the magical arts, so I call wind to our sails! It is a very beneficial exchange. It was actually in that moment when we started working together at Fish On, Fish Off, a great tavern. It didn't take long for us to fall in love." He started to stare off into the distance.

"I know of druids," Allarie said, rolling her eyes. "I also know of magic—although, again, rare here. You two really, really need to be careful. Magic here? I'm looking at the individual who grows wings. I called you a seagull because you are seafaring folk. I didn't mean it literally."

Martimil let out a slight sigh. "Yeah, I can do magic. But as you can see, we are stuck here. So, clearly, I'm not one of the best mages you've seen. Where do you think the flames came from earlier to cook us the food? My mind tells me to cook the gruel if that is what I am stuck with, and the flames appear. At least Ella, as a bird, can go to the shore occasionally and catch a nice fish for us, but it is quite the haul and too dangerous with the smell.

"Do you have a tent to sleep in tonight? After those trolls, I believe we will have a few empty tents. A heads-up—might find a fairly clean one." He started to poke around and opened a few tents, revealing tired villagers who stirred restlessly. Finally, he found an empty one. "I feel less bad—I mean, I still feel bad, but I didn't really know them," he concluded.

"Out of curiosity, why trust me so quickly?" Allarie followed Martimil and dropped her things in the tent he showed her.

"You have the skills and the wherewithal to possibly get out of here," Martimil said. "We don't have much of a choice. When there's water in the desert, you drink it."

Ella nodded in agreement.

"Where is your tent located from here?" Allarie looked around, seeing very little other than a small bedside desk, the one piece of furniture in the tent.

Martimil brushed the tent door as he peered in. "We are located a few paces from here. They put us in the thick of the miners."

Allarie found a quill and some parchment in the desk. She marveled at how the small desk had been dulled by existence and worn with ages of just sitting, a place for this person's parchment and quill. The parchment had what appeared to be various scribbles, long lines, and loops for letters. She read the following:

Captain's Log

I know not what day it is. I just know that the sun is out. Today is going to be a good day. I can feel it. When I went to the feed truff, I got the best part, I believe. Back corner, I believe less hands have been there. Keep your head up; tomorrow will be new. Trolls are coming, they said. I will write again soon.

Your Captain

Allarie looked at the note intently. Her eyes shifted, staring at the piece of parchment and then at nothing. A frown formed on her face. She folded the note and placed it back in the small bedside desk.

"The nursemothers like Haan have taught the miners and guards how to read and write. Ella likes to circle above and watch them work with each other as they spend their days drawing in the sand. There isn't much to do—can't watch me swing a pick all day, not for nothing. But I appreciate that she cares so much." Martimil was lightly clapping and making small sparks in his hands. "How have you been able to sneak in and out of here?"

"The guards here are not the brightest, so I was able to slip past them. I have been watching for a little while now. I know we shared food, and you seem genuine. I could be wrong, but, then, so be it. I have enjoyed getting to know the two of you. After all, you have been nothing but a help, and also you are not from around here. Your attachment isn't here, so you shouldn't hinder my mission."

Allarie took a seat on top of the bed mat facing Martimil, who was dancing some flames in his hands and flashing his fingertips for the flames to mock their movements. She glanced over to the side, and behind him was a seagull. He was right; she did look rather out of place here.

Light from his fire fingers gleamed in Martimil's eyes. "I believe we said something earlier about Greyson. We haven't been here for long, but that guy goes for escaping often. Like, he solidly produces—that boy is strong as an ox, so his production is off the rails. He should have been a guard or in the army. I am getting this much, and I have only been here for a couple moon turns. But from what the others say, that guy doesn't quit. And the guards give him leniency. They feel bad for the guy, for some reason, and he is genuinely liked, except by a certain few."

One moment there was a random seagull in the desert, and in the next, there was a fully formed woman who immediately began to speak. "Greyson has had three wives, and, no, I do not, not know the details pertaining to them. All I have heard was he was supposed, supposed to have two children by now. Which leads me to believe, believe they did not make it through childbirth. That is sad, sad. I believe they believe him to be cursed, and they do not kill him out of fear, fear they might obtain his curse, as well. The two wives dead from birth; then, what happened to the third really sealed the deal, deal in their heads. And why bother to chance, chance it when he is well liked and brings in plenty of ore for them?" Ella had spat the information out as if she had been holding on to it for a while, awkwardly clearing her throat afterwards. "He is interesting, interesting."

"All right, all right, dude. Keep it in your pants," Martimil told his wife.

"Just stating the obvious, obvious," Ella retorted. "He'll find you again, again." She looked back over at Allarie.

Allarie tilted her head at Ella. "You think?"

"Hands down, absolutely, absolutely, you are his type," she responded. "He has his issues with authority."

Allarie looked at the tent roof and changed the subject. "I need to get some sleep. I look forward to seeing you tomorrow. Hopefully, we can figure out something about our current situation."

She tried to get as comfortable as she could in the tent, shifting about awkwardly, and then giving up and moving herself back into an upright position. Most of the villagers were asleep in their quarters. Fires could be seen flickering along the walls as cleanup crews were still picking up the mess in the dirt roads.

"What did happen to his third wife?" Allarie couldn't sleep now even if she tried.

Ella was watching in amusement. "You know, I was about to leave. She had tried, tried to escape with him. A jealous guard killed her. He really doesn't give up, up, but I guess his attempts are getting more pathetic. I think she also had something to do with that. We have clearly enough time to wonder about the guy, since he is literally the best drama around here. Why I had to warn you—women get the same eyes, eyes you did for him. I figured you should know."

Allarie digested the story while she started to sharpen her daggers. "I am not here for romance—actually, quite the contrary." She looked up and fixed her gaze on Ella. "Greyson has his story, and to be honest, he is a moving target. That is why it is not hard to hide behind that guy. For some reason, luck is just in his favor. In that regard…" She was clearly trying to soften the blow of how Greyson, somehow miraculously had luck under his circumstances. To Greyson, it was clearly a torturous existence that he was trying to escape.

"What is the contrary part, then?" Martimil asked, brushing his thick red beard.

"How much do the two of you know about Karnaugh?" Allarie was still sharpening her blades, being sure to sharpen both evenly.

Ella's and Martimil's faces met, each furrowing their brow. Martimil shrugged his shoulders. "We should have guessed. Someone like you doesn't come out of nowhere here," Martimil said. "He is always surrounded by his boys, you know."

"Oh, do I know," Allarie stated. "But he is the reason I am here. With all that has happened, I have not seen him in ages, which is utterly disgusting after this troll attack. Where was he the whole time?"

"Ella said he galloped with his boys towards the outer hills. You can't really miss them with their shiny armor. But they left in a hurry. They can't have gone very far—I couldn't imagine those lazy oafs going very far, always avoiding as much responsibility as they can."

Martimil looked at the ground, clenching his jaw and narrowing his eyes. "This isn't something new for them, either. We hear the stories of how he bullies the villagers and flaunts his gold. He is a lazy man, but what happened with the trolls makes no sense to me. They were coming from the desert, where Karnaugh usually sends his boys. In the back of my head—I don't want to really think about it—but I think he held them off on purpose."

He gave an exasperated sigh and looked over at Ella. "I am lucky Ella loves me. I am so sorry that we got stuck here."

Ella sent a tired look back to her husband. "Buck up, son, son. You are acting like we will be here forever, and, boy, do I have something to tell you. Allarie over there is gonna help us get out of here, here. We have been here for maybe a few moon turns, and I am all set here. I can't stand, stand watching you eat gruel, even when you have the mushrooms and flames. You are better than that, Martimil." She exited the tent and leaned on a rock formation nearby, casually changing her arm into a lengthened and muscled furry form. "I won't, won't have it."

"Ah! What is that?" Allarie pointed at the out-of-place furry arm on Ella.

Ella laughed. "It is my ram's leg. I can also transform into a ram, ram." Her eye's flashed excitedly. "The isle of the druids is a magical place that has a large mountain with a steep waterfall. Rams congregate in the area, scaling cliffs and showing overall happiness. The druids were curious about the happiness and the hardiness of those rams, so they decided to become them."

"You two are a strange lot."

Ella brushed off the comment. "When you are stuck, stuck on a boat with one another, you learn ways to entertain your-self," she said. Her face was now fully in the form of a ram as she looked at Allarie.

The village was becoming more and more quiet. The rhythm of clattering gruel slabs and pans being sorted and snores of the sleeping could be heard throughout. The guards had finally finished their cleanup of the area and were following suit, getting ready to chase dreams with the sleeping villagers. A few guards grumpily marched their way to the walls to start the first shift of the night watch.

The miners and guards had never experienced such mistrust of one another. They had to work together in order to survive and for the whole thing to work, but the guards were failing the people by not doing their job. So, there were miners who kept post outside their tents, watching as others slept.

For whatever reason, the guards were missing the night prior to the troll attack. The flames for the torches had been lit, but the guards were nowhere to be found.

But on this somber night for the village, there they were again, all along the walls.

5

"Eat you alive, ya old ham!"

Karnaugh was on his hyder, gliding along the hillside. His armor and his hyder's armor were bright gold with a red-checked drape showing his beer-mug standard. He looked at his men smugly. "Have any of you spotted a boar? Or heard of anything from that shit village?"

No response.

Karnaugh spurred his hyder's sides with great force and trotted farther into the woods, well away from town. He got to the entrance of the woods and dismounted, his gallant armor shifting. He took his hand, placed it on the hilt of his blade, and stooped down to inspect the nearby ground.

"Forgar! I need you here. Find the boar!" he erupted.

A hulk of an older man strode forward on top of a rather poor, smaller hyder that was a gift from Karnaugh. The hyder trotted forward slowly and laboriously, clearly not pleased to exist. It went over to where Karnaugh had dismounted, and Forgar leaped down as well, not as nimble as he once was and stumbling due to his massive size. Shaking its sandy mane, the hyder appeared to be physically relieved.

Forgar shifted a small backpack on his giant back, causing the vials of oil contained inside to clank and jingle together. He headed over to where Karnaugh stood, and he bent over to look at the ground, searching for any tracks. The sands were soft enough to reveal telltale signs for the eye that would allow for tracking. He reached out and rinsed his meaty hands through the sand.

Forgar's skin was leathery, a sign of the time spent putting in work for the expansion of the South. He had dark-gray eyes that were dulled by years of following the younger Karnaugh. A huge hunched back on broad shoulders completed his bulky frame.

"Think we gotta go farther in," he muttered.

Karnaugh called over the rest of his crew.

They followed in a column and halted their hyders side by side in a straight line before dismounting and then hustling over to where Karnaugh was standing. They performed every movement in unison; they moved together so efficiently that one would almost believe they all shared the same brain. The men formed a line in front of Karnaugh and stood at attention.

Their formation stood in front of the nearby forest. Tall, twisted, and gnarled trees that were nearly lifeless served as sentries on the outskirts where the desert started, and the men stood in a grim face-off with the looming forest. The eye could see a wall of dying vegetation where some of the forest had receded into the sands.

"At ease, boys," Karnaugh barked. He had begun to march in front of his crew. "It has come to my attention that the target is in this area. I am giving you all a mission: Find this boar. Then, we shall eat well tonight! Dismissed." His march ceased at front and center.

Karnaugh's crew looked visibly unfazed by what was said, and they moved out as soon as the command was given to find the wild boar. One of the men marched to the front and called for a lined search of the area, so they spread out and moved in unison to check out their surroundings and see if there was any movement in the brush.

Karnaugh walked back to Forgar. "So, how much do we know?" He looked up to his large companion.

The massive man had taken off his backpack and was stuffing his oversized hands into it, creating noise. He took out a vial of oil and popped the cork before handing it to Karnaugh, who consumed the substance eagerly. After the liquid had gone down his throat, Karnaugh's eyes glazed over and his head nodded. Forgar reached out and retrieved the vial, stuffing it back into his bag.

Karnaugh took a few more vials and handed them out to whoever was left and hadn't gone on the hunt just yet. The few who had hung around were particularly thirsty looking, anxious as to what Karnaugh and Forgar would have them do next.

"Better to keep them entertained," Karnaugh said to Forgar.

Forgar then followed the line of boys. "Come along now. They need to see you in the hunt."

Karnaugh started to jump up and down, his armor rattling as he pumped his fist. Sweat dripped from his brow.

"I am so ready!" He cracked his neck and let out a few rhythmic grunts. "How many times must I tell you that you need time to hunt. It isn't just go, go, go, as much as you like that form of play," Karnaugh said rapidly, his aggression starting to show.

Forgar unstrapped his crossbow. "Come with me. Grab your bow, as well." Forgar looked at the squad of boys, searching the area with a frown.

"You know there is a better way," Karnaugh called to Forgar's imposing figure.

Forgar walked into the forest and bent down several times to check the ground. Karnaugh was at Forgar's heels, following his movements back to back, mimicking him as he scanned the surrounding underbrush of the area.

"Hold it." Forgar stood straight up, showing his full, impressive height. "You need to leave behind all that shine, or we will be looking forever." The eyes of both men darkened. Forgar fixed his strong gaze on Karnaugh and nodded.

Karnaugh frowned. He rolled his eyes as he took off his armor. "Let's get this pig." He whooped.

Forgar took Karnaugh farther into the woods. They tracked some hoofprints, some fur that had been scratched on the bark of a tree, and finally some pellets. The boar was close by. Forgar attempted to sneak on his approach, but he snapped a branch, causing the pig to squeal and run off deeper into the woods.

Karnaugh leaped forward, crossbow at the ready, but Forgar steadied Karnaugh's grip. They had come to the nest and could hear the family grunting and squeaking in fear. Karnaugh licked his lips in eager anticipation. "What luck do we have here!" He lifted his crossbow until it was level with his shoulders.

Forgar steadied his stoic eyes on the family of pigs. "Take aim at the mother. Remember to squeeze the trigger on exhale."

There was a metallic clank, and then a bolt sliced through the air and struck the chest of the large sow. The pig let out a wheeze and dropped. Karnaugh took his time torturing the boarlets before finally killing them. "This is a special sauce," he whispered to the piglets, and they were stabbed with his sword, which was dripping in oil. Karnaugh laughed hysterically before calming himself down. He cooed to the pigs while he snapped their necks in a casual manner, as if he were uncorking one of his oil bottles.

Karnaugh gazed at the pig corpses with glee. "Bacon is back on the menu, boys!" he yelled in a thunderous voice to the line of men who were searching much farther away. He had Forgar carry the boarlets, carrying the massive mother himself so that he could flaunt his kill in front of the boys.

"Assemble!" Karnaugh shouted.

All at once the group did an about-face and headed towards Karnaugh. They made a formation in front of Karnaugh, and he inspected them. They were still wearing their armor, which was extremely polished and shining brightly in the afternoon sun.

"We are heading back. We have our prize."

Forgar stepped out, following Karnaugh. He was cuddling the dead animals and speaking softly to them. "I thank you for the meal you provide." He continued to think about the boar family, how it might not have been large enough. "We only have enough meat for us. We haven't been here longer than a few hours," Forgar stated, still gripping his crossbow.

"I want to hear the screams," Karnaugh sneered as he started to smack the dead pigs. "Time to head back. Maybe there are still some living!" He started to put his armor back on. "Forgar, can you get this buckle?" Karnaugh had loose-fitted armor hanging from his body since he couldn't buckle all of the pearl clasps.

Forgar sighed wearily, his colossal body shifting notice-ably up and down. He lumbered over to Karnaugh and adjusted his master's gleaming armor. "We need to return with something more than this, or we will see issue."

"And what will they do? Malnourished, tired from working the mine? They need to eat, and we have plenty of gruel. Why not reap the rewards of what we have now? We worked for this." Karnaugh smiled in smug satisfaction. He then placed the pig carcass on the rump of his large hyder and tied it down.

The brightly armored hyder neighed in anticipation.

"Mount up! Time to ride, boys. I have a harem to get to." Burdened by his excessive regalia, Karnaugh had to use a tree stump to boost himself onto the hyder. "Time to see how those weak pick throwers are doing against the trolls." He immediately kicked his hyder into a gallop towards the village.

His men prepared their mounts. Forgar led with his small hyder, followed by the rest of the crew, and they started their journey back.

"Reports state that they are overwhelmed at this point, sir. I do not believe there will be more combat to be had," Forgar said while riding next to Karnaugh.

"Cleanup? Suffice to say, I am impressed." Karnaugh leaned back in his saddle. "Do we have a damage report?" He gave Forgar a devious look.

"It was half of expected exterminations, but it isn't over yet," Forgar said.

Karnaugh's face immediately scrunched into a childlike pout. "Those miners are stronger than I thought." His grimace slowly gave way to a smile. "I guess we should stay out here a bit longer. Who knows? Maybe more will die."

Karnaugh turned his hyder around and started to gallop down to his men. "Listen up!" he shouted, confidence booming in his voice. "We need to head back out and gather more food for everyone! It is time for another hunt!"

His crew all looked stoic as they turned their hyders around and headed back towards the forest. Karnaugh's soldiers moved to wherever he needed them, without question. His proud smile never left his face when observing his men in action, as they uniformly did an about-face while marching. Forgar handed out vials to them as they passed.

They all trotted back to the woods where they had originally hunted. Forgar was looking over the troops and helping them get ready to resume hunting when there was a sudden shift in the sands.

Forgar paused before saying to himself, "And there he finally is."

He waited for the ground to collapse on itself to reveal a man-sized scorpion blocking their way. Its armored form was black with yellow highlights on its head.

"Forgar, has there been any other word?" Karnaugh asked, ignoring the scorpion.

The scorpion's head elongated as its legs folded in and began to attach themselves. The sound of cracking bones and bending ligaments echoed. The creature went into a ball, and, moments later, a human form appeared in its place, sitting in a fetal position. His armor matched Forgar's—silver decorated with curling green vines and Karnaugh's beer-mug banner at the center. He was a tall, blond-haired man with an ample chin and a nose that was long and round. He had a stoic, glazed look about him, and he spoke in a silky-soft way. "I bring word, ha-ha," he said.

Karnaugh finally paid attention. "Report, Crix!" he called.

Crix sighed, stretching and flexing his joints. "They are still on the premises; however, it appears as though they are being fought back, ha-ha."

"Well, did they eliminate or take enough of them? I cannot keep up with them anymore. They breed like rabbits, but they're not providing food like rabbits. Other mouths to feed. We have to find another pig now, I guess, in celebration or whatever."

They continued moving towards the forest line.

"Reports that I have heard—they have taken a dozen or so people, as well as a number of other things that were not agreed upon…" Crix's voice trailed off at the end.

"How many have fallen?" Karnaugh asked.

"From the count, I believe only six. Many more were captured instead, ha-ha." Crix shook his blond locks and started to walk with the group.

"Fucking-stupid trolls." Karnaugh took a swig from his canteen and showed his wine-glossed teeth.

Forgar grinned, which raised the ire of an already displeased Karnaugh.

"What are you so pleased about? It is coming out of your pay," Karnaugh stated. "Matter of fact, it appears it is coming out of all of your pay!" he then shouted.

Karnaugh's group frowned and grunted in response.

"Now, the villagers are going to request a rescue… Ugh, gross." Karnaugh sounded disheartened and shook his head in shameful disgust.

Forgar's grin remained. "They are strong. This makes me happy."

"Happy? Forgar, don't forget—you said that we are behind this season financially, and that this was the best possible option, or else we would be in trouble." He smiled wickedly at the large man. "Wars are not free, big man. Who knew the newest guards and miners could handle that?" Karnaugh had anticipated a valid reaction from Forgar. After all, Forgar had a soft spot for the villagers.

Forgar's smile dipped to a frown. He gripped his massive war hammer tensely, his knuckles whitening. "So, we are in trouble again."

"Are you getting angry, Forgar?" Karnaugh's smile widened. "Perhaps a spar?"

"Why is that always your conclusion?" Forgar lifted his hammer onto his shoulder. "Now is not the time." He sighed and walked towards the forest.

"Not the time? Isn't now the perfect time? Boys! Keep hunting. I wanna spar." Karnaugh went running back to his hyder in eager excitement. He then shuffled through his equipment and grabbed his shield.

Karnaugh's group had gone back to hunting, leaving Forgar and Karnaugh standing with the hyders at the forest's edge.

"Okay, time for you to get that hammer swinging. I am ready for it." Karnaugh motioned with his hands for Forgar to approach him. He then adopted an aggressive posture with his sword and shield.

"This is fine," Forgar said. Steeling himself for combat, Forgar took his hammer and started to trudge over to where Karnaugh was standing by the hyders. Forgar did not notice the single drop of oil on Karnaugh's sword. "Away from the hyders now; one sweep and we are all walking home. Crix, we will catch up to you. We are having a disagreement here."

Crix motioned for Karnaugh to move away from the hyders, and the two men walked farther down to the forest's edge.

"We will succeed, ha-ha." Crix took lead of Karnaugh's crew to go hunting again, gaining distance from Karnaugh and Forgar. "A crystal has been found. It is currently with Reevus." He continued to walk towards the boys.

Karnaugh's wicked smile curved on his face. "Very good, Crix. We shall meet back at the village and reap the rewards after this spar."

Karnaugh swung his sword in a circle and brought his shield forward, protecting his chest. After he made his full arc, he pointed the sword at Forgar. "That should be enough. I am prepared."

"Whoa there, Karnaugh. We need to stretch first." Forgar began to stretch. He then paced forward and made an about-face to his opponent. He gripped his humongous hammer in both hands. By all appearances, Forgar stood like a statue with his hammer.

Karnaugh walked towards Forgar, his pace speeding up as he drew closer. He pulled his arm back with his sword, still holding his other forearm with the shield forward. With a jerk of his arm, his sword stuttered, and he slapped Forgar with his shield.

Forgar spun away and shook his head as he stumbled back from the shield blow. He had been prepared only to deflect a jab and instead had gotten the shield. "Why the face every time?" He took his hammer in one hand as he was rubbing his face with the other.

Karnaugh was already jabbing at Forgar. His strikes were faster than the hammer, but Forgar's armor was able to deflect the blows. Forgar grimaced as he defended against the forceful salvo of aggressive slashes. He stepped back and wound up his hammer, and he then proceeded to execute a large across-the-chest swing.

Karnaugh had to duck out of the way; the force of the swing would have cleared him off his feet.

"I felt the breeze in that swing!" Karnaugh said. He was still kneeling after dodging the swing, but then leaped at Forgar with his shield leading. "You are still too slow, Forgar," Karnaugh jeered as he threw his shield-strapped arm into Forgar's chest repeatedly, scoring a few more blows.

Forgar once again needed to shake off the hits from Karnaugh's rapid assault. "Do not fret. You will get yours."

Forgar held his hammer straight out in front of him and began to walk towards Karnaugh. He thrust out the hammer several times, spun it around, and then moved it quickly to try to catch Karnaugh off guard.

Karnaugh had to take the blow from the hammer that time. He blocked it with his shield, but Forgar's force still lifted him from the ground, knocking him back towards the tree line. His body rolled on the ground, limbs and shield tumbling over one another, until finally coming to rest near a broken tree. Karnaugh lay motionless with his eyes closed, recovering from Forgar's brutal hammer strike.

The giant man lumbered to the shade of the split tree where Karnaugh lay facedown. "I know you are not dead. Get up and move."

Karnaugh lay lifelessly.

Forgar bent down and turned him over from his facedown position.

Karnaugh quickly rolled over and shot a fistful of sand into Forgar's eyes.

"All of these cheap tricks! This is a spar," Forgar yelled.

Karnaugh scrambled to his feet and then ran behind a tree. "Does this mean you give up, then?" he asked cautiously as he peered over at Forgar from his hiding place.

Forgar's hand was yet again rubbing his face. "No," he said as he took his hammer in both hands and heaved it in a downward swing, crushing the ground next to Karnaugh.

The man yelped before grabbing on to the hammer's shaft and using it to propel himself deeper into the forest.

"Let us just do this right," Forgar said as Karnaugh sprinted into the woods.

"Well then, you proud bastard, I'll do it right. Come and get more punishment!" Karnaugh shouted from the woods, bursting with confidence.

The trees had full leaves in this area, forming a lush canopy over the ground covered by moss and stone. Particles of sand could be seen dusting the surrounding foliage, as the winds brought the desert closer. Whatever forest critters that might have been in the vicinity had surely vanished at the presence of Forgar's elephantine body crashing through the undergrowth.

He held his hammer straight up and down in front of him, his hulking frame too wide to fit between trees. Birds flew away as he walked through the brush and shook the nearby leaves. "You would head into the forest," Forgar said glumly. What will he pull this time?

Karnaugh's bright-gold armor flashed in Forgar's eyes as it glimmered between the trees. Forgar rotated his hammer into a defensive position, his eyes trying to find more of the golden blur. Then, Karnaugh sprang from a tree branch with surprising agility. Forgar swung his hammer at the ball of gold coming at him, hitting Karnaugh with only the shaft, but knocking the wind out of him. Karnaugh was on the ground, trying to catch his breath and wheezing desperately.

Too hard. Forgar carried his hammer in one hand. "Are you going to be able to breathe? Actually, do not speak. Regain your breath." He paused.

"This isn't over, Forgar," Karnaugh rasped. He got back on his feet, clutching his chest. He uncorked his vial and sipped a few drops from it.

"We really do not need to continue. If we continue anything, it should be this hunt." Forgar started heading towards the desert. "Did you want more oil?"

"Hold, Forgar, I need your shoulder," Karnaugh said as he strapped his shield onto his back. "You win this round."

Forgar walked over and wrapped his arm around Karnaugh, but as soon as he did so, Karnaugh jerked his sword and sliced open Forgar's cheek.

Forgar immediately recoiled. "Again, why?"

"Because I can. You'll be feeling weak soon, there, big man." He then wiped his blade on a nearby leaf. "I really do apologize, Forgar. You must understand. I have my way."

Forgar began to feel his strength fade. He dropped his hammer as his arms failed. His knees buckled, and he fell forward as his legs failed, too. The mighty Forgar spoke between sharp gasps as he collapsed onto the ground. "What have you done? I cannot feel my arms." Drops of blood appeared on his cheeks.

"Forgar, you know you will always outmuscle me; however, I will always outsmart you. I think the treasury is doing well again." Karnaugh smiled to himself smugly.

"What do you mean?" Forgar asked as he spit blood on the ground. "Wha ith hap…" His motor functions were going haywire, and he stared at Karnaugh in disbelief.

"Forgar? Forgar!" Karnaugh shouted. After grabbing Forgar's pack, he headed towards the desert.

Forgar was unable to move, unable to speak—just glazed eyes of panic, blinking, looking at Karnaugh as he walked away.

—————•—————

A troll was lingering by the hotbox. It appeared to be feasting on a charred corpse. Further from the hotbox was the area where the villagers incinerated their deceased, a perfect place for a troll buffet.

Greyson gripped his sword tightly. The more time he spent with the blade, the better it felt in his hands. He had been followed by some of the town's guards. Sergeant Killmead showed up a little while later, armed with a sword that was far too big for him.

Greyson and Sergeant Killmead stood next to one another, peering cautiously at the troll that was devouring their fallen comrades. As they approached, more trolls on the hill near the outhouse were shambling towards their feasting companion.

"I firmly believe we should allow this troll to dispose of these bodies for us," Killmead flatly stated in a low tone.

Greyson cocked his head. "I think we should respect the bodies, but the dead are dead. That is a lot of work that is being taken care of. I think I agree with you."

They stood side by side and stared at the grisly scene until the trolls finally noticed them. They each wondered why they had stood there idly watching as the trolls feasted, but the men couldn't help being transfixed by the gruesome image.

"I also believe we have gained its attention," Greyson said. He raised his sword over his head, put a smirk back on his face, and took off in a run.

The troll then charged, as well.

Killmead stood in disbelief, watching as Greyson fearlessly bolted headfirst. Sergeant Killmead called his town guards over. He started to give out orders: "We need to get moving. Listen in. Fend off the trolls, fight them, and make sure that guy stays alive—he needs to take the last hit with that sword. If he falls, grab the sword." Killmead had seen earlier how Greyson sliced through the trolls with little effort. "If that is not an option, be sure to light your weapon on fire. Can I get an 'agreed'?"

"Agreed," the guards repeated.

They were dismissed by Killmead and went after the charging Greyson. Each had his own armor or whatever they could piece together for protection. They did not have the same equipment as Karnaugh's soldiers. Each one was hooting and hollering, chasing Greyson into the fray, banging their weapons on their shields.

This bold assault distracted a couple of the trolls. Their course steered away from heading towards Greyson and over to the charging guards.

Greyson swiped his sword at a troll. The troll deflected his blows quite easily. Greyson was sloppy when fighting off the troll. Try as he may, his swings were too wide or too short.

Sergeant Killmead advanced towards Greyson. He unsheathed the greatsword strapped to his back. "Greyson, stay back and watch," he commanded. His right hand was located near the cross guard, and his left hand was at the pommel of the blade. He charged in as quickly as his short legs would carry him, and the troll went on the offensive, attempting now to throw pieces of dead body at Killmead.

On seeing the troll distracted by Killmead, Greyson lunged forward.

"Greyson, wait!" Sergeant Killmead shouted as he caught Greyson out of the corner of his eye.

The troll swung a corpse leg in a large, sweeping motion to hurl it at Killmead, but hitting Greyson on the way. As the body part soared through the air, Killmead smacked it aside with the flat of his blade. He spun around and continued towards the troll. Killmead looked absolutely graceful, despite his short stature and tall blade. He came up on the troll, which lashed out wildly at the little man, and Killmead deflected blow after blow.

Soft chunks of flesh were penetrated by the blade, but the troll did not relent. The wounds were upsetting the troll, more than hindering it. So, it attempted to pick up more body parts to hurl at the nuisance.

Killmead was quick enough to step with the troll to where it was picking up its fleshy ammunition. He sliced cleanly through the troll's wrist as soon as it had a grip on the leg of a cadaver. Its severed hand writhed in the sand like a crushed bug.

"Greyson, it is important that you watch their movements. Be aware of what they could possibly do next. This troll was outmatched, and it started to panic, so the first thing it went for was some kind of weapon to level the playing field. Since the troll used the bodies before, that would indicate that the troll would probably do it again."

Sergeant Killmead was tutoring and battling at the same time. His vocal pattern barely changed as he was swinging and speaking. This was a different Killmead, one that was hyperfocused on battle. His movements with his blade were dynamic and precise.

"I will need you to make the finishing blow after I cut off its other arm."

Killmead then swiped his blade across the troll's chest, raised the sword above his head, and swung downwards, chopping off the opposite arm. The blade passed through the arm, and once the troll's defenses were down, Killmead pushed back and shouted, "Greyson, now!"

After hearing the call, Greyson executed a swift slicing action. The blade had a white-hot edge as it passed through the troll's neck.

"We have to move to the next," Killmead sputtered.

The other guards were doing their best to defend against the two remaining trolls, parrying blows and moving at different times. One of the two trolls had been wreaking the most havoc—picking guards up and tossing them, brutally gashing most who were involved in the bloody fray.

"The big one!" Killmead cried as his legs pulled him towards the large troll, sword at the ready.

Greyson's face was bright, and he couldn't help but smile. "I don't think my body wants to stop right now." His adrenaline was pumping. He took off in a run at the larger troll, joining a few of Killmead's soldiers.

The troll had one tooth that hung outside its mouth, which looked out of place and was very noticeable. It had a large, square face, with larger ears and an even larger nose. Its mouth had an entire human torso hanging from it. The troll let out a bellowing scream: "Retreat!" The corpse twisted like tender meat as the troll broke off an arm from the torso it had been chewing on and flung it at Killmead. This throw was a lot harder and faster than the previous one, and it caught Killmead off guard, knocking him to the ground.

Greyson was able to catch up, and two guards broke off from fighting the other troll to come and assist him and Killmead. One dropped next to Killmead to see if he was wounded, while the other went to fight the troll with Greyson. The guard charged in before Greyson was able to get there. He was skilled and was able to deflect the first blow with his sword, but the large troll was able to get its other hand in on him. It lifted the guard up with one hand and then brought in the other hand to get a full grip.

Greyson and the guard both screamed in terror as the troll violently twisted and tore the man's body in different directions, creating a cacophony of sickening snaps and crunches. The troll dropped the guard's crumpled, lifeless body, and turned its ugly, wide face to stare directly at Greyson.

Greyson fumbled with the hilt of his sword. His regular smirk turned to a look of shock at seeing the mangled body fall. Out of the corner of his eye, a furious Sergeant Killmead came bounding over, his legs rotating like the wheels of a wagon. With his giant sword leading the way, the sergeant jabbed at the troll.

The troll gave a toothy grin and caught the giant sword between its enormous hands.

Killmead had to let go of the sword; he wouldn't be able to outwrest it from the troll's strong grip. He released and rolled away.

On the sergeant's roll, Greyson turned his blade and made a leaping jab at the troll, slicing into its hand and chopping off a finger.

The troll screamed and held the hand up to its face, staring at Greyson with utter contempt before taking a giant leap and landing behind the outhouse. There was a brief moment of peace, and then flying dead bodies began to be launched through the air at Greyson.

Greyson moved towards the troll while dodging flying body parts as they flew, finally rounding a tent corner to see the troll standing next to the burn pit. The troll was chewing on a foot, its square head with overly large orbs staring right at Greyson. It picked up a rather thick and bony leg, more than likely a soldier's, and chucked it.

The leg came spiraling at Greyson, who instinctively chopped at the projectile. His sword deflected it with a thump before being pushed back from the force of the throw, which made the broadside of the blade smack him in the face. Greyson shook his head after being dazed by the throw, reorienting himself.

Killmead circled a corner, advancing to where the troll was hiding. Still infuriated by the brutal slaughter of his guards, his face began glowing a bright red. He swung his large blade. "Same as before, Greyson. I will try to knock it down, and I need you to deliver the fatal blow."

The sergeant wheezed, struggling to breathe with a lung that might have collapsed. He turned his blade and tried to slash at the troll again, scoring several hits. The fiend recoiled at the slashes, but it then bunched its fists and started to hammer down at Killmead. He immediately dove out of harm's way and rolled around to avoid the ham fists thrown by the troll.

Greyson stepped in, and the troll had to divert its attention from Killmead to this new threat, as it knew that Greyson was the one with the dangerous sword. The troll noticed that the wound was sealed where its finger had been cut off, not growing back as would normally be the case for trolls. It screamed and leaped again, this time towards the wall.

The giant troll began its retreat as Greyson and Killmead quickly followed it to the wall. They were able to see a group of fleeing trolls that had climbed over the wall, carrying some of the villagers with them. The gigantic troll grabbed a screaming, hapless villager as it leaped over the wall and escaped.

The last remaining troll in the village could be seen crumbling in a fiery ball in front of the rest of Sergeant Killmead's onlooking guards.

6

"Pass me the mead. We're going for a kill"

Allarie could not sleep in someone else's bed; it felt too strange. She looked out at the sleeping village through the tent flap and spied a troll as it leaped and climbed over the wall, to disappear into the desert. It slowly faded off into the distance, and all that she could see then were two figures near the wall.

She decided to go over to them and ask about the troll. She didn't know who the figures were, but much to her surprise, one of them was Greyson, who was inspecting the portion of the wall where the troll had escaped.

Greyson saw Allarie approaching. "I know her," he shouted to Killmead, who wasn't paying attention. Greyson waved and said, "By any chance did you see where a rather large troll ran off to? He is big and fucking dumb looking."

Allarie walked towards Greyson. "I did get a glance at your troll. He climbed over the wall and took off into the desert somewhere." She made a waving motion with her arms. She then shifted her eyes to look at Sergeant Killmead. "New friend?"

"Sergeant Killmead is going on a hunt for trolls with us. He knows it is the right thing to do," Greyson said confidently. "We have to get outside the walls, Sergeant."

Killmead was still kneeling beside the crumpled, dead body of one of his guards. The body was properly mangled, lifeless. The sergeant had his head bowed and a hand placed over the guard's eyes. He said something softly in prayer. He then stood up and walked over to where Allarie and Greyson were standing.

Killmead didn't hesitate to discuss the situation. "We know where that last troll went off to? I can only assume the location. I know where they come from, if that is where you think they are headed."

"Allarie said that it went over the wall and into the desert. Can we head outside these walls to hunt it?" Greyson asked.

"I am a guard; you are a miner—we have no business going hunting for trolls, as much as we would like to. That being said, let's go." He slapped his heavy blade on his palm a few times and then strapped it to his back. "I am going to tell my squad that I am going with you to get revenge for our fallen comrade. I doubt there will be an objection. Let's move out," Sergeant Killmead said with finality.

"Greyson, we need to grab some people before we go. I believe they could help us immensely on this mission. They are not from around here," Allarie said.

Martimil and Ella came out of the tent village, holding hands. "I hope you don't mind, but we came along, anyway. We will be accompanying you," Martimil said.

"Allarie, we need to speak." Greyson took her hand and walked away from the group. "Hey, listen, I know you made some friends, but this isn't some walk in the park. I have been trying to get out of here for years. They look like a very sweet couple, but…"

Allarie motioned with her hand at Martimil and Ella, gaining their attention.

"I can't risk this mission because you made some friends," Greyson added quickly.

Allarie saw the look of desperation in Greyson's eyes. "Greyson, get to know these people before you judge so swiftly. You have taken me on, as well. I choose to bring them. I believe they can help me with what I am doing, Greyson. You and I still have drastically different missions here."

"I do not believe we ever discussed what exactly you were doing, anyway. Skilled with a blade in such a way, one would think you were using magic when you fight." Greyson knew he wouldn't have gotten this far without Allarie's assistance, and this was the closest he had ever come to escaping the drudgery of the hellish mining village. He took a swig from his water pouch. He looked at the couple and then to Allarie, then back to the couple before looking at Allarie once again.

Allarie rolled her eyes. "He uses fire magic. She can fly. Logic, Greyson. We use what is available, and, luckily, like us, they want to get the hell out of here, too."

"Fine. I am sure everyone would like to get out of here, and Sergeant Killmead and I—we're buds—have a troll to catch. They are welcome to follow." Greyson motioned for Martimil and Ella to come.

Ella let go of Martimil's hand and stepped forward. "I have seen you before, before, Greyson. I just hope, hope the rumors of your curse are not true."

Greyson let out a sigh. "If I had a copper piece for every time I have heard about that damn curse, I could buy my way out of here. It is simply untrue." He walked towards the couple. "Hey, Marti! Long time, no see. How's your spot in the mine? Shit, I got to a softer surface, and, let me tell you, cave of my own." He exaggerated with the use of his hands. "And hello, lady who hopes I am not cursed."

Ella spoke before Greyson was able to talk further. "Fair enough, enough. My name is Ella, by the way."

Martimil stepped forward. "Well, you see, now I have questions."

Ella turned Martimil around to face her and stated, "Enough time spent here, here. Let's get moving." She spun him back around.

"We'll talk later…," Martimil said in an undertone.

Greyson and his companions headed outside the gates.

Sergeant Killmead saluted a few of the guards along the gate walls. They passed a formation of other guards, and Sergeant Killmead took off to go meet with them. After giving some instructions to his leftover guards, Killmead made his way over to a sand horse stable and spoke with the owner. He called over to the rest of the crew and instructed them to grab hyders. They quickly outfitted the hyders with supplies and bags, and the once-naked beasts were soon prepared to depart.

"We will bring these right back, I promise, sir," Killmead said.

"But that's what you said the last time!" cried the hyder breeder, an older man with a rectangular face and patchy beard.

"At ease, soldier. This time, it will be different." Sergeant Killmead then took a running leap onto the back of his hyder, immediately taking off. The rest of the group had to follow and catch up; they left the poor breeder flailing his arms in frustration.

Greyson caught up to Killmead, who had slowed down well away from Haneserrath. Killmead pulled the reins as he looked back at Greyson, causing his hyder to stomp the dry ground impatiently.

"I believe I know where the troll is headed. We have to be careful. The place could be treacherous after the order from Karnaugh. I haven't heard a report from there since that time, either." Killmead pointed to a tall hill between some dunes in the distance; it was covered with an abundance of cacti. "Over there," he said. "We should set up camp. I have some things I would like to discuss."

They had ventured out quite a distance. The scenery was dull in the desert, away from the village and away from the woods. Those who did venture out into the desert could see the windy waves on the dunes, the little bit of beauty to be seen in such a desolate place. With little or no vegetation in sight, such venturers often succumbed to death from dehydration. The only source of water was the cacti that were heavily protected with prickles. Unfortunately, no cactus farms were developed out in the middle of the desert, as it was way too dangerous.

The group set up their camp on the eastern side of the hill so that they would face the sun when they woke up in the morning. Although they had only one tent among them, Killmead had come prepared. He had some tinder that he used to light a fire in the middle of their camp.

"Only a few of them can actually speak. Whatever that troll was, it has been around for a while—from the reports, it was able to speak and even screamed, 'Retreat.' Greyson, you should stay back. I will not be there to advise you in battle. Swordplay is something you learn over time, miner man." The soldier gave a sharp chuckle.

"How good of a teacher are you?" Greyson asked. "I am not going back at this point, and I believe your boys are too busy to stop me from finally walking on out of there. I feel since I am helping out, you should give me a pass. I want to learn."

Sergeant Killmead gave Greyson a stern look. "I agree to the terms...on one condition: I need your help to finish these trolls, as you have luck on your side. I messed up, allowing for this travesty. I can't believe I allowed it."

———————•———————

Til'lock watched the villagers. The troll had watched as the humans brought their defenses down in the village, as was agreed; however, it did not anticipate an undefended village being able to kill so many trolls. Til'lock had leaped away just in time.

The puny one with that sword—that one hurts. Til'lock rubbed where it was now missing a finger because of the magic blade. The trolls were reckless this time. Stupid humans, they are weak. We need to gather in greater numbers before we go back. Forget the agreement—this ends now. Nasty humans.

The humongous troll headed back towards the portal where other trolls had come from, a gathering place before wandering the desert. In the midst of the desert floor's broad and monotonous expanse was a dim pit of ugly trolls that were hitting, punching, and ripping each other apart. Glass stairs led to a ripped-open portal, the desert troll's Keep of Morhoth.

Til'lock could recall a wizard's face with a shaggy beard —the face disappeared as quickly as it had appeared, leaving Til'lock and a group of other trolls inside of a pit. It was Til'lock's home, and those inside listened to him. Luckily for Til'lock, bigger was better among trolls, and he happened to be quite large.

Til'lock casually walked among them. He growled at any threatening look, but mostly the other trolls cowered. On occasion, trolls stepped up to challenge Til'lock's authority, but their skulls were eventually crushed by the mighty troll. Til'lock walked by a group of trolls greedily ripping apart a dead animal. One appeared to have more of the animal than the other, so a brawl started. A raging troll punched one of the others square across the face, giving a satisfying crack of its jaw.

The entire keep was filled with a seething mass of troll bodies, their faces stuffed with animal parts and spattered in blood. Til'lock decided to address the trolls after they finished feeding.

The troll keep was a large, winding, walled circle with stairs that led to a pit in the center on the lowest level. The pit contained plenty of bones, and the trolls were constantly cheering as fights broke out all day, either between the trolls themselves or between trolls and various beasts they had captured.

Sometimes, the trolls were lucky enough to capture a human. Humans always put up a fight, so they were highly desirable trophies to a troll. The savored taste of human flesh made them a delicacy, as well.

One of the trolls approached Til'lock. "Back so fast," it said as it wiped blood from its chin.

With a toothy frown, Til'lock glared at the troll. "I have weakened them. We must go back—end them, eat them." Til'lock went to the meat pile and picked up a leg, dipped it in a pool of blood, and then ate it down to the bone.

"You failed, Til'lock!" It laughed, pointing at Til'lock with a long, thin finger.

Til'lock grabbed the extended finger and snapped it. "You have failed, Minow. How many more trolls have amassed since I left?"

Minow winced in pain and slapped the ground. "That was not the plan."

Til'lock looked at the trolls ripping each other apart in the pit at the center of the keep. They were generating more of themselves. They fought—and it was painful—but the more they tore each other apart, the quicker they would multiply. The bigger the piece of troll that fell off, the quicker they would spawn; the bigger the chunk torn off, the louder the crowd would cheer.

There were not many trolls left after the unsuccessful raid of the village, and the crowd was much smaller than usual.

Til'lock had lost more trolls than it had thought possible, and now they must wait. Luckily, humans do not multiply like trolls do.

The pit had traps, as the trolls liked to see suffering and danger. There were falls from great heights—for seeing a good fall was entertaining, as well—and walls that were pronged to impale those that were pushed against them. In the center of the pit was a dark black crystal. They loved the crystal; it told the trolls to fight, to multiply. The trolls smelled like rot and death, as they should, for the whole place reeked with the sickly-sweet smell of rotting carcasses. Other than bones and refuse, there was very little adornment in the keep since trolls are not interior decorators. Trolls simply enjoy eating, lazing around, and, down to the core of a troll's soul, they always want battle, but on their time and their terms..

Til'lock stood up, cracked fingers on one hand, and glanced at Minow. "I will get my revenge." Til'lock turned towards the other troll abruptly. "Time to do some of this myself," Til'lock said angrily before leaping from a balcony into the arena of the pit. The troll started to grunt and yell, "I need more volunteers!"

Another troll leaped down. It was on the taller side, with skinny, long arms. It was about seven feet in height, shorter than Til'lock, but clearly ready for a fight, as it was grunting and punching itself in the face.

Trolls are notoriously aggressive, and when they are not aggressive, they lie about, never doing much. Very little thought goes into what trolls do, and they do very little besides eat, fight, and sleep. They crave superiority over each other, and they want the chief to be the strongest, no matter what. The troll in the top spot gets to enjoy the most luxury and have minions do their bidding, and they are able to crush whomever they want to destroy.

The pit was where they spawn their minions. The more a troll tore off the other, the more offspring they would have, free to plunder the human land.

Til'lock and the troll opponent squared off, circling one another and sizing each other up. Til'lock started with a low kick that swiped at the troll's legs, swiftly knocking it to the ground in one sweep. Til'lock then jumped behind the other troll and put it in a headlock, spinning the troll towards the ground and twisting its head.

The troll, with its backwards head, bent its knees and kicked away at the last second. As it stumbled away, the troll put its arms up to throw a few jabs, but its hands were smacked away by Til'lock as they were flailing in an attempt to connect. The troll rotated its head back to continue more jabs, but Til'lock grabbed at the troll's waist and threw it back to the ground. The troll smashed a fist into Til'lock's nose, spraying a stream of green liquid into the air.

The infuriated Til'lock wiped the blood oozing from its face. It speared its hand right through the opposing troll's upper arm, trying to slice it apart. The shorter troll recoiled and gripped its now-dangling arm as it was huffing and moving away from Til'lock.

Til'lock knew the offensive had to continue, as the other troll was weak. Also, a follower was dangling there—Til'lock could feel it—another troll would spring from the arm. Til'lock rushed the other troll, its hands stretching to grab at the dangling arm and bite off the rest. The troll pushed Til'lock's face back and smacked it with the limp arm.

Til'lock knew to get back in there before the arm started to repair itself. The troll tried to close the ripped flesh with its other hand, not at all deterred by the severe pain. Since its arms were occupied, the troll desperately tried to kick. Its foot was caught by Til'lock, and the troll was tossed to the ground. Til'lock started to stomp where the other troll fell, but it rolled until it was able to get back onto its feet. The troll kicked and struck a leg, making Til'lock buckle back.

The troll's arm had almost repaired itself. Once Til'lock started to fall backwards, the injured troll threw punches from its still-functioning arm. The other arm was making pathetic limping motions as it was growing back.

The troll overextended itself. Taking advantage of that, Til'lock was able to lock on to its shoulder, gripping and using the fatigued troll's weight to pull up and then bite down deep into the torn arm with long and sharp teeth. Til'lock then used its other hand to tear the troll's arm off and tossed the battered appendage aside.

Wicked laughter and tormented screams echoed throughout Morhoth. Trolls leaped down from the balcony and scooped up the severed arm. The smaller troll was getting its face beaten in by Til'lock, and the relentless assault did not stop until Til'lock was satisfied that the troll was sufficiently knocked out.

Til'lock went to work at piecing out the troll's body into how it wanted to establish a squad. As per usual, arms and legs were made into separate trolls, and a cut could be made along the stomach to split the torso into two trolls, or the torso could be left intact to get one larger troll. The head would be left to regrow itself so that the original troll would live on to join the winner of the fight or to live in shame. To be utterly picked apart, just as Til'lock was doing to this troll, was the ultimate disrespect, but it was still highly preferable to join the victor's crew than to live in shame. That was the troll way.

Til'lock was known to be a conqueror and had done this many times before. Many human villages had been fed to the hive.

Til'lock raised the troll's head by its hair. "Who is next?" Til'lock shouted while scanning the crowd. The victorious troll slapped a large, solid, hexagonal crystal that rested on a glossy pedestal of what looked like clear glass, about five feet from the ground in the center of the pit. "Who wishes to join me?"

The humans had been stronger than anticipated, and Til'lock hadn't advanced into the village as far as the troll thought it would. Til'lock did not have time to spare, but there was a need for a larger troll presence to finish the humans off. The trolls wanted blood, and Til'lock wanted the village to be wiped off Amerthine.

Greyson stirred awake. He had been sleeping next to the embers of the fire that the group huddled around to save themselves from freezing in the cold desert night. Allarie woke up next to him. They groggily looked at each other and then at the rest of the snoring group. By far, the loudest one snoring was Ella, but Martimil was still snuggled right next to her.

Allarie motioned for Greyson to follow her, and they headed a short distance outside the camp. "You do know that you could run at this point, right?" Allarie yawned at Greyson.

"What are we doing out here?" Greyson replied. He picked up a stone and tossed it a short distance away. Greyson scanned the desolate landscape. There was nothing for miles around the barren hill.

Allarie gave Greyson a stern look. "I am going to have to go back after this. I have some unfinished business in that village. Obviously, I do not wish for you to come with me…" Her words lingered.

"I didn't even ask you to come, or did I?" Greyson scratched his head. He looked back at the others, who were now budging as they began to wake. "If you need to get back, then go back to the village." He shrugged with seeming indifference. "But if we're being real, I know you will be taking point. You appear to know what you are doing." He smiled again.

"Karnaugh's gone. I don't know where he went, and now I feel the need to help this village. They deserve so much better than him," Allarie huffed. She stabbed the sand with her dagger.

"You should just want to help. It is the right thing to do, after all. Just think of living with the what-ifs. If we do accomplish something here, think what it would mean to everyone else!" Greyson had stars in his eyes as he looked into the distance.

Allarie just looked at him, dumbfounded. Who is this guy? "Greyson, get your head out of your ass for a moment… even though it's sweet. I think I will need your help to get what I need done. Right thing to do, correct?" Allarie was watching Greyson's face expectantly.

He nodded, and her expression immediately changed to a look of concern. "These people trust you, Greyson. I think we can come up with something to get to Karnaugh."

"As much as I hate the guy, that is a steep target. He does need to be removed, but that is way out of my scope. Such a challenge. I am lucky to even be here right now—I was mining yesterday." Greyson leaned a hand on the hilt of his sword. "Life makes me want to help out, but reality is telling me, 'Hey, man, this really can't be it,' you know?" He was avoiding her eyes.

"I think I need everyone here, Greyson. I don't think I will be able to do it myself. I think he already knows I am coming to kill him." Allarie started to play with her shorter dagger, her green eyes still locked on Greyson. "He knows I am coming."

Greyson looked at her curiously. "Why, Allarie?"

She frowned at Greyson. "Karnaugh is an evil man. I didn't believe he was evil to his core. He was so confident. He dragged out how he would take over a village, become someone that could build the place up, make it great. I ate it; he said it so convincingly."

Greyson shook his head. "You thought that was him, Allarie? The fuck?"

Allarie's frown deepened. "I know, but what if? And also, not like I had a choice in the matter. They had betrothed me to marry him, as per custom for Southern ladies."

"He kills humans for fun, Allarie. You had to marry that guy? Just awful. Glad you are here." He chewed on his mustache. "We need to figure out the trolls first."

Greyson headed back to the camp. Everyone was standing.

Sergeant Killmead exited the tent, looking way more awake than the others. "Top of the morning to all of you." The nostrils of his slightly upward-facing, pointed nose were flaring to take in a whiff of the morning air. "Was anyone able to get some morning rations?" He sniffed emphatically. "This smells like air!"

Everyone responded to Killmead's candor with a glare of resentment.

"Good morning, Your Majesty." Greyson gave a bow. "We ready to find this troll?"

"Do yourself a favor, boy, just call me Sergeant. Helps me distinguish who is speaking to me." His face turned towards Greyson and went from disgust to stone. He started to take the stakes out of the sand so that he could pack the tent.

"Do you know where we are going, Sergeant?" Greyson said the sergeant part in an exaggerated, flat tone.

Allarie looked at Greyson strangely.

"It's the only way he will listen," he said, looking back at Allarie. "We are missing a key component to the sergeant here: Nursemother Haan."

Allarie nodded her head. "Appeared that way. Why is that?"

"Besides the whole raising him, I think it is also because she treats him like a human," Greyson said.

Killmead fished some bread from his pack and ate. "Are we ready to move out?" he said, bread flakes shooting from his mouth. "We have quite the run. We should be there in half a moon's time." The others had already headed for their hyders, and Killmead called after them, "Time to head out, then. It is quite the distance. Better get your riding legs ready for this one."

"Do you know where we are headed, Sergeant? I would hate to be wandering randomly in this desert. We do not have the supplies for that." Greyson's stomach was growling due to the lack of gruel.

"Eat. You need to learn to use that sword." Killmead's voice softened. "I know that there is not enough time, but watch me, and do your best." The sergeant paused and cleared his throat. "We begin training tomorrow!" he boomed loudly… as if he wanted Haan to hear.

7

"Hyde Away"

The venture went on, and the hyders kept trotting along the monotonous desert land until Killmead motioned for them to stop.

The sergeant peered into the distance. "I believe the troll lair to be near that hill. At least from memory, that is where they previously took us," Killmead said as he patted his hyder reassuringly. "We take a pause first. Dismount, Greyson."

They and their companions formed a circle around the bottom of the mound. Killmead and Greyson dismounted and approached each other while their companions remained on their hyders and observed, stern looks upon both of their faces.

"Draw your sword, Greyson." Sergeant Killmead unsheathed his large sword from the scabbard on his back. "I hope you are a quick learner. Swordplay isn't perfected overnight." His sword reflected the unrelenting glare of the harsh desert sun.

Greyson drew the sword from his belt. "Let's do this." He postured his body awkwardly, with the sword outright, his legs wide in a squat position. He placed one hand over the other on the handle and pointed the sword at Killmead.

"How are you still alive, boy?" Killmead looked at Greyson in disbelief. "Look at that posture. I remember it from when I was ten."

Greyson dipped his outstretched sword. "So cocky. Come at me."

"I do this for a living, Greyson. Your pickax is no sword," Killmead stated matter-of-factly. "We don't have time to waste. Let's go from the start."

Greyson rotated the blade sloppily in his hands, fumbling the sword before straightening himself out. "Fair enough. Where do I go from here?"

Sergeant Killmead held his sword before himself, pointing it directly at Greyson. "Now, posture your lead foot to help balance, stretched in front of you, pointed in the direction of your attacker."

Greyson readied himself into position.

"Now, mimic this position, and try your best to maintain posture—vertically preferably."

Greyson got into position, making his best Killmead impression.

"Block this overhand." Killmead advanced with a rapid downward stroke.

Greyson postured in the best way he could manage, lifting his sword to block. Rust and dust vibrated off his blade as it struck. The impact of the blow was jarring to Greyson, but it was dampened due to his braced positioned.

"You will not be perfect by the end of this, by any means, but at least you can block a simple strike." Killmead withdrew his sword and repositioned into another striking stance. "When charging an enemy, be certain that you bring your sword forward. If an enemy were to strike"—he moved his sword swiftly into a parrying position—"you will be more effective in deflecting a counterattack."

Greyson nodded. He turned his blade and attempted to perform an overhand strike like Killmead's.

"Go for the neck when you strike. It is more difficult to parry that way." Killmead deflected Greyson's shoulder-high swing. "Now, if you see an opening, of course, you go for that." He rotated the blade and sliced across at a speed that allowed Greyson to shift his blade to block. "Need to be quicker. You have a smaller blade than me, but I can be much swifter than you. Learn to handle your blade."

They began to train together with more sparring techniques. Greyson still fumbled with the sword.

"If I see more dust and rust come off of your blade…" The sergeant shook his finger. "Clean it. I will be inspecting," he grunted as another blow was swung.

"I will get this," Greyson said as he lifted his sword again.

There was a sharp clang of metal, followed by several more. He overextended on one swing and was smacked by the flat of Killmead's blade.

"You are getting careless the more we fight. Have patience," the sergeant chided.

"We can give it another go," Greyson said as he puffed in exhaustion, leaning on his sword that was now stuck in the sand.

Sergeant Killmead, looking tired, shook his head and crossed his arms at the sight of Greyson. "You have got to be absolutely kidding me. You are going to start out lazy. Okay, okay." Sergeant Killmead was now orbiting around Greyson. "Get your lazy ass off of your sword!" he yelled into Greyson's ear, letting spittle fly free from his mouth. "Again, Greyson? Do you enjoy this? Do you enjoy getting yelled at? Get off of your weapon!" His volume grew louder; his voice cracked.

Greyson dropped the sword and put his hands on his knees.

"You had better not drop that sword to the ground." Killmead was in Greyson's ear now.

"I don't believe I can do this. I am out of energy."

"Better find a way. You do not drop your sword like that." Killmead's voice was insistent. "I have to let you know, Greyson; I am disappointed in you. This is not a mining pick."

Greyson got into a plank position, as Killmead had been pointing to the ground. "Clearly," he sighed as he placed the sword over his hands so that it did not touch the ground.

"Oh, speaking back, now? Not in the mines here. You'll get a crisp five more for that. I would say ten, but we are strapped for time." Killmead sheathed his sword.

Greyson started doing push-ups. He did them quickly and then leaped back onto his feet. "May I ask a question?"

"You may." Killmead stood with his chest puffed.

"Will you teach me as much as you can with the sword?" Greyson was now making sure the sword was clearing the ground. "I need to make a sheath of some sort. Check out how badass this is." He slid his fingers along the runes on the blade.

"I believe that sword is another reason I need you. I should just snatch it away from you. But you seem eager, so I will give this a go." Killmead nodded to himself, as if agreeing to a conversation in his head. "I was fairly curious as to why it had cut those trolls so easily," he mused. "I think you have picked up something of magic, Greyson."

"You'll never guess where I found it. That dirty bastard Ragz was leaning on the rusty thing this whole time. Always thought of it as a useless old relic, but the protector of the mines now makes a lot more sense."

"Give it here. It isn't my style of weapon, being smaller, but the swordplay is similar. Just follow my lead in the next combat we have, and we will spar along the way. There isn't much time, so I will not expect perfection. I know guards who could easily replace you." Killmead was looking at Greyson intensely. "But I need them at the village. I feel responsible. I need them to defend the people. So, we must go. And you are helping. Just a heads-up—this is most certainly a suicide mission; we are heading into the hornet's nest. But honor demands me to go."

"It is madness, but, honestly, why not? Let's give it a go." Greyson was feeling optimistic; it was either combat the trolls or be in the darkness of the mines.

"You act like you have a choice at this point," Killmead stated. "I know your heart wants the fight. I felt that, too, getting this position."

The group took a rest. Allarie asked about the home of the two island dwellers, and the couple were cheerful to respond, as Greyson and Killmead continued talking.

"Also, my hyder-riding skills," Greyson said, his voice wavering.

Hyders are desert horses. Their frames are in the shape of a normal horse, but they have skirts of wispy-looking sand falls that make them look as if they are gliding over the desert. The skirts appear only when they are standing on sand; when on normal land, they have slim, unflattering lower halves, and their efficiency in moving is diminished.

"You are not the sharpest weapon in the arsenal, but we will make it work. You have ridden a hyder before this, correct? You have been doing well."

"Well, you see the vast fields to ride these hyders under the mountain. It's quite the spectacle—" Greyson started.

"No time for dawdling. You are really going to have to learn fast and in a hurry, Greyson," Sergeant Killmead said.

"Once they had me ride a hyder for entertainment—'Give the miner a ride.' They volunteered me for it. The guards."

Killmead's mouth folded in on itself, and he cracked into a smirk as he snorted. "At least, you somewhat know how to be atop a hyder."

"It was so painful. It still is. But I am just too into being here," Greyson said.

Greyson handed Killmead the harnesses after he got the hyders ready to go. Killmead had equipped the hyders for a longer ride, placing dried fruits and other provisions in the pockets, along with some tinder and a rope. "Always be prepared," he told Greyson. "The desert is unforgiving."

They rode farther into the desert, towards the center of lower Amerthine—a collection of dunes, cacti, and some rolling tumbleweeds. The cacti in the desert were different from the ones that were farmed, as they had not been cared for and properly nursed. They were wild and, as such, had a wild appearance.

"Do you know where you are going?" Greyson asked, trotting up next to Killmead.

"I have taken this path before. There are specific things to look for to get to the target. I should have known back then that this was bad." He scratched his square head. "Three more dunes, two cactus plants, and, finally, a large metal rod sticking out of the ground close to another hill." The words marched out from his mouth.

"I am going to tell you here and now—my memory will not be able to retain that. But I will try." Greyson laughed nervously.

They continued on hyderback. Greyson heard a call, the first indicator, as they passed a dune. I got this. This is the first dune.

There was nothing of substance to remember about the first dune. And then, flatlands for the longest time, a strong breeze whipping their faces and slowing the progress of the trotting hyders. Another dune, then the third dune just beyond it. What looked like buzzards flew overhead.

"You see, this is why you can't turn into a bird, Ella!" Martimil yelled. "Look at the size of that thing." He pointed to where a massive buzzard was circling.

"You don't see me flying, flying!" she replied, bouncing up and down on her hyder.

The hyders slowed to a stop near a pair of cacti with wide flowers on top that were wonderfully blooming in a brilliant red hue.

"Do you think it is wrong, wrong if I pick one?" Ella dismounted and walked over to the cacti.

Killmead dismounted as well. "If Greyson is unable to remember these, you all need to remember. Know your way back."

Martimil nodded his head. "Don't touch it, Ella."

"Don't touch it Ella, Ella," she mocked, smiling. She ripped off a piece of cloth from her purple dress and then started to search the ground.

"You all need to know the way back. Who knows if we'll make it, but I would like to make sure that one of you is able to figure it out." Killmead's voice was serious.

Martimil raised his hand. "I think I have it, so far. Not too complicated, and I have the general direction of the village down already."

Allarie was looking up ahead. "It isn't much farther, correct?" she asked.

"Patience, Allarie. I think you really need to know how to get back. Everything out here will look the same when you leave that portal. Memory also tends to wane for some," Killmead said.

Allarie stomped a boot, and a frown formed on her face.

Greyson smiled at her. The others had gone to check out the cacti absentmindedly. "Whoa there, chief. I know we want to get going, but what are we running into?"

She cocked her head at him and started to pace.

"We will be fine. That was a significant number of trolls we dispatched. We just need to finish them off, or they will spread. And they are already so filled with hate." Killmead scratched his head as he looked into the distance.

Martimil and Ella were looking at their surroundings, making observations of what they could find in the area. They had both taken seriously what Killmead said. Martimil's face brightened with a grin.

"What do you know of this place, Killmead? Also, how?" Greyson asked.

Killmead sighed noticeably. "I wish life was easier than this," he said, looking at the flowers on the cacti. "When Hanes died, I felt the shock wave. The guards lost faith, became irritated, became evil."

"I could have told you that way back," Greyson said.

"I lost so many men to the changeover. They all tucked tail and ran as soon as they heard the name Karnaugh." Killmead made a fist and punched the palm of his other hand, shaking his head in frustration. "I thought we would be fine if we just followed orders. How wrong I was."

Greyson rolled his eyes. "Bro, that was your job. The fuck were you doing?"

"They gave us a celebration, rolled barrels down to the station. Told us to stay inside as we celebrated. Ignore what was happening outside, and we would be rewarded. They took us up to Karnaugh's tent. I made a mistake; they fed me and my guards an oil. I know what you are thinking—why would I partake? Well, when you are front and center with your men and then get asked by the leader of the village to take a swig, you do." Killmead's mouth formed an uneven frown.

"That sounds exactly like how I thought he was—just a dickbag," Greyson said angrily.

"Where do you even come up with that terminology?" Killmead asked.

Greyson smirked. "I am really going to miss my friends. I am trapped in a mine all day. All miners do is talk shit on you guards and the wannabe-king boys. The lot of ya. That is working in the mine. You and I aren't so different. You just have tools to hurt people—funny how it could change someone." He took his sword from his belt and swung it around.

"I hear you, but to continue my story—we can't change the villagers' attitude like that, not after how we neglected them. A large contingent of us were not there for the majority of the attack. It isn't like a few of us didn't want to help, but we just knew it was too late. We came out to see the aftermath of what happened."

Greyson was fidgeting with the pommel of his sword. "All of you," he said.

"Indeed, a great number of us were called," Killmead said. "I made a mistake."

Greyson was stringing some pieces together. "So, all of you had been convinced by this guy to leave our town in the middle of the troll-infested desert, defenseless. Haan saved you. No wonder why you are here. We mine day in and out, and you have one thing to do. Protect us."

"I grew careless when Karnaugh came to power. When all of the good-hearted guards—the honest ones—left, our accountability left with them." Killmead shook his fist.

"I do not blame them for taking off, Killmead. Look at us. Look at where we are." Greyson's arms did a rotation, motioning to the surrounding desert. "You know as well as I do that these people need hope, not some drugged-out lunatic."

"As I have been told, as well. I just wanted to change things up a little, you know?"

"Killmead, you? Out of everyone, you were the last I would have assumed would go along with the asshole that is Karnaugh. Should have hung in the mines with me, instead of that other douche. Not that you are one."

"The sergeant of the guard doesn't go to the mines. I felt obligated to follow orders; however, those orders appear to have affected everyone negatively. I will do better."

"The sergeant of the guard is not better than the mines," Greyson retorted, changing the subject. "You should have stopped in. I am sure the other miners would enjoy a sword show! They certainly enjoyed my hyder show."

Killmead laughed. "I will make it a point to stop down. I'll take my squad, as well. Maybe we'll share some gruel and cactus mead."

"You see, Killmead; you should have done that right away. All good. Here we are in the middle of the desert." Greyson looked away from the sergeant.

"I hope things can change," Killmead said.

"Same," Greyson said as they continued onward, the others not far behind.

They finally came upon a large rod sticking out of the ground. It was made of some sort of smooth black stone; it rose as high as a troll and was as thick as one's arm. The group could see a sandy hillside that loomed over them. Killmead said the pit with the portal in the center was on the other side.

The five companions sheltered behind a large rock, and they carefully looked over it to the pit below, being sure to hide their faces. They looked down at the glass stairs that spiraled to the bottom of the pit. A few trolls could be seen wandering the grounds around the portal, picking their noses—the large, ugly behemoths that they were. The portal shimmered metallically, expanding and collapsing as trolls went in and out.

They stalked the trolls for a while, discussing the best time to strike and following Killmead's orders, nodding their heads in agreement at his suggestions. Three trolls were meandering around the portal—one was swinging its legs in and out of the portal, and the other two were talking with each other near the end of the glass staircase. Greyson wanted to bum-rush the portal; however, Sergeant Killmead had other plans.

"Divide and conquer. Trolls are hard. Let us make it easier on ourselves by splitting the fight load. Ella distracts the aloof troll hanging on top of the portal, and then the four of us will divide the others, making it a two-on-one. Key to this is for Martimil to set them aflame with magic or to have Greyson finish them off using that sword."

They agreed to their next moves, and Killmead continued, "Martimil and I will take the one on the left. Greyson and Allarie will take the one on the right. Remember how we can finish these." He was staring straight at the trolls, not moving his head as his mouth spilled plans.

"Are all of you ready for this?" Killmead asked.

They all said yes.

"Ella, you first for this."

Ella crouched down, and her face hardened, turning into a beak. She then sprouted wings as her form crunched and shortened, becoming smaller and more birdlike until she fully changed into a seagull and flew over towards the troll on top of the portal. She stayed out of arm's reach of the troll and proceeded to squawk, enticing it to follow her. Trolls are not known for their intellect, so as planned, the brute flailed its arms and lolled its tongue as it followed the bird.

Killmead charged in as soon as the troll and Ella were out of eyeshot, followed by Greyson. The two trolls appeared confused for a moment as they looked up and saw the crazed humans charging at them. Then, they began to hiss, baring their claws. Killmead delivered a fierce overhead swing of his sword at one of the trolls, but it sidestepped and moved out of the way just in time. He continued running, and the troll gave chase.

Killmead eventually stopped, and Martimil was standing behind the troll with balls of flames coming out of his fingertips. Martimil began his motion to launch a bolt, gathering the flames from the tips of his fingers into his palm.

The troll was now running straight at Martimil, its full focus on the new threat. The approaching troll got almost close enough to touch the tip of Martimil's button-shaped nose, but Killmead once again sent an angry overhead shot. This time, he hit his intended target, severing the outstretched arms.

The troll screeched, its head gyrating. Its motions were wild, spraying troll's blood everywhere, and its arms were now crawling like worms on the ground. Killmead went back in on the now-nubbed troll as Martimil ignited the writhing arms with his magical flames.

"If a ligament separates, tell me, and I will light it aflame," Martimil shouted.

The appearance of Greyson's sword had changed. The rusty exterior caked with sand was gone, revealing a clean blade that had runes etched on it. Although the sword was in better condition, the user was still lacking in skill. He tried to imitate Killmead's downward blow, but he ended up stumbling, allowing himself to be smacked by the troll.

The troll was not able to do too much as its arms had to keep up with warding off the danger of Allarie, who was already flashing her daggers. The troll was attempting to defend itself against Allarie, but her strikes were too sudden to block. Troll blood seeped from the large gashes sliced into its ribs, arms, and legs. The troll gave a series of shrieks and flicked its tongue, the veins in its neck pulsating.

Greyson was back on his feet now. He turned around to see the shrieking troll and charged back in. This time, my swing will strike the loud bastard.

The troll was giving full attention to attacking Allarie. She was deflecting as much as she could, but the drooling troll was able to dig its sharp nails into her flesh. Out of the corner of her eye, she saw Greyson charging. She ran in the opposite direction so that the troll wouldn't see him coming. The troll was desperately grasping for air, trying to get to her.

Greyson was trying to keep up with them. Did she not see I was just knocked down? Have quite the run here. They were going way too fast for him to catch up so that he could slash at the troll.

She eventually stopped, and the troll immediately went back to attempting to slam her with its fist. Greyson was panting, needing to catch his breath before charging back in on the troll. He knew he didn't have too much time, as these things appeared to be tireless. He took one big huff of breath and started a run at the troll, both hands on the hilt of his blade.

As the troll was throwing a series of blows at Allarie, Greyson swung his sword. He missed his mark but nailed the troll's leg, slicing cleanly through it. The blade landed on the ground with a thud, as Greyson's swing had eventually dipped.

With a leg now missing, the troll lost its balance and fell, landing on its side. It had not seen Greyson's attack coming, and it stared up at him with a look of shock and agony on its face. Allarie backed off from the thrashing troll, which was now attempting to block the blood flowing from its stumped leg.

The wound wasn't healing and wasn't scabbing over; it was just gushing a fountain of green troll's blood. Its severed leg lay motionless on the ground nearby, not squirming, alive, and ready to create a new troll. The troll's ugly face with its lashing tongue looked helplessly at its body, which was losing blood and weakening rapidly.

"Greyson, you need to finish it," Allarie said. They were quite a distance away now from the others. She had not taken into account Greyson's stamina. She was lucky that he was a miner; he had more in the tank than expected, at least she hoped so.

Greyson heard Allarie and struck his sword right through the troll's head. Its writhing immediately ceased, the face displaying a slack jaw with a tongue hanging out.

Greyson withdrew his sword and turned to Allarie. "Anything serious?" he asked, nodding at her leg.

She shook her head. "'Tis but a flesh wound."

They both looked up to the light of fireballs being flung in the air, then shifted their gaze to a small man spinning a large sword at a gruesome troll. They nodded at one another and started to head towards their companions.

Martimil continued to send small fireballs. He avoided hitting Killmead, occasionally missing the troll on purpose because Killmead was positioned in the way. The fiery bolts seemed as if they were shifting the troll's movements. Their tactics were not as efficient as those of Greyson and Allarie, as Killmead had to brush flames off himself from the splash of Martimil's tosses. But the plan was still a solid one, and Killmead was easily able to defend against the troll. It appeared the troll was getting tired, as its motions were slowing down.

Killmead took an upper swing at the slowing troll. The swing was intended to remove the troll's arm, but instead the sword lodged in its armpit. With the sword now stuck, the troll used its other arm to grab at the small man.

Martimil responded by delivering a powerful gust of wind directed at the troll, bending the arm back with several snaps of its bones. The troll was sent spinning backwards with Killmead still hanging on to his stuck sword. Martimil grimaced in weariness and disgust, but his expression changed to a smile when he saw Greyson and Allarie approaching. He waved his scorched hands. They must have dispatched the other troll.

Greyson clutched at his ribs, as he was suffering from a cramp. Allarie ran ahead of him so that she could assist Killmead, who was now wrestling with the troll on the ground.

The size difference between the two was substantial, but the diminutive sergeant seemed to know how to defend himself against the oversized troll's attacks.

The troll's tactics changed; it started trying to suffocate the small man under its substantial bulk. Killmead had been good at ducking and diving away from the attacks, but finally the troll got him, pinning him down under a leg. Killmead's oxygen was cut off, and he blinked rapidly as he was losing consciousness.

Greyson was still a distance away.

With her blades drawn, Allarie was able to slip near the troll and strike. She could see the troll smiling vindictively, still distracted by the suffocating sergeant, who was helplessly swatting in a desperate attempt to free himself. She dashed behind the troll and lifted her daggers above her head before plunging them into its neck.

The troll wanted to scream, but oxygen had been cut off by the blades. It diverted its attention away from Killmead and towards the new assailant. The troll gripped the choking daggers until it was able to pull one of them out and launch it aside. Allarie had to roll away from the wild swiping of the troll's arms.

The scene was interrupted by an incoming word train from an awkward and angry Greyson. "You nasty fucking creature, vile piece of shit, fuck you!" Greyson shouted at the troll. He swung his sword in an unsteady motion due to his fatigue.

The troll was able to shift its weight to dodge the attack. Its breathing was still labored by the dagger lodged in its neck. The troll was grasping at the embedded blade with one hand while swiping at Allarie and Greyson with the other.

Allarie retrieved her other dagger that had been carelessly lobbed by the wounded troll. She then dove forward and stabbed the troll in the leg, making it buckle over and expose its neck.

Greyson realigned himself and chopped with his sword—an effective move, it appeared to him. The sword severed the head cleanly.

"Ella incoming," Martimil gasped.

The companions turned to see the soaring bird.

A panicked seagull was flapping its wings desperately at the four, who were now just sighing in relief that the two trolls had been dispatched. A troll was hot on its tail, clapping hands and attempting to slap the bird. The seagull was flying from one surface to another.

Martimil went sprinting toward Ella and tossed fireballs. The flaming bolts went streaking at the troll, one landing at its feet and the other knocking into its shoulder. The fireball burst on the troll, but it did not ignite.

The others then attacked. Martimil went towards the exhausted seagull as Greyson and company went to finish the last troll off. It went from a hungry troll to a very angered troll, and being hit by the fireball didn't help. The troll then saw its two comrades dead on the ground, and it went into a full sprint at the portal, attempting to avoid the humans.

Allarie took her bow out and pulled an arrow back. She unleashed the projectile, which soared right past the troll and landed near the portal. The others rushed at the troll after the arrow was sent. Allarie then set up and shot another arrow that pierced the troll's knee, and it collapsed right before the portal.

The five of them quickly approached the portal, scanning their surroundings for any threat. The portal had runes along the borders, arced in a wide circle. The area inside the border looked like fuzzy water, a light-blue glow that was interspersed with shadows.

Greyson stepped on the troll's back as it was gripping its leg and trying to squirm up to the portal, but it was too far. He sank his sword right into the troll's chest, ending its pitiful life.

"Do we just head straight in, or do we have a plan of action for this portal?" Martimil asked. He had his hand resting on Ella's back.

She was by his side, catching her breath. She brushed it off. "The hand is quite warm, warm."

Sergeant Killmead stepped forward. "We should come up with a plan of attack. I know as soon as we enter the premises, there will be hordes of them. They will be ready to pierce us with their spears! We must be prepared for battle." He swung his blade in a circular motion. "I am prepared for this. We can have the bird and the fiery-hand man stay in the back. I will charge in with Greyson, and the girl can come with us."

"I have a name—Allarie. And, honestly, starting your speech off with 'we are all headed to our deaths' is not the wisest of strategies. As we saw, there were bursts upon entering and exiting the portal. I couldn't really tell how long before they were able to exit again. My suggestion—and I will go first—is to go in, and if it is dangerous, we will leap back out. Only issue is, we are already here, so we should do this together."

She paused and looked at the rest of the group. "I'll fire a single arrow through, and then we run in," she said with finality. She nocked an arrow and then sent it soaring through the portal.

"Let's go," Greyson said.

"We go," Allarie said.

"We go," the group repeated.

They were all at the portal entrance, staring and waiting for each other to make the next move.

8

"Morhoth"

Allarie was first. She proceeded through the portal while the rest of the group carefully approached.

When Greyson stepped in, a rushing, cool sensation came over him, and he then appeared in a strange location. He was surrounded by walls of flesh. The walls looked as if they were made of raw muscle and tendon, and the area was lit by a cloudy red sky.

There was a hollowed man sitting in an unimpressive chair near the entrance of the portal. The man was pale, having not seen the sun in many years. This man was truly broken, and his sole purpose seemed to be to serve the master troll.

The man sat motionless and stared with blank eyes. "You shouldn't be here," the hollowed man said. "They will come for you. They come for all of us." His eyes were dead, his voice monotone.

"Where are we?" Greyson responded, unfazed by the man. Greyson was observing the blade in his hands. It was like a whole new weapon—he thought he did a good job of cleaning it, but the sword appeared to be flashing with brilliance, as if it were a new blade in this place beyond the portal.

The man's hollowed eyes turned to Greyson. "This is the last place you want to be."

Drops of blood fell from the walls. The surroundings were painted in red from all the blood, the scarlet sky doing nothing to dampen the vermilion environs. One thing that no one could miss was the stench of rotten flesh, a sickly-sweet smell of death, lingering in the air that was truly nauseating. Shouts could be heard in the distance, echoing off the walls—more than likely a human prisoner, trapped. The floor was bloodstained sand littered with remnants of body parts and other items that had fallen off hapless victims of the trolls.

The man deadpanned, "It is a troll pit, Morhoth. The desert trolls. Run." He just sat there, expressionless.

Greyson continued to look around, trying to hear if any trolls were headed to the portal entrance. Other than the attention of the hollowed man sitting in his chair, they had not appeared to raise any alarms in the pit; no trolls were coming. At any point in time, he knew Killmead would come barreling in, followed by Ella and Martimil. Greyson had seen Allarie's arrow that was shot through the portal, as it lay a little distance away. The liquid energy of the portal seemed to slow whatever passed through it, which was good news concerning Killmead.

Like clockwork, Killmead came charging in with his sword over his head. Killmead had gone through the portal with his eyes sealed shut; Greyson called for him to open them. Killmead's senses shocked him for a second. The sergeant sliced down with his giant sword, sinking it into the red desert sand.

He slowly opened his eyes, his mouth slack—he thought he would be heading into a mob. Killmead finally looked around at the sight that was Morhoth, the trolls' spawn pit. He had been told of the place and where it was located, but he had never been inside. "The fuck were the wizards doing here?" he said with a gravelly voice.

"You all really should not be here unless you are followed by an army," the hollowed man said.

"Unfortunately, no army is on its way." Killmead looked around and saw Allarie's arrow. "Where are they?" he asked as he walked over to the arrow and picked it up, his eyes scanning the surroundings for potential threats.

"They are making new trolls," the sitting man said in a monotone voice. "I just told you where you were."

An enraged Killmead spun around and approached the hollowed man. "Why are you even here?"

Despite being yelled at, the hollowed man simply looked up at Killmead. "You really shouldn't be here." He didn't budge from the seat.

The portal burst twice more as their remaining two companions entered. Martimil seemed to experience the momentary sensory shock, but for some reason, Ella was unfazed.

"The fuck is this guy?" Killmead said.

Martimil shook his head, then observed the walls, and spoke, "He is their slave, a hollowed man." He walked over to the sitting man while still observing the area. "He won't move from this-here spot."

Martimil examined the man's face closely, which was sunken and covered in pockmarks. Then, he wrinkled his nose and shook his head at the absolutely repugnant smell of the hollow man. "Stay back from this one, Ella; you might catch something." He started to backtrack, a slight frown on his face.

Ella nodded. "All set, set on that."

"Do you know if a large troll has passed through recently? He has a square head, ugly fucker," Sergeant Killmead asked the hollowed man. "We are on the hunt for him."

The hollowed man just sat there, staring at the opposing wall.

Sergeant Killmead redirected his tactics and spoke to the man pleasantly, "Come on, man, just show us where. We are about to go in blindfolded. Whatever these trolls did to you, we're about to end them. Point the way, chief."

The hollowed man's face looked up. His mouth twitched. "Was I just called chief?"

"Indeed, you were. We just need a direction. It is all red here." He pointed to the rest of the pit.

"Are you real?" The man looked at Killmead.

Killmead puffed his chest and stomped the ground. "As real as the chair you sit upon."

"Left, downstairs, right, back upstairs, take another left, and then down, down, down. They are in the arena area, last I heard. They are busy." The hollowed man looked straight ahead again. "Best of luck to you."

Allarie, who was scouting the area, took a pause to approach Killmead, and he handed the arrow to her. "That is more complicated than I would have assumed a troll's lair would be. You have all that, Killmead?" She placed the arrow back into her quiver.

"Are we ready to go?" Greyson looked at the group. "I think I remember what he said."

"Greyson, we are not at home. If we take a wrong turn, it could be the end of us," Killmead said.

Greyson shrugged as he proceeded. "Sergeant Killmead, we are in a troll keep."

They headed for a corridor to the left of the entrance to the portal. The adjoining room had a few large, open barrels full of rags. Pieces of broken glass, weapons, shields, and bones were scattered among large mounds of sand. Some of the mounds were shaped into makeshift couches; it would appear as though the trolls were using this room as a lounge for relaxation, as the sand was indented by their large body shape.

They continued onward, finally coming to an interesting hole in the ground. It seemed as if a chunk of land had just disappeared, and there was a glass staircase going down into the hole.

Allarie went ahead and looked down to the bottom of the steep stairs. She peered down a few levels, noting they were empty and lit by torches that indicated the floors. The group began to take the stairs down to the lower floor. There were no windows—only darkness, torches, and red walls with claw marks. They were about to descend farther down the stairs, but troll voices could be heard. Allarie warded the others off by signaling pushes with her hands.

Killmead looked at her indignantly and went barreling ahead down the stairs, his chest puffed.

Two trolls were very surprised when a large arcing sword seamlessly sliced one of them down its shoulder blade and came out the side of its abdomen.

Shaking her head at Killmead's impatience, Allarie immediately unslung her bow, firing two shots into the other troll.

The second troll shifted from a state of shock to one of rage and threw a couple of haymakers in Killmead's direction. It missed with the first blow, but then scored a hit with the next one, sending Killmead flying.

Greyson ran in ready for battle, the runes on his sword glowing. The troll had fear in its eyes when it saw the sword. It tried to run from Greyson, but he was too quick for the lumbering troll. Greyson chopped at the troll, which attempted to block the swing with its arm. His sword struck the scabrous limb, and it was cut off cleanly. Before it could make a squeak from its maw, Greyson slashed the sword back in an upwards motion and severed the troll's foul head.

The first troll had almost recovered from Killmead's assault, and Allarie was firing arrows at it while Martimil was sending in fireballs. Meanwhile, Ella was annoying the troll by flying overhead. The troll was swatting the air and lunging at the attackers. Then, Allarie scored a shot right into one of the troll's eye sockets. The feathers from the fletching of the embedded arrow were sticking out of the bellowing troll's face.

"Aim for the arrow!" she shouted at Martimil.

Martimil projected a soaring flame from his fingertips. Two shots hit the troll's chest, and a third fireball struck the feathery protrusion coming out of the troll's eye, setting its head aflame. The desperate troll made a few futile attempts to slap out the flames before collapsing and falling down the glass stairs.

The air in the room calmed, and the group looked at one another.

"We need to follow that down," Sergeant Killmead insisted. "Ready yourselves." He nodded at the others.

The group crept down the stairs, wary of any trolls that could have been alerted by the clamor of the fight. Luckily, the two trolls were dispatched before they were able to shout to alert the others in the pit.

They turned to the right at the bottom of the steps, entering a foul dungeon where there were prisoners moaning and shouting—a dozen or so people, all in very sad shape. Dirty faces stricken with hunger looked pleadingly at them. An entire caravan of people had been trapped by these trolls.

"Free us, please!" a caged woman said, followed by a chorus of similar chants.

"We need to know where we can find the spawn pit," Killmead said bluntly, "and the leader of the trolls."

The woman had a look of panic and pleaded, "Please, water!"

The group was in quite a predicament now, as they did not have enough water for all of the prisoners.

"Please understand. We need to face one problem at a time. I cannot get you water with these trolls still around. Where can I find them?" Killmead said.

The despairing prisoner wouldn't stop begging, clearly in a form of shock.

Allarie approached the distraught woman. "Could you help us out?"

"Is there anyone who will speak to me?" Killmead called out to the prisoners.

A child approached from behind the woman, clutching at her dress. "Sir, we need water." The ragged little girl was shaking, tears welling in her eyes.

The whole group got out their canteens for the kid, even Killmead in all of his stoicism. Allarie gave her canteen to the girl and turned to the woman who was most likely her mother. She drank from the canteen a little and then handed it to the woman.

"I am going to fucking flatten this place," Greyson muttered between gritted teeth.

"Right there with you," Martimil said.

Ella nodded her head in agreement.

Allarie put her hand on Greyson's shoulder. "It seems like we are already underground, but I get where your head is at. We need to keep moving."

The rest of the group gave the prisoners what little water they could spare, which barely left any for themselves. Allarie spoke lightly to the child, stooping to her knees. "Do you have any information on the biggest troll you have seen here?"

The child looked at Allarie cautiously and gave the canteen back to her. She licked her dry lips, which hadn't seen liquid in a long time and were very chapped. "Trolls chanting a name...Til'lock. Lower." She continued to gaze in awe at Allarie.

"Oh wow! Thank you for the information," Allarie said, smiling at her. "May I ask you another question?"

The girl nodded her head.

"Who are the people with you?" She pointed to the other prisoners. "Would they be from the village, too?" she asked in a pleasant tone.

The little girl shrugged. "No. Haven't seen them before."

A long-nosed man with parted hair spoke up. "Just get us out of here now. We have been here far too long already," he huffed.

Allarie ignored him. "I know I am asking a lot of questions! I just want to get to know my new friend. What's your name?"

"Ally," said the little girl.

"No way! My name is Allarie. Oh wow, thank you. I promise I will be back." Allarie gave the girl a smile, and the girl gave a hopeful grin back.

The companions had to keep moving, heading back up another set of glass stairs on the other side of the prison. Along the stairway were bones set in a line, as if a troll had decided to work on some kind of bone art.

"We take another left at the top, correct?" Allarie asked, taking the lead. The stairs opened up at the top to a large, open room littered with trash, bones, and broken pottery.

"Did you want to talk about the prisoners?" Greyson asked.

"They seemed rather, rather strange," Ella said.

Greyson continued, "Besides the villagers that we recognized, what of the others?"

"The hooked-nose prisoner who approached us seemed pretty awful," Martimil said.

"The village will fix that," Greyson said confidently. "I can't see the miners dealing with that bullshit." He shook his head. "And, Troutus forbid, the guards."

"We unfortunately do not have time for this. Let's get moving," Allarie said as she nodded in agreement. "We will talk with them when this is over."

Killmead snapped his fingers. "Attention! Let's move."

The group searched the sandy floor until they came across a hole with another glass stairway. They could see a very interesting sight through the glass staircase; several awkwardly sized and odd-looking trolls were pulling at each other and moving up towards the group.

The companions went into a smaller, adjacent room, hoping to avoid attention from the arguing trolls that were climbing a couple flights of stairs down. The group huddled to plan what to do next.

These were new trolls that hadn't yet had enough time to fully regenerate, so they were half trolls with oddly sized parts. The deformed oddities could be seen using their lopsided appendages. The trolls with larger legs hopped on one foot, while other trolls used their arms to ambulate. A few troll torsos were unable to move on their own, as the arms and legs were too short. These trolls were moving in unison, as if they had shared one brain at some point.

Every so often, one of the trolls would pop, and an appendage would grow a little. Again, however, not enough time had passed for these little ones to grow, but they were large enough, like a full-sized appendage with a small body attached. There was a big head running around with a small body—the ringleader, Frank—that repeated its own name several times. It agreed to be one of Til'lock's pawns that would march back to the village.

These developing trolls were called brolls.

"Over there, we must go," the torso broll called out.

"Where must we go?" said the left-leg broll.

"Over fro! Over fro!" The smaller arms of the torso broll reached out in the air.

"Want a little blow?" asked a small body attached to a large right leg that was holding a blood-filled skull. It took a quaff of the blood and then jumped in excitement with a little front flip and a blood-drunk landing.

"Focus!" said Frank, the full troll head on a toddler-sized body. "Look who has arrived," it stated in an oily voice as it beckoned towards the entrance to the smaller room.

The other brolls finally noticed the group of humans after they stopped distracting each other. They all said, "Frank!" in unison as they rotated to see the new arrivals.

The torso started to crawl towards a column on the far side of the giant room, and two brolls—one with the left foot and the other with the right—were hopping on their longer legs.

Greyson and his companions prepared themselves for the brolls to make their next move.

The legs moved forward, jumping towards them. The leg brolls each had one leg that was larger now, but an opposing leg that was about toddler length. The fists of the larger arm brolls were smacking the ground as the small rest of the bodies lifted off the ground.

Frank came forward, its face full of an ugly smugness. It flashed its tongue at the humans and waved the fellow brolls forward. "Look how confident they are."

A few of the other appendage brolls echoed these words.

"Confident."

"Confident."

"Confident."

Ella's bones cracked as she hunched over, her face becoming furred as horns grew from her head. Allarie nocked an arrow and then sent it sailing through the air, but the broll with the oversized head and small body rolled out of the way.

The party all headed towards the stairs after the shot.

"Dammit," Allarie cursed.

The arm brolls pushed forward, propelling their smaller bodies through the air and making their way sideways as their limbs dragged them. The leg brolls kicked powerfully, jumping high. Their ringleader now posed with its arms crossed, snickering in the back, where it had rolled away from the arrow shot.

Greyson's group moved together initially, but then divided, taking on what they could, and whatever body part flew their way. The left-leg broll did an overhead ax kick targeted at Greyson, who had stepped ahead of Allarie after her shot. Killmead forcefully pushed Greyson out of the way and tossed his body into the leg broll, which sent it down with a crash. He swung his large sword at the leg broll, but it hopped over the top of the wide arc of the blade.

The same broll came forward and sent some short-arm jabs at Killmead's face. Left jab, right jab—they were smaller arms, but hard smacks, nonetheless. Killmead had his hands full with the barrage of incoming attacks, swinging his sword wildly in all directions.

Suddenly, the leg broll was slammed by a blur of gray. Killmead looked over to see Ella, now in ram form, snorting viciously and leveling her horns at her next intended target. The arm brolls bounced in. With a single fluid movement, one took the other's hand and sent the arm broll soaring through the air. It extended its larger arm, coming at the ram as a straight arrow.

Martimil stepped forward, his cheeks puffed with air. He sent a billowing wind, changing the trajectory of the arm broll with his exhale. The right-leg broll made a leg sweep at Martimil, and he was knocked down. Just as he collapsed, Ella changed her charge to be directed at Martimil's attacker. The broll tried to roll away as Martimil sent fingertip fireballs at it while Ella's ram went charging.

The arm brolls then shifted their focus to Allarie and Greyson. Greyson was swinging at the brolls, trying to get them to avoid his strikes. He was wild, while Allarie slowed them down with a flurry of precise cuts. Greyson was being slapped and scraped by the brolls' long nails. Spinning and thrashing, he was barely able to fend off their strikes. But over time, Allarie's blows sliced them to the point that their longer arms were no longer responsive, and their running turned into jerky walking.

Sergeant Killmead was still brushing himself off after receiving so many short-arm punches to the face.

The left-leg broll galloped towards Killmead, readying itself into a crouch during its run. Just as Killmead turned to notice it, the broll bounce-kicked right at him.

Greyson slashed at the right-arm broll. It weaved its body to dodge the slash, using its large arm as momentum. The large arm scraped the ground in an upward swing, but the swing missed, allowing Greyson an opening. He cut its throat. The broll collapsed and died.

Frank found a sharp rib in the bone-ridden room and threw it at Greyson. It struck him in the shoulder and punctured his skin. "Got you!" Frank cried.

"Leave it!" yelled Allarie.

Greyson had his hand over what was the handle of the makeshift bone knife. The injury was unbearably painful, and it gave immense pressure to the rest of his arm, not allowing it to have full motion. "I can handle this," Greyson said in a dark tone. "See how your strange friend died. I'll make work of you next." He left the knife, but scoffed at the grinning, big-headed broll. Taking his gleaming sword, he went at a full sprint towards the smaller broll, but out of the corner of his eye he could see the thick torso broll gathering more bones.

The small, big-headed broll looked over at the torso broll, which tossed two more sharp rib bones. Frank turned its big head to focus its attention back on Allarie, who had danced her way over with her blades extended to attack. The broll blocked her blades with its bone daggers. Two swipes with the left, two hard right jabs, then one jab with a twist of her wrist, and her dagger dug into the broll's arm, causing one of the sharp bones to fall from its hand. She rolled and stabbed her dagger forward, which made Frank stumble back. The broll parried the thrust wildly, and the remaining bone dagger cracked. It tossed the cracked bone blade from hand to hand.

"What are you doing here, Frank, Frank, Frank?" said the oversized troll head.

"It is time for the trolls to get theirs," Allarie replied quickly.

Allarie thrust her blades a few more times before having to spin out of the way of a bone toss from the torso broll. "Greyson!" she shouted. "Get the thing hiding. It cannot move well!" She pointed at a now-terrified-looking torso broll—it should be an easy enough dispatch, one less thing to worry about. She saw Greyson start moving at a gallop.

Killmead was taking on the left-arm broll, which had gone on the offensive. It dodged a sweep from the large sword and slashed its claws at Killmead, scraping his face but not making solid contact. A leg broll then kicked at Killmead and smacked him in the face with a long, clawed foot, leaving a gaping flesh wound on his cheek. Killmead was visibly wincing in pain, his hands unable to be removed from his blade, and blood covered his face from the grievous wound.

"Back away!" a wild Martimil shouted in desperation.

Fireballs were sent the brolls' way. The leg broll had to leap out of the way, but the left-arm broll was still standing over the fallen sergeant. It lowered its meaty left hand onto Killmead's head, stuck its claws into his neck, and removed the head from his torso in a single sick, ripping motion.

"Oh fuck, he's gone!" Greyson screamed.

The companions were shocked by the gruesome scene.

Killmead's body was still gripping his sword as it fell to the sand. The broll was holding his head with a portion of the spine still attached, cheering in victory. It screeched at the humans and tossed the head aside as if it were nothing.

The rest of the party did not have time to absorb the loss. Greyson stabbed the torso broll in the chest as it was smiling and winding up another bone dagger to throw. The broll crumpled immediately.

"The little one with the big head, target that one next," Allarie shouted.

Greyson gritted his teeth. "Easier said than done. One at a time, dear."

Greyson started swinging his sword at the left-arm broll. His swings were strong and swift, but the broll was able to dodge them. It picked up bones off the ground to deflect some of the strikes, but the sheer strength of Greyson's blows shattered the bones, leaving the broll weaponless and screeching.

Allarie stabbed and kicked at the big-headed broll. All of its limbs were the same size, and it was more agile than the others.

"Just give up. We killed your leader. Frank, Frank, Frank." Its voice was acidic.

Allarie pointed her bow at the broll. She lit an arrow on fire and then launched it, but narrowly missed the smaller broll.

"Motherfucker, his name wasn't Frank." She reached for another arrow, hoping to ignite it before the broll approached.

"You missed. How mad are you?" Frank jeered. Brandishing bone knives, its small arms reached for Allarie.

Ella soared in as a seagull and flapped her wings in front of the broll's eyes, temporarily blinding it and allowing Allarie to reposition herself.

The broll managed to grab on to the seagull's legs and was getting ready to chomp down on a feathered surprise, but Allarie was able to fire off another shot. This time she scored true, and the flaming arrow was caught in the creature's wide-open, massive maw.

Its face went from an obscure smile to an ignited look of horror. The broll let go of the seagull and made a futile effort to slap out the engulfing flames.

There were three brolls left: the legs and the left arm. The brolls gathered together and locked their smaller arms with each other. Using the longer legs in unison, the connected brolls approached the group of humans, who had shifted their focus to face this new behemoth of broll bodies. The brolls flipped over and spun around, using the long arm of the left-arm broll to hold themselves up while the two leg brolls sent out a volley of kicks aimed at the group, who had to duck, spin, and jump out of the way of the large limbs.

Martimil barely avoided being hit before sending out his fireball fingertip shots at the large broll conglomeration. They cartwheeled away, dodging the balls of flame, and then turned around and headed back towards Martimil.

Ella charged at the spinning brolls in ram form. They saw the incoming ram with is lowered head ready to smash into them, and the brolls hastily split from each other. The leg brolls leaped to either side, and the arm broll launched itself at Allarie.

"Watch yourself!" Greyson deflected a long swing from the arm broll with the flat of his blade, unable to angle it to make a cut. The broll grunted at him, still barreling its arms.

Allarie regained her footing. She sheathed her daggers and took her bow from her back, launching an arrow at the attacking arm broll. Her movements in transitioning from the daggers to the bow were flawless. She scored a hit, and the broll hissed at her as the arrow sank into its body.

"It needs to die!" Allarie nocked another arrow.

Another arrow flew right over Greyson's shoulder. Her arrow hits had disabled the broll's massive arm. Greyson got up on the broll, his sword in his right hand cocked back while he gripped the broll's small neck with his left hand. The broll glared at Greyson and reached for another bone, picking up several with its long arm, but nothing of substance.

Greyson had a rage-filled look on his face as he gave a chop of his sword. His blade pierced its shoulder blade, cutting down across its chest and cleaving right through the broll in one sweeping motion.

"Help!" Martimil screamed. The leg brolls appeared to have pinned Ella and Martimil; they were attacking and holding them back. The left-leg broll leaped into the air and landed a kick on Ella, the heel of its foot landing directly on her head, turning her from ram back to her human form as her body lay motionless. The broll went from trouncing Ella to punching at Martimil, as the right-leg broll came to assist.

Greyson had repositioned himself after delivering the final blow to the left-arm broll. His attention was now on Martimil, who was fighting off the other brolls. He saw the leg brolls striking Martimil with concurrent jabs while Ella was down.

A red-faced Allarie sent another arrow streaming.

"Try your best to hold them off!" Greyson shouted.

Allarie turned towards Greyson. Her leg was bleeding from the injury she had sustained in the previous troll fight, made worse by all the motions she had made, and now her movement was slowed.

Greyson rushed over to her.

"Greyson, you have to get to them. I will try my best to fire from here. What are you coming this way for? My leg will be fine." She motioned him forward.

Greyson did an about-face and started towards the troubled Martimil, who was defending against the two leg brolls. Ella was still on the ground recovering, and Martimil was frantically scooping sand and attempting to throw it in the faces of the brolls, a feeble attempt at stalling them.

Shaking from blood loss, Allarie shot another arrow, this time going wide.

Greyson threw his weight behind his sword, but the swing was too wild, and one of the brolls slapped him in the face, cackling.

The brolls linked arms, rotating so that one was lifted off the ground and could start to swing its long leg. It swung at Greyson. He was moving to better position himself, but wasn't quick enough. The broll leg struck Greyson's chest, kicking him a distance, which caused him to stumble and lose his footing.

Martimil checked to make sure Ella was okay. She was gripping her knees, letting out deep breaths, her body littered with bruises. She needed to rest. Martimil clasped her shoulder and nodded his head in reassurance. The man had never felt such anger in his peaceful boater's life.

He rose from her side, holding his arms out wide. With invisible force, he pushed the air into a forceful gust of wind that blasted at the brolls. They lost balance and fell over, separating from each other and tumbling a distance away.

Greyson was regaining his breath after getting the wind knocked out of him.

"Everything still together, Greyson?" Martimil asked while breathing heavily.

"Together," Greyson replied. He coughed a few times and spit out a wad of blood as he turned to Allarie. "How many more of those arrows you have in you?" He started at a sprint, and she sent an arrow ahead of him.

"That was my last one!" Allarie shouted.

The arrow streamed through the air and made contact with a broll's neck. The broll clutched at the wound while the other one turned and yanked the arrow's shaft from its neck, bringing a gush of green blood. They both turned to see the man they had just kicked, now sprinting at them with sword in hand.

Greyson's face was a mess of sweat and red sand. The adrenaline pumping in his veins pushed him to go back in and finish the job.

The brolls went from smiling and cackling to looks of concern and anger. They lifted each other up and braced for the man who was charging at them. One kicked at Greyson as he approached, and the other was lining up to get a jab in.

A furious storm of fire bolts came at the brolls, one after another bursting, until one of the brolls was finally engulfed in flames. The last broll stood with a stupid look on its face, now surrounded by its fallen siblings and completely unaware of its surroundings. It stood over the smoldering leg broll for a moment and then leaped into the air.

Greyson was prepared for the ax kick this time and raised his sword above his head. As the leg attempted to crash down upon him, the sword sliced right up the center of the foot, exiting the broll's body through its upper thigh. Greyson's swing had followed through, and he spun his wrist to cut the broll across its sternum.

The broll immediately collapsed as it clutched its mortal wound. Its eyes looked frantically around, and then it was lifeless.

The four companions were now standing still and staring at each other.

"We need to keep moving," Greyson said, his chest rhythmically rising and falling as he was still breathing hard.

Allarie walked over to the downed Ella. "We might have to take a pause or rally somewhere safe for now. We need to catch our breath," she said.

"We do not have time. If you want to, you all can stay back. I can do this," Greyson said solemnly.

The group stared at the sergeant's body.

9

Til'lock was standing over the trolls that had sworn fealty. They had agreed to accompany Til'lock for a follow-up attack on the wretched human village. One of the trolls had a fat face and a round stomach. It can be a general, Til'lock decided.

"What is your name?" Til'lock's long face approached the pudgy one.

"It is Hug." The lumbering troll stood lazily, slobbering on itself and looking back at Til'lock with dull, vacant eyes. Hug was the last brawl's winner, and the opposing troll had been torn to pieces.

Til'lock's mouth grew into a smile. "What a name, what a name. How long ago were you born?" Til'lock was slinking around Hug, sizing up the other troll. "You are a survivor. Are you prepared to attack?"

Hug picked its nose. "Bored," the troll grumbled.

"Trolls follow you?" Til'lock smacked itself on the chest and rotated an arm around, gesturing towards the small collection of followers. "They are fresh. They will listen."

Hug scraped its hands together. "Yes."

Til'lock was satisfied, as that outcome was what the troll wanted. The initial plans with the village leader were almost successful in Til'lock's eyes. Then, that shawled figure and that crazy man ruined my plans. We had the upper hand. We should finish the villagers off or take them as slaves. That portal man is useful. This was just a holdup in the plans.

Til'lock was peering over the rest of the trolls—larger, full-sized, unlike the young brolls. The brolls should be ready enough when we head back. Those brolls were last seen recovering in the meat pit. They should be coming back soon. I need them to be whole before heading back. More human flesh will help with their growth, as well.

Trolls had seen the humans come attacking several times over the ages. They had always been a foe, along with everything else—specifically, anything with meat. The trolls had never gone so far as attacking the village, and there was an agreement between the trolls and the human leader. Til'lock intended to change that.

That last time, I was so close to ending the village's rule. This new leader that they have has relaxed the protections, allowing us trolls to feed even farther inside of their walls. It was so simple—the small human didn't even want to be there.

The lack of leadership was apparent when Karnaugh first showed his face to the trolls. The shouting bravado over the usual combat, the freedom of the desert he gave to the trolls in order to get them to settle down. It is truly amazing what these humans can be told to do, how they just follow. They are soft and weak, and we are so hungry. This will be easy.

Til'lock scraped its long troll nose before sitting down on some stolen furniture and grabbing a slab of dead cow leg. There were scraps of bones everywhere around the large, lopsided wooden chair—a bone throne, one might call it.

Hug was standing nearby, staring blank-faced, and Til'lock called the troll over to share the cow. "Do you have others that follow you?" Til'lock asked, spitting chunks of fat out of its mouth.

Hug grunted loudly a few times, and five more trolls stepped forward. "Mine," Hug said with a grin. The troll was proud of its small group of followers.

One of the trolls—a larger troll like Hug—carried big bongo drums. It had a wide nose and eyes that were close together. Another troll carried the largest femur bone that Til'lock had ever seen. And, lastly, there was a troll with two smaller trolls that looked very similar to the large one. That threesome appeared to all come from the same troll and had very similar demeanors. The largest of the three was clothed, which was rare for trolls.

"First, need you to head to the humans," Til'lock grunted to Hug, flicking a finger at the other trolls. "They will go with you." The trolls were wandering the area, picking at bones here and there. "For your backup, I will take the brolls and head to the village."

"We go." Hug turned towards the center of the grand hall.

Til'lock finished the cow leg, watching as the other trolls left.

Greyson was standing over the last broll as it crumpled to the ground after he finished it off with his sword. He turned away from the dead broll and saw his companions nursing their wounds.

Ella had some type of healing salve that she was applying to Allarie's leg wound. She ended up tending to each of them with her salve; the fight had taken a lot out of them. They were all staring again at Killmead's headless body.

"Any last words for Killmead, here?" Greyson said. "Not to be insensitive." He took Killmead's hefty sword and scabbard. "At least he can rest. I will get this done."

"I can only speak for myself. I do hope he rests in peace. The trip was honorable, his intentions sincere, and now I would like to see it through," Martimil stated.

"I did not know him, but I am glad he helped." Allarie winced a little as Ella dabbed more salve on the puncture wound.

"It is wild, wild. We need to look after ourselves." Ella looked absolutely exhausted, her eyes still lingering on the body. "May he swim with Troutus, Troutus."

Greyson glared grimly at the descending stairs. "I am going to continue on. I know I just need to go down there now."

"Being honest, Greyson, we should probably head out. I know how you feel, but this is it. Look at us," Martimil said in exhaustion. A bruised Ella was still applying the salve to Allarie. They were banged and beaten.

"I suggest the three of you head out, then." Greyson gave them a nod. He gripped his sword tightly in grave determination as he headed for the stairs.

Martimil grabbed on to Greyson's tunic. "Where the fuck are we? This is way over our heads. We will end up like him." He motioned over to Killmead's corpse.

"I would rather end up like him than go back and die in the mine," Greyson responded.

Martimil bowed his head.

"Martimil, look at me. None of that timid shit. I saw how fired up you were earlier. What is the reason for any of this? Each other. We all saw those prisoners. My intention is to get them out. In my life, I need to try." Greyson snagged his tunic out of Martimil's hand. "Take them and go."

Allarie stood despite holding her salve-covered wound. "Greyson, I'll go with you."

"Don't. Your leg needs to heal. Get out. I will see the end of this. You fear death the most, correct? You dance around fearless, but it is apparent. Death is a part of life. What kind of story will you write? I just want to be seen as someone who tried. Death is a lot easier to accept when you live a life you can and should be proud of. Fuck the mine."

Greyson's voice trailed off as he turned and began walking away. He bounded down the steps a few at a time. His footing wasn't perfect, and he slipped on some sand on the stairs. He stumbled down the first set and leaped to the next. Down, down, down.

Greyson finally stepped into where the brolls were spawned. It was the troll pit. It had been emptied except for one troll that was standing next to a black crystal in the center of the arena.

Til'lock was petting the crystal and staring at it. The troll orbited around the crystal with a slow and steady swaying motion. "I hoped it would be you." Til'lock's long nose pointed at Greyson, a sharp smile appearing on the troll's face.

Greyson's eyes followed Til'lock.

Trolls started to march back into the pit, and they were forming a circle around both Greyson and their leader. Til'lock was still stroking the crystal in the center of the pit and appeared to be whispering to it. The troll's fingers started to glow. The other trolls in the pit started to chant Til'lock's name over and over.

"Hear those chants?" Til'lock crowed. The troll's hands were now brightly lit, and it stared at its luminous mitts as it withdrew them from the crystal. "Are you ready? The crowd appears to be ready." Til'lock was waving its hands at the cheering trolls.

Greyson looked in awe as he was being surrounded by absolutely hideous creatures, separated from them only by what looked like a stone fence running alongside the walls. He started to nervously spin the blade in his hand as he realized he was alone. The situation seemed fairly hopeless, and he tried to ignore the noise of the chanting trolls around him. Greyson stared at the remains of long-dead creatures half-buried in the sandy floor, the only things in his world as he steeled himself for the inevitable confrontation.

He stopped the sword's rotation with the handguard perpendicular to the ground. He gave it a twirl and rushed to the center of the arena.

Til'lock's face turned from delight to seriousness as it prepared for Greyson to strike. Greyson went at the troll in an overhead arc, and it lifted its hands. Instead of slicing right through the fingers, as the sword would usually do when met with troll flesh, it clanked as if the sword had been reflected by metal. Greyson's hands shook as the sword clashed. Panic struck his face as he withdrew the weapon.

He shook off the unexpected block and turned the blade as he steered it in for a jab. As the sword went plunging in, Til'lock cocked its arm back and unleashed a sweeping blow to Greyson. His sword was able to deflect the blow, but the force behind the strike sent him staggering.

Til'lock started a barrage of strikes as it followed Greyson's retreat. The more vicious the attack and counterstrike by Greyson, the louder the reaction from the onlookers in the chamber was for Til'lock. Greyson did his best to deflect whatever attack was sent at him.

The surrounding trolls were cheering ever louder as Til'lock landed more blows, and they yelled when it looked as though Greyson was going to slither away. Til'lock pushed aside the blade and punched Greyson, sending the dazed human stumbling backwards.

The other trolls caught him as he went towards the fenced walls, their arms protruding into the arena. They swatted at him and pushed him back into the center of the room.

Greyson stumbled, desperately trying to recatch his footing. Til'lock clawed at Greyson, and he had to roll out of the way from the hard downward slap. The troll was much larger, but it was quicker than he had anticipated. Its glowing hands deflected blows by Greyson's sword and had cut wounds in the flesh. Blood dripped from Greyson. The troll was relentless, and Greyson had to constantly duck and dive out of the way.

I need to find an opening.

The troll's energy didn't wane, and, one swing after another, its assault wasn't slowing. Til'lock balled its hands into a single fist and attempted to bash the human. Greyson tried to deflect the fists, thinking that his blade would cut right through the troll's hands and forgetting that they were able to brush the sword away. The troll continued to strike at Greyson. Its fist hit his stomach, and he was sent reeling back into a pillar in the middle of the pit. He gasped for the breath that the blow had forcefully pushed out.

The crowd of trolls hollered and hit each other in excitement as they eagerly watched the struggle. Til'lock pumped its raised fists in the air, and the other trolls followed suit.

Greyson felt his head throbbing. His eyes blurred, and Til'lock was a massive smudge. This is starting to feel hopeless. He rubbed his face with his free hand, still holding a loose grip on his sword with the other. His body was bruised, and his fatigued hands were feeling weaker. The last hit had taken a lot out of him.

"Kill him, Til'lock!" one of the trolls shouted.

This guy is just a piece of shit. Greyson used the pillar to get back onto his feet. Is there a time when I am not falling down from these oversized assholes? Frustration showed on Greyson's face. He was tired, demoralized.

Its legs—I have to slow the troll down, somehow get a hit away from the glowing hands. His breathing was labored, and sweat was burning his eyes. He picked up one of the many bones protruding from the sand and charged back in.

Til'lock started to smile again. "It is over, puny one. There is no hope left here." The chants became increasingly loud. "I grow bored of playing with you." The troll cracked its knuckles. "It is time to end this." It began to walk over to Greyson, who was now leaning on the pillar, his chest slowly rising and falling as he was taking deep breaths.

"Better end it, then," Greyson panted. "I will not stop till you are dead." He was now on his feet, bracing for a strike from the troll.

Til'lock took its time waltzing over to where Greyson was standing. The troll was strutting and making a show for the crowd, with its monstrous body fully outstretched, soaking up the attention it craved. It reached out its hand, and it was deflected, but just as one hand was hit away, the other was able to knock Greyson down.

Til'lock full-on palmed Greyson's head and kept hammering away, smashing his head into a bloody, swollen mess. As Greyson's head bounced on the first slam, light flashed in his eyes, and pain shot through his skull. Looking up, Greyson saw the hands that had encompassed his head.

Slam…again light flashed in his head…more pain. Over and over.

The troll's attack did not stop.

Hug and his contingent of trolls were climbing the same staircase that Greyson had gone shooting down, albeit they had started from another path in the pit.

Allarie headed down the same way as Greyson, while Martimil and Ella went to help the prisoners escape. The sloppy and loud approach of the trolls could be heard. With the clanking of their oversized weapons and their babbling and shouting at one another, Allarie couldn't miss the amount of noise they made.

In a panic, she searched for a suitable hiding place. There wasn't much in the staircase other than bones, but then she spied a collection of vases in an alcove along the stairway. She decided to hide between a few of the larger vases, squatting down into a kneeling position to better fit. They should walk right by me; surely, I look just like a vase.

The trolls were chatting amongst themselves on their way up, pushing, shoving, speaking obnoxiously. "This cow… now, this cow…it was huge," a troll—very much larger than the others that were laughing—rumbled.

A troll smacked one of its companions, and that troll, in turn, lost its footing on the sandy staircase. The troll collapsed and fell down the stairs, slamming each step on the way down, one after another, until it finally landed right in front of Allarie's vases.

She looked directly into its eyes. It screeched, and the troop of trolls on the stairs immediately ceased moving.

"Are you being a baby again?" a troll said.

They turned back and looked down on their fallen comrade that was now parallel with the vases.

Allarie used one of her daggers to smack the troll in its gaping maw with a swift, downward blow. The blade sank right through the troll's cheeks mid-screech. She rolled over the troll and continued down towards the bottom of the stairs, leaving her long dagger lodged in the troll's mouth.

The other trolls had seen the fallen troll stabbed in the mouth and then a shawled figure roll over its body.

"There! It is moving towards the pit!" a troll screamed. "She is mine!"

"No, she is mine!" the troll with the large bone weapon said. "You got that fat cow."

The two trolls got in each other's faces, flexing their muscles. One troll grunted and the other responded with an angry punch. Then, all of Hug's crew were scrapping.

The bongo-drum troll was slapping its drums and yelling at Hug, "The human is mine. I am so hungry!"

The drum troll started to shift down the stairs. One of its large drums knocked into Hug, causing the troll to stumble. The stairway wasn't large enough for the feuding trolls. Hug then grabbed on to the drum troll's legs to stop its momentum, but it was too hard for its feet to stabilize, and it lost its footing on the staircase. The staircase was so narrow that the trolls had to either jump over or start rolling with Hug and the drum troll, as they had both fallen hard. The smaller trolls that had been heckling the large-femur-bone troll dropped and were scooped into the falling bodies. The stairs were steep enough to get them all rolling at a solid pace. They tried to stop their rolls, but besides the occasional alcove, there was nothing for the trolls to grab on to that would slow their descents.

Allarie was trying to quickly limp down the staircase. She could hear the trolls yelling at each other. All of a sudden she heard several crashes, and a ball of scraping, clawing trolls came tumbling down the stairs at a rapid clip. Eventually, they caught up with the first troll that had fallen and knocked into it. They continued to wrestle each other as Allarie sneaked farther down the stairs.

Allarie came upon the steps to the pit. Her eyes turned to see Greyson's limp body and a large troll clutching his bloodied head. He was a bloody, crumpled mess. Allarie was shocked as she witnessed Greyson get knocked over and over. Out of arrows, she turned her remaining dagger upside down, took aim, and let the blade fly.

Til'lock was distracted by its relentless assault on Greyson, and the dagger scored right into the side of the troll's chest. It clutched at the wound and screamed as the other trolls in the arena roared in anger and frustration.

<hr />

Greyson could feel something besides the pain. Thank goodness for adrenaline. It was his heart. It kept pumping, as scrambled as his brain was. He felt it. He needed to live.

The blade was resting on the floor, his palm on the hilt. The sword can't hit the ground.

Til'lock was attempting to withdraw the embedded dagger, clearly agitated and clawing at it.

Greyson wasn't recognizable, his face a bloody pulp. But his body moved on its own. He swiped across the troll's stomach, pouring out its contents. The sword glowed as brightly as the sun.

"Thuck it," Greyson mumbled through his swollen lips.

The cocky look on the troll's face turned immediately to disbelief. The crowd went absolutely wild, and a few trolls were jumping and climbing the gates, then sprinting towards where Greyson was on the ground.

Guess this is it.

Greyson's head was pounding as he collapsed after his last blow to the troll. The blade was still pulsating and glowing, the runes shining and radiating light as one.

The trolls were going wild—tongues, arms, and other body parts flying as they tried to get to Greyson, reaching into the arena.

Allarie sprinted over and scooped up the sword. She raised it above her head and then smacked the crystal with a strike that she put all her weight into.

The troll lair began warping around her; everything flashed and became visually distorted. The world shook. Frustration showed on Allarie's face as she desperately swung again. This time, she cracked the crystal and shattered it. The world around them blurred and flashed into darkness. They all blacked out of existence, their bodies drifting up from the solid surface before being abruptly dropped to the ground, right back into the pit in the desert.

Greyson lay on the desert floor, his head pulsing from the adrenaline crash. He screamed in agony.

Ella, Martimil, the prisoners, and what looked like all of the bones and miscellaneous human items were scattered on the desert floor. Everything looked as if it had been dropped from a great height, but there was not a troll in sight.

Every person's face was fraught with confusion. Then, suddenly, a single person laughed. Soon, the whole camp of prisoners erupted in giddy laughter, at least those who could do so.

Greyson lay in the sand a little farther away from Allarie, across from the perplexed prisoners. He was knocked out, and she approached him on the ground. She gave him what little water she had left.

Greyson eventually stirred. "Are we alive?" he asked with slurring words, his body shaking. "My head aches. Really badly." He shivered.

"We did it, Greyson. Somehow, we closed a gate." Allarie was in disbelief. "We came to kill that troll, but we ended up closing a whole gate. Those crystals…" She paused and looked around, deep in thought.

They were still in the desert pit The sand had collapsed in on itself, and the glass stairs had fallen or been swallowed up by the ground, but the portal was gone.

"Not to dismiss your injury, but we are alive." Allarie looked around again.

All that was now in the vicinity were things taken from humans or their surrounding area, and nothing from the portal—bones, half-eaten corpses of animals and humans alike, and things that appear to have been taken from wanderers and small villages in the desert.

Allarie stayed by Greyson's side, calling Ella and Martimil over.

"You all right, Greyson?" Martimil had a relieved look on his face, and Ella had an exaggerated grin. "That you bud?"

"I can't believe, believe we did it!" Ella was looking at the desert floor that was now littered with troll trash. There was nothing of the trolls but the things they had looted. Her eyes were rotating around, looking for the child and her mother. There were people still strewn out across the desert floor —about a dozen or so—confused, disoriented, and still very much dehydrated. They all looked lost but relieved that they were away from the trolls, including the long-nosed man.

"Well, it is about time." The long-nosed man started to tap his foot. "We were already supposed to be at the village by now. They told us of a grand tent, not of trolls."

Allarie bit her lip. "Real quick, what's your name?"

"Oh, it's Tyler." He turned his nose up again.

"Well, Tyler. It seems like you have some energy, and everyone looks super hungry and thirsty. You can go ahead and look around for some supplies."

"Of course, I can!" Tyler said sarcastically, rolling his eyes taking off.

Allarie nodded her head as he left. "We need to get more people to look for things we could use. This is a lot of trash." She looked around sternly. "I didn't know the trolls would keep so many useless things."

———————•———————

Allarie walked around, gazing across the barren desert. Few things looked unique. "Killmead knew the area. Do we even know how to get back?" Her face that had been full of optimism now grew concerned as she spoke to the group. She walked over to a pile of looted items—rugs, paintings, and other things that seemed very strange for desert trolls to take, as they are not known for their appreciation of the arts or refined culture.

The hollowed man from the entrance to the portal found them. "They appreciated it because the wizards had," he said.

The hollowed man had been around during the Time of the Wizards, and time didn't pass for him as it did outside. So, the man had sat there and endured the trolls for years.

He turned his gaunt face to look at the group and continued to speak, "I do not know how you have done it, but I owe you a debt of gratitude."

"Would that be a slight grin on your face, you gaunt-ass man." Greyson smirked. "I cannot remember what Killmead told me about directions. My brain has been rocked."

The hollowed man stared back at Greyson. "My feelings are appreciative."

Allarie rose from a pile of plundered art. "Would you happen to know the way back?"

The gaunt man turned his face in her direction. "I haven't left that seat in a long time. I do not recall how to get anywhere outside."

"They kept you alive somehow. Do you know where they got food and water for you?" Allarie had been watching the group of human prisoners, and they all looked too feeble to move. "We need to get back to civilization for these people, and for our sake, as well."

The gaunt man had a frown on his face. "Whatever I received was from their hunts. We are lucky that trolls, for whatever reason, liked human belongings." He started to fidget.

"We need those who can move to search these piles. Find anything we can use as supplies!" Allarie called to the dozen or so prisoners.

A few of them actually started to move towards the piles that lay in the sand.

"I will start to go around and look for things we can use," Allarie said to her companions. The three others looked at her as she started to limp away to look for supplies.

"Sounds like a plan, plan," Ella stated. She slowly got to her feet, as well.

"I think we have run out of that healing salve," Martimil said as he looked through his own belongings. "We should look for someone who might be able to guide us towards other humans. Ella could fly ahead and see if she can scout for a direction. We gotta start looking around, too—can't be lazy now. Look what ya done!" Martimil smirked at Greyson.

Greyson's face was swelling badly. "My face is in so much pain." He rose to his feet. "Where is that little girl? I feel like she might remember, or her mother may have words for us." He was squinting, peering around. I don't think I even remember what she looks like.

Martimil gritted his teeth. "She is the only kid here, and who the fuck do you think you are? You were just in the mines with me. Give yourself a break. I'll look for the child and her mother. We'll find our way back. Your face is so swollen you look like one of those trolls."

"I have some questions, Martimil," Greyson mumbled through his now-puffy lips.

"You are becoming indecipherable," Martimil said matter-of-factly.

Greyson's puffy face tried to morph into a grimace, but it looked warped because of his injuries. He started to join the search, but Martimil stopped him.

"Those people back there, you gave them life. Each of them living unique lives of their own." He was waving his arms at Greyson. "Now, they are free again. They could have experienced a terrible fate. They'll remember me, and they'll remember you. That is what matters." A slight smile showed on Martimil's face. "Haneserrath is not a wonderful place, but it is no troll lair. We need to get everyone back, including you. So, rest up—we have a distance to tread."

10

"Get us home"

Allarie was on top of a pile of troll junk. Mostly, she found bones and artwork. Although the art was beautiful, it was useless and not needed. There were also a few weapons, including one of her long daggers that she gleefully retrieved. Skulls with spears piercing them lay on the ground. She shook off the bones and gathered what she could.

Her eyes were still scoping the piles when, in the distance, she saw a bowl. The bowl contained some fruit—bruised fruit, but still some kind of food. She bounded for the bounty.

Ella was flying around, looking for anything other than desert. She found nothing but hilly sand, and she knew she would have to venture out even farther to be able to see anything. She was unable to smell any signs of civilization, either. Outposts of civilized life smelled potently of cooking gruel or wild animal, smoky fires, and, worst of all, humans themselves. But the only humans she could smell were the ones that she already knew. I should report that there is nothing to be seen just yet. The out-of-place seagull took a dive towards the group of humans below.

"Has to be something else." Allarie had a couple of apples, tomatoes, strawberries, and potatoes—the traditional Southern mix of Amerthine. Some of it was beginning to go bad.

As she was searching one of the piles, a small head appeared near some paintings. "Come out," Allarie said to the little girl spying on her.

The girl held her hands out to Allarie, who was still holding on to the bowl of fruit.

Allarie picked some of the healthier-looking items from the bowl. "I need you to do something for me, okay?" Allarie waited for the girl to acknowledge.

The girl nodded.

"You need to take this bowl and share, especially with those who look like they can carry these." Allarie patted the clustered spears she had found. "Do what you can, Ally, and find me when you are done."

The girl nodded, a smile appearing again on her dirty face, and then she ran off with the bowl in her hands. Allarie was satisfied with what was available to eat.

Well, found the girl. Now, for the mother. I have to figure out who these people are, more villagers to know. She was still searching among the piles of rubbish, knowing that the bowl might have been all there was to be found. Allarie's eyes followed the child as she ran towards her mother. Nice. Allarie started to head that way.

Ella landed next to her, morphing back into human form. "Do you honestly, honestly believe her mother might know the way?" Ella asked.

"Suppose that means disappointing news from above." Allarie went back to poking around the mostly useless items and bones. She crossed her arms in frustration. "Think we are fucked, Ella." She looked around quickly at the empty vastness of desert, putting her hands to her face.

Ella placed her hand on Allarie's back. "We'll figure it out, out." Ella walked towards the others, who were now gathered around to split the small portion of fruit that the little girl was holding. "Or Marti will. He is the compass guy. Usually, usually I just follow him, and it works out."

"This is, by far, not enough!" Tyler screamed upon seeing the bowl of fruit. His hands were reaching to the sky dramatically. "We will not survive!" He began to whimper.

Allarie walked over to the man and gave him a solid smack to the back of his head. "Is that a way to act in front of others?"

Tyler looked at her in contempt. His demeanor changed, and he was no longer whimpering. He balled his hand into a fist, shaking it at her. "Who do you think you are?"

"My name is Allarie, and if we would like to all make it out of here alive, I suggest being a bit more rational."

Tyler dwarfed Allarie, and his hooked nose pointed down at her. "We need food, water, shelter." He was shaking.

"First of all, all, get that booger, booger-encrusted nose away from my friend here." Ella puffed her chest and squared her shoulders, mocking the man.

The man's face changed once again to a look of confusion. Then, a frown, a smile, and anger once again. He raised his fist as if to strike Ella.

With a swift motion, Allarie hit the crazed man over the top of his head with the pommel of her dagger. "I just do not know if everyone deserves saving, sometimes. Just look at him."

Anger swelled on his face.

"Let him sweat, sweat it off." Ella smiled. "Do you believe there to be anything else to find?"

"Over here!" one of the former prisoners shouted.

Allarie and Ella headed over to where the group was standing around the shouting man. The man held his hand in the air, a reddish liquid streaming down his arm and covering his grinning face. Large gourds of wine were on the back of one of the carts that was yoked to a single bull; the cart looked as though it was once pulled by multiple bulls, but just one remained.

Allarie walked over to the bull. "You must have hidden. You'll be strong enough to lead us back." She patted the beast.

People standing around the man were staring in awe. A few appeared to be very parched as they brushed the man with their feeble fingers, begging for some liquid.

"Hold, everyone! What is the liquid the man drinks?" Allarie shouted.

"It's wine from that gourd." A woman pointed at a container.

There were a few similar gourds on the cart, along with some smaller ones, all elegantly decorated with pictures of the sea and white birds that looked like Ella's seagull. They had been stolen or taken from Ella and Martimil's island home.

Ella ran her hand over the painting of the sea depicted on one of the gourds. "I do wonder, wonder where these come from. An abundance of wine." Ella uncorked a smaller gourd and took a small swig. "This tastes like straight-up juice, juice."

"Toss it here," Allarie said. The gourd was launched by Ella and caught by Allarie. "This, indeed, tastes freshly squeezed. We need to get this around to people." She set her gourd down and walked over to the man taking the long, hard swigs of wine. "Easy there, sport. Need to save yourself." She placed her hand on the gourd that was being chugged from. "We are going to have to boil one of these." She slapped the gourd that she had placed on the ground.

"Now, why in the hell would you do that?" The man scratched his head.

"We need to get the alcohol out of these somehow. From what I have heard, I believe we can boil it out."

"Now, why in the hell would you do that?" he repeated.

Her patience with the man was waning. "We are going to get out of here, and we will not be able to, drunk with just wine." She slapped each of the gourds. "Do you think Martimil will be able to boil these?"

"Wouldn't be the first, first time he has boiled liquid," Ella said.

Tyler was stomping his feet while eating a large piece of fruit. "I hope you know you are going to have to pay for all of that."

Allarie looked at him. "Are you seriously back for more?"

"This stuff was given special to me...and only me," he said. "Being that it is mine, I can sell it if I so choose."

"No need to be a jackass," Allarie said with a grin. "Your wine can work. We can do this." She shifted her glance to the others, who were now focused on her. "Oh…"

The woman had reappeared with her child. "Thank you again for helping us out of the troll prison. We also appreciate being looked after. It is extraordinary how humble you are being with these supplies. Why?"

Allarie looked past Ella, a grin still on her face. "We are all out in this desert together, correct?"

"Your chance for survival would greatly increase without us, however." The lady had a serious look on her face.

Allarie sighed. "I guess today is the day I tell you the world isn't all doom and gloom." She picked up some rocks and started to juggle them. "I think we should set up camp and head out to find civilization again in the morning. It would give us time to cool the hopefully alcohol-less wine. Again, we need longevity out of this less potent wine; the trip could take some time."

The woman's face brightened, and the grip on her child loosened. "I think you are right. We might just make it out of here." She lightly shook the little girl, and the child looked back at her quizzically. "Do you hear that? We might be able to go back home," she said happily.

The girl saw how cheerful her mother looked, and she mirrored the same smile.

"You see that, Ella? That is what this is all about." Allarie snapped her fingers.

"Your confidence is inspiring," Ella said straight-faced.

204

Allarie stared back at her. "Do you repeat the words on purpose, then? I apologize, but I just have been wondering. I do not know if this timing is correct, but you are wonderful."

Ella stared right back into her eyes. "How did you guess, guess?"

They started to walk away from the child and mother. Greyson and Martimil were chatting while walking towards them.

Martimil looked up from talking with Greyson. "Did you ask any of them for a general direction? If not, I will figure it out," he shouted over to Ella.

"We completely, completely forgot!" she shouted back, a smile on her face.

"Let's set up some spots to lie down...and a fire. Nights are still going to be chilly. Is there any cloth available or a way to make a makeshift building with all this junk?" Allarie's eyes never stopped moving, and her mind could be seen running.

The guys exchanged glances, a goofy grin on Greyson's bruised face and a look of positive panic on Martimil's. "There might have been some clothes dropped off somewhere that haven't been taken by the breeze or have been caught by some of these cacti here," Martimil said.

Greyson walked over to a sharp cactus tree that had caught a long, dirty cloth. He ripped it from the cactus. "Well, here is one so far."

"Directions! Focus." Martimil thought out loud, hammering his fist into his hand. "I need to remember which way we were facing when we initially came."

He reached inside of his vest and produced a small compass. On first look, it appeared to be a normal silver compass, but on closer inspection, there was artwork on the inside that depicted the sea, and the shape of the compass resembled a ship's wheel.

"Oh shit, yeah, Allarie, where we going?" Greyson was wrapping the cloth around his arm and then unraveling it again.

"Neither of you remembers where we are going? Even the direction man himself?" she responded.

"Time doesn't work the same coming from that portal, either. However long you believe you were in there, time outside has not passed," the gaunt man said.

"Troutus!" Greyson said abruptly. He and Martimil both visibly recoiled. Greyson clutched his forehead. "Highly recommend you do not appear from the shadows. Do you have a name?" Greyson managed to get out.

"Trolls are lazy, unless they have a goal in mind." He paused and then started to tap his forehead. "I do not remember my name. I haven't been called my name in centuries...or what felt like centuries." The man looked to the clear blue sky, where a seagull was circling around.

"Do you remember even the first letter or a sound of it?" Martimil was now looking curiously at the man, patting Greyson on the back.

"I believe it might start as da...however, I could be mistaken." The gaunt man looked solemnly back at them.

"Dan the man. It is settled, then," Greyson said with a chuckle.

"I really believe that is something possibly an infant just says initially. However, if Dan works…" Martimil now grinned at the man.

Dan was staring at his palms and whispering, "Dan," while the other two laughed.

"I'll figure out how to get us back," Martimil said confidently. "That way." He pointed northeast.

They were still in the pit, surrounded by a wall of bone. Some of the group were working together to establish a base of sorts, finding rags where they could and making a patchwork tent, while others gathered wood to make a fire in the middle of the makeshift camp. Allarie pointed in different directions for people to move, shouting orders to carry large bones to prop up the temporary structures. Everyone's spirits were rising, and the evidence of this could be seen in their faces and heard in their chatter.

"Let's start a fire for one of those gourds—that way they can cool through the night. Get something possibly potable," Allarie said.

Greyson was continuing to pace, as the former prisoners were following orders given by Allarie. "If I stop moving now, I might just pass out."

Martimil was also watching as Allarie was orchestrating the group to set up camp, her face rotating until it stopped while facing him.

"I need fire," Allarie said. She started to trudge his way, but he was quick to move himself over to her.

Martimil snapped his fingers and produced a flame. Allarie ripped some extra cloth that they had been using and set it afire.

"Not to be a poor sport here, but you might have to set that flame of yours on the pot yourself. We don't have enough tinder." She cocked an eyebrow at him.

"Let me get my bag. We have cooking materials. I do not need scraps of cloth. Ella! Where are our things?"

"I think she might still be in the sky, but so far she hasn't been able to see humans. Things might change since lights tend to appear during the evening." Allarie held her arm above her eyes to shield them from the setting sun.

"I was just asking out loud. I usually am the one to carry that type of stuff."

Martimil found their hyders nearby, and he rummaged through the supply packs. He then fed the hyders and gave them water. The beasts didn't need much, and they shook their sand-filled manes as a sign of contentment.

Martimil got out a coiled contraption. "All righty, let's get this going now." He grabbed one of the gourds and placed it on top of the coiled contraption on the ground. Martimil lay on the ground with his arm stretched out and snapped his fingers, producing a burst of fire that engulfed his hand. He then pressed his lit finger against the coils, which quickly turned a glowing red, like wine filling a goblet. "Give this a good ten, or if you want, I can shorten the time and get you some mulled wine?"

"Whatever can get this dryness out of my throat and hopefully not make me unable to function." Allarie started to smack her lips. "But really, though."

"Patience, then. We take it off now, the alcohol won't have boiled out," Martimil replied.

"Greyson, what will you do now?" Allarie asked. To Martimil, she said, "Get that to the main tent when it is done boiling. I would like to get it out of the sun," she stated flatly.

"Chill, Allarie. You know to just ask, not tell, right? Whatever I please, to answer your question." Greyson grinned at her.

She gave him an annoyed look. "You know what I mean, and you know you have to tell people or else they will not listen," she said matter-of-factly.

"If they hear you holler, though, things change fast. That right?" he retorted.

"A change of tone does make things move faster." She nodded her head. "Pretty basic stuff."

"I see you. What, Captain?" he said mockingly with a sneer. "I see how they are listening to you. The same way that the guards speak to one another—very authoritarian. Had me ready to do things for you from a distance!" His sneer turned soft.

"I have been in the presence of authority before. I reflected on it, hoping to get the same reaction. And that is how it works." She averted her gaze.

"And look at you now! Fighting side by side with a miner," he said smugly.

"It is much the same as fighting alongside anyone else." With those words, she evaporated his smugness from the air. "Now, answer my question."

"I am lost in the middle of a desert. Even if I knew the way back, this is still a large desert. Better that we are together, shoot for questions." Greyson replied.

"We will get back. You do know that, right? Give me the follow-up, what then?" She was staring at him insistently.

Greyson adjusted the sword on his belt. "Well, if we do... when we do," he corrected himself, giving a knowing stare back to her, "I might follow Martimil and Ella to the shore. Anything to get away from looking at the color of sand." He took Killmead's sword and strapped it to his hyder.

"I think you are needed for a bit more than that, Greyson, or else that particular sword of yours is. In order to get you out of your current situation, I need you one more time if another situation occurs."

She moved her eyes over to the people constructing shelter and looking for sand creatures to eat, watching as they all huddled together in a group. "What is going on down there?" She took a wide stride forward towards the group.

Allarie moved some people aside; Greyson followed behind her. Two scorpions were battling, and the people were cheering.

"Which one are we cheering for?" Allarie asked a particularly enthusiastic man.

"Believe it or not, the smaller of the two! It has the energy. I can tell it!" The man cheered.

"A heads-up: we can cook these, add a pinch of salt," Martimil observed.

The smaller scorpion was leading with its stinger aimed at the larger scorpion, flailing it wildly, as the larger scorpion was scrambling, trying to back itself up a rock surface. The larger scorpion then fell and flipped over the top of the other scorpion. They both paused and circled each other menacingly. The larger scorpion was trying to strike with its stinger, but it had overextended itself, the last strike causing it to fall over, exposing its stomach. The smaller scorpion sprang at the exposure of the other, and it lashed its stinger, scoring blows that made the larger scorpion curl in on itself.

The small group of people that had once seemed lifeless were now erupting in cheers for the small scorpion.

"All right, now we cook them." Martimil stepped forward.

<hr />

After a short celebration, Greyson and Allarie walked away from Martimil.

"It's not good-bye. I'll be back. Plenty of assholes in the South who have these portals. You are an inspiration to watch. These people love you! An absolute asset to humanity, triple-A, if you will," Greyson said.

"That was deplorable," Allarie responded. "You all right there, guy?"

"They don't listen to me like they listen to you, just saying," he insisted.

"Humans are better with direction—you see them working together. We will make it back, but things are not as they should be." She smiled, looking at the new group.

"I completely agree with you, which is why, when we are back, I will take the road to the water." He was kicking the sand now. "Do you want to spar, maybe?"

"A spar?" She smiled at him. "Never thought you would ask." She withdrew her daggers from their sheaths.

He settled into his best spar stance. "Ready when you are."

She had a light skip in her step while approaching the en-garde Greyson in a half-circle motion.

Greyson struck first, leading with a sweep of his sword. Allarie blocked the blow with both of her blades. She then withdrew one and went for a poke, but Greyson spun out of the way.

"Look at you, getting quicker." Her tone was gleeful. "A fancy spin, to boot!"

"You are dangerous!" He lifted his sword above his head. Leading with his front foot, he moved his sword in a downward arc.

Allarie swiftly moved her arms to slap the sword aside. She spun this time, and her dagger was against his neck. "About that, you are correct. You need to move faster, still."

"How"—he tried many more strikes—"are"—tried another slash—"you so quick?"

Allarie dodged all of his blows. She dipped, rolled in the sand, and deflected blows from Greyson. She slapped him a few times with the flat of her blades. "Each time I hit you, you'll have to realize those are wounds."

"None of those count," Greyson said stubbornly. "You are much faster than Sergeant Killmead, by the way."

She flashed her blades at him, and he was able to get a better look at them. One was, indeed, larger than the other, and both had been sharpened. The handguards were finely decorated. The shorter dagger had a pommel in the shape of a diamond and a small mushroom etching, and the longer dagger had a glossy pommel with a wide green stone embedded in it. Those are some fancy daggers.

"Let's do a point match!" she said excitedly, changing subjects. "Let's say three—I wouldn't want to tire you out too much." She smiled, a sparkle in her eye. "I like to be fair."

"I agree to your terms." He positioned his right foot to face Allarie, his sword pointed in front of him. "What, do we bow first or something?"

"No, you just strike. Come now, you know how to spar." She sent a flurry of blows from her daggers.

He grinned as he swung upwards and down in a fanlike motion, trying to deflect the blades.

"You are leaving openings. Block one aside, and position yourself to better deal with two blades. You will not be able to keep up with both." On an upward swing of his sword, she was able to get a hit to his hip. "I will count that as one."

The little girl had started to cheer, followed by the rest of the group. Martimil and Ella were now watching, as well.

Allarie twirled her daggers in her hands. "Don't hold back now—we have an audience," she said.

"Still not completely comfortable throwing full-bore weight behind a friendly duel." Greyson matched her twirl with a spin of his sword.

"Don't be a coward, and do not dismiss my own ability. Matter of fact, throw your weight around recklessly like that, and there will not be any strength in your blows if I adjusted slightly, or you will violently miss your strike." Allarie was still circling him, daggers outstretched. This time her pose was the short dagger in her left hand and the long one held overhead in her right.

"You asked for it." Greyson lifted his sword and swung across the chest. Allarie deflected the strike with the short dagger and tried to tap him on the head with the long dagger. He just barely dipped out of the way of her attempt at the head tap. Greyson backhanded the flat of his blade and slapped the side of her leg. "You see! You're getting careless!"

There was a noticeable boo from the crowd.

"Oh, come on." Greyson looked incredulously at the crowd as he shrugged his shoulders.

"It appears they have picked a favorite. Score is one to one." Allarie was nodding her head, pushing out her bottom lip with her tongue. "I will not let you get another one of those. I will admit I let that one by."

"Keep talking, I'll keep getting those hits," Greyson shouted, nodding to the crowd. "Let's make a show of this."

Allarie smiled. "It appears we have a fair match!" She now spoke loud enough for the small crowd watching.

The mother sat next to her daughter on a sandy dune. "Watch them dance," she said to her child.

"Wonder if they are ready for the funniest dancing man?" Greyson said in a voice loud enough for the crowd to hear. He picked up his sword and did a couple of obnoxious lunges at Allarie.

She was able to easily skirt them side to side. She made sure to slap his blade a few times, the connections making loud clangs of metal. She leaped back, her short dagger still leading. He threw the flat of the blade overhead at her shoulder, and she easily deflected his blade and hit him several more times side to side with her long dagger. "One, two"—she tapped him once more—"three, and I win." She turned to the small crowd and took a bow.

"Well, hold on one second. That counts as one." Greyson looked indignantly at her. He started to clutch his head. Frustration was rising.

Allarie was eating up all of the cheers. She waved to their small audience, and everyone appeared to be distracted by the duel.

"Finish him!" the little girl yelled. The mother had a questioning look on her face.

Allarie's expression turned to a frown. "Hold up, Greyson." She put her blades in their sheaths and walked over to where the mother and girl were watching.

The little girl looked positively gleeful that Allarie was approaching her.

Allarie matched the child's smile and got down on her knees. "Hey, listen. This is a friendly dance, just competitive. We are certainly still friends."

The little girl nodded.

"All right, Greyson. Let's finish this up. I am not going to lose now." Allarie rose from her knees and spun to find an en-garde Greyson.

She started at a jog, heading towards him with her daggers drawn.

Why am I so angry? Greyson was trying to anticipate her maneuvers, but she was moving faster than before. She spun in a quick flash, dagger after the next dagger, and he was able to parry both swings. He felt sorely outmatched, so he began to wave the sword, flailing in an attempt to deflect the strikes.

"Do not get overwhelmed," Allarie warned. She was still throwing shots at him. Her breathing was paced, just fine, even with her speaking during strikes. "Again, concentrate on one blade. Just be aware of the other."

Greyson had been dodging, deflecting too many blows. He rolled away. Distraction. "I am prepared for your strikes. That small dagger is quicker than the large." He wound up, and with a strength that he had not put into his previous blows, he swung at the hand holding the small dagger. His sword caught the guard and lifted the dagger from her hand, launching it at a nearby dune.

Allarie watched the dagger fly. "Greyson! You have disarmed me. Good thing I have two." She matched his own battle stance with her longer dagger.

He had a smile on his face. That went way better than I anticipated. "See, now we are on equal footing weaponwise."

She held the longer dagger out in front of her at shoulder height. "Well, then, come at me."

Greyson spun his sword until the hilt was perpendicular with the ground, the flat of the blade still exposed. He swiped across the chest, and Allarie sidestepped the attack, shoving him with her now-empty hand. He grunted in response, and the sudden force of the shove caused him to step back. His foot got caught in the sand, and he collapsed. The look on his face turned to panic on losing his ground.

Allarie then threw her own overhand blow at Greyson, who was clutching his blade while he was scrambling to his feet so that he could be in a better position. Her strike almost nailed his hand but was halted by his blade. He was stronger than she and lifted his blade, tossing her, as she was leaning her weight into the strike. She got some decent air, but was able to land on her feet and immediately roll forward in one deft motion, knocking Greyson's sword aside. Her dagger met sand as Greyson was quick to get back onto his feet and grab his fallen sword. As they had switched positions, Greyson rushed and tapped Allarie again with his sword as she attempted to roll away to grab her dagger.

The people were still cheering, and Martimil was pouring out some of the weakened wine that was now cooled.

"We all tied up again?" Greyson said with his typical grin.

"All right, two to two. May I grab my other dagger?" She stood back up and brushed off the sand.

"You'll need all the help you can get." Greyson had a skip in his step as he brandished his sword, readying for the next round.

Allarie retrieved her dagger. "I will be happy to take home this win."

Their audience numbers drew down, but some were still observing.

"All right, let's kick this off, then."

Greyson came at Allarie with a forward lunge, making sure to lead with a slapping motion of his sword. She deflected the attempt with her short dagger, going for another head tap with the longer dagger that he had anticipated. He swung the sword again in an arc, but she pivoted out of the way. Her first swing led the way to strike at Greyson, but she barely missed her mark. She then lightly brushed him with her longer dagger as he countered with his sword.

A wide smile spread across Allarie's face. "Ah!" she shouted at him. "Ah!" she shouted again. "Winner. Say it with me now!"

The small crowd clapped and cheered, and the little girl ran over to Allarie with her arms up. Allarie picked her up and spun her around.

"I do not accept these results," Greyson said with a smile on his face. "Ya cheated."

Allarie was still celebrating with the people who had been watching. Martimil finally brought out the wine, pouring it into silver goblets found in the sand among everything that had dropped from the troll keep.

"Congratulations. You certainly do not know how to take a break." Martimil handed goblets to the two thirsty competitors before picking up one for himself.

"Hey, Marti, where is Ella?" Greyson asked.

"I would assume still up in the sky. She really dislikes the desert." Martimil groggily stared at the sky as the sunlight began to wane. He took another chug. "Don't tell her I started without her." A rivulet of wine was dripping from his mouth.

"I do not blame her at all. I am sick of it here." Greyson took a seat next to Martimil's wine gourd and continued to drink. "We have time. What is the sea like?"

"Do you even know what a large body of water looks like?" Martimil was suddenly very attentive. "Do you even know what a fish is?" He was looking at Greyson quizzically now.

"Yes, we were lucky to try fish once. We had a whole public dinner and everything. Absolutely stunk afterwards—the number of days we had to wait to get the stink out."

"The sea has those, when they are alive. Also, fish in a trough sounds absolutely horrid. How do you even put up with that?" Martimil was still looking at Greyson with bewilderment.

"So, yes, I agree. It is absolutely awful. The thought of it, the lack of choice—indeed, it is terrible. I want to change that so badly," Greyson said in grim determination.

"I worked at a tavern before. Do you know what that is?" Martimil asked.

"I have heard of them. But the way we live, we just do not have access to them. I want to try more of the food you make. Those spices you use, they are wonderful. Our village has always promoted efficiency. If we were to attempt to stray from our everyday routine, everyone would suffer. That is what they told us."

Martimil gave him another quizzical look. "You try to escape. Are you not contributing to your own suffering, then?"

Greyson sighed. "There are reasons why no one does the things I do." He held his fist out with one finger extended. "One, people seem to like me." He put a second finger out. "Two, I have dealt with much worse before than the sad punishments they give me, and from what I have seen, other people have not been affected; it is like I am a ghost." His third finger extended. "And, finally, the third—we all suffer from this one—boredom. Just look at their faces now that they are free, that genuine feeling—I crave it. We live unfairly, but in a way, that keeps the river flowing. You know, kind of like what that fish god keeps spewing." He withdrew his fingers and started to pick one of his scabs.

"Do you get captured on purpose? From all appearances, those guards do not seem that bad, either. Just all stuck in an awful situation like the rest of you. I am not staying there," Martimil huffed, assisted by his wine. "You do know there are other places with better ways, correct? Awfully cocksure. Why does no one else try to escape?"

"You do know we are in the middle of a desert, correct? Also, without you guys, I would still be getting my butt kicked. Life here already sucks, and no one wants to further their suffering," Greyson stated matter-of-factly. "Your misfortune of sailing into that storm really worked out for me." He shrugged, picking up his goblet for a toast.

Martimil's goblet met Greyson's, and they clinked cups. "That wasn't a yes or a no. It really sucks in your village."

"Layered questions, Marti." Greyson shook a finger at him. "Of course, I know there are other places. You are next to me. Safer? I do not know." His goblet was running low again. "Captured on purpose? What do you think?"

"To be honest, at first"—Martimil paused and took a deep breath—"I thought you to be suicidal. Then, looking around at everyone's reaction to you, it set me at ease. Not everyone was dead there."

"You see! That was the whole point. That really wasn't everything. And lo and behold, here we are." A look of excitement was on Greyson's face.

A seagull flew down from the sky.

"Oh shit." Martimil chugged the rest of his wine.

The seagull shifted. Its wings and legs extended and morphed, looking more humanlike, until Ella's body was back. Her head was the last to change, making for a brief animal-human form until she was quickly back to her full human self.

"Starting without, without? I will let this one slide. It has been a long, long day. Now, give me that goblet."

"Hey! I want a refill, as well," Allarie said.

Greyson was feeling better upon waking up the following day in his makeshift tent. His head had been feeling shaky since the closing of the portal, and he was still regaining his bearings. Allarie was brushing his hair, staring at his once-mangled head, which was healing.

"If this is death, then all right." Greyson emphasized the last two words.

"You are, in fact, dead. A congrats is in order," Allarie replied.

"Yes, yes, of course. A fulfilled life. Is that wine still around?"

"A bit early for that, no? Well, now that it is good and early, I have to tell you something."

"Oh Troutus, here we go. Anything to help with this headache."

"Don't do that." Allarie nudged Greyson. "On a serious note now, I came here on a mission. This ended up being extra, and I am so glad I joined you," she whispered to him.

"This is hands down the greatest surprise of my life. I am so glad you joined me, too," he immediately responded.

"Greyson, I am a Southern princess. Remember, I was set to marry Karnaugh," she stated. "As soon as he acquired the village, I was to come with him here."

"Oh, word," Greyson replied, placing his hand on his face, nostrils flared.

Allarie disregarded him and continued, "He was set to have this desert village after his mother passed." She paused. "He poisoned me, thought I died, and ran to Haneserrath."

"Hold up. Did you say you died? What was it like?"

"I'll fucking stab you. Yes, the asshole tried to ditch me when he acquired that village."

"Yeah, I could totally see him doing that." He rolled over and turned his head towards her. "Do not stab me for saying that. I, too, hate the man. He killed my former wife. I know we are dropping some daggers here."

"I thought a guard did that, and something about two others died in childbirth."

"World is wild here." He chuckled a little, his face struggling to maintain composure as his frown widened. "No, my wife was pregnant. She disappeared one night when she was summoned to the big tent. I know it was him."

"You chuckle at the strangest times."

"Discomfort will do that." Greyson's face crept closer to hers.

Allarie realized his intentions and went in to kiss him. "It's okay."

When they stopped, he looked away. "No."

She took his chin and pointed it back towards her. "It's okay."

"Really, Allarie, it's been some time. Family is just not for me. And, anyway, that village is no place to raise a family."

"You know I want to change that. I want people to feel good, feel happy in this life."

"That is just not the way of that village." His face turned a hue of red.

"Help me, please." Her eyes followed his.

"With what?"

"Take him out," she said with vindication.

"You do know he has an entire entourage of well-armored men that follow him everywhere... Wait, of course, you do."

"Don't be a wiseass." Allarie sat up and began to get dressed. "Having gone through this, I really do not think I can finish my mission alone anymore." She gave him a concerned look. "It's a lot to ask, but this could be the next step, Greyson."

"Next step to what?"

"Your life maybe? I want to make a change. And you appear to have the gall to do just that." She went from sitting up to opening the makeshift tent flap.

He got up and put on his pants.

"You do know you jump and mumble incoherent things during your sleep." She put her hand on her hip. "I can't sleep with you thrashing about."

"I'm working on that."

"Dude, how?" Allarie turned on her heels as Greyson approached. She was playing with her short dagger.

"What's up with that dagger? What is on the pommel, a mushroom?"

"Do not deflect. But this is my favorite yummy, little brain tree." Allarie held the pommel up to her eyes, biting her tongue. "It was also a gift from my late mother. She wanted to turn the tide, but she turned to me instead. Believed that I could make this a better place. She was royalty, after all, just in a difficult position." Her voice faded.

"What happened to your parents?" Greyson asked bluntly.

"They do not give you sensitivity training in that mine, do they? They took ill one night and passed. Again, my family were royals, and as such, I was given to Karnaugh, who was to take me to the village. He needs to die. He is no leader, but a self-serving man." A stern look was on Allarie's face.

"And that is when he got you. Those are some pretty hard hits," Greyson mused. "I feel like that would be the correct thing to do—to continue following you." He smiled.

The ground began to rumble.

Greyson immediately frowned. "Oh fuck. Dune crawler."

<hr />

The surface rumbled. Shouts were heard throughout the caravan as the tents and spears were being torn from the ground. Crowds of people were looking around, confused and frightened.

Allarie, grabbing her bow, ran out of her tent and jumped on top of the wagon. She looked down at the ground and shouted, "Crawler!"

Some of the villagers had taken arms and readied themselves.

The crawler crashed through the desert surface, attempting to engulf the villagers in a wide swallow. An eyeless worm—several carts in length, its maw full of spindly teeth—cut through the sand. Sand was ejected through the crawler's porous skin, allowing the beast to glide through the dunes effortlessly and mash up whatever was in its path. The worm smashed what it could and then crashed back into the sand, reentering the sand.

The people in the caravan tried to move farther away from the crawler's underground burrowing.

"What would attract the crawler!?" Martimil shouted back to Allarie.

"The wine from the cart," Allarie said.

Over at the bull-pulled cart, one of the barrels of wine had leaked, a steady drip was coming from the container and soaking the sand below the vat.

"We have to move!" Allarie was shouting. "Move away from the wine cart!"

Still, the villagers ignored the orders. Some were looking at the ground while holding spears; others were sprinting as fast as they could, moving erratically since they didn't have a specific direction or destination.

"Move!" Greyson shouted in support.

Martimil and Ella were standing by the leaking cart.

"Oh no. Coming this way was a mistake," Martimil whispered.

The ground rumbled below them. Ella held on to Martimil as he returned her embrace. The crawler emerged from the ground, smashed the cart, and swallowed the couple whole.

"No!" Greyson and Allarie shouted in unison as their companions disappeared.

———————————•———————————

The crawler's deep, tendriled mouth gnashed at Martimil as he held the smaller Ella in his arms. The digestive process had started as the two started to fall deeper into the acidic, sand-filled esophagus of the worm. They were rolling and tumbling, but Martimil's embrace never loosened.

The tendrils kept prodding him, and he started to glow like a bright-orange ember. Grunting through stabs, Ella let out a cry. In turn, Martimil took a deep breath of dune-crawler air, and his back began to expand until he looked like a bubble filled with molten metal.

The worm was leaping in and out of the ground in wave-like motions, swallowing and crashing through whatever got in its way. Allarie fired off fruitless shots, the arrows sinking into the ground below her.

Then, on one of its leaps from the ground, the crawler's body appeared to be a deep-red hue. It never ceased its movements, but the worm exploded as Martimil became engorged and encompassed by flames. Ooze from the dune crawler went everywhere. The couple's appearance was sudden, and the demise of the dune crawler was quick.

Villagers and companions all rushed over to Martimil and Ella.

Martimil turned his head skyward and let forth a burst of flaming-hot air, decreasing the size of his engorged back. His complexion gradually lightened from its shade of deep red.

"What was that, Marti?" Greyson called to the blood-soaked Martimil. Greyson was mystified by what he had seen and had a look of wonderment on his face.

"Are you both all right?" Allarie asked as a follow-up.

Martimil placed his hands on Ella's shoulders. "We good?" he said quietly as he looked into her eyes.

"We good, good," Ella replied. She let out a long sigh.

A look of relief washed over Martimil…and then horror. He was grabbing his skin, attempting to tear at it. Ella snapped around, looking at the panicked Martimil scraping at his skin, blood spurting from his exposed wounds.

"We need, need my bag. Where are the hyders? Quickly!" she shouted.

Allarie looked around, spotting the hyders not far away. She shouted to the closest villagers, telling them to grab the satchels from the hyders.

Martimil began to groan in agony, his hands bloodied from scratching, and Ella tried to keep his nails away from his exposed skin. Greyson held him, as well, helping her out by holding one of his arms down.

"Little time, bud. Just need to give us a little time," Greyson spoke softly to Martimil.

A villager came running over to Ella and tossed her the satchels from each of their hyders.

Ella popped the first one and tossed it aside. She took her water container and cleared the mess around the wounds with it.

"That stings!"

"Do you want, want to rip your back off?" Ella took out a vial from the next satchel and swirled it in front of her eyes. "We don't have a lot. This is for jellyfish sting, stings from the water." She ripped a dry piece of her dress off and uncorked the bottle, soaking the cloth. She dabbed the panicked Martimil's skin; he looked relieved by the touch of the balm. "Get what you can," she added.

The villagers, too, all had a look of relief now that the dune crawler had been disposed of. They relaxed and took seats in the sun.

"Now is not the time to relax. We have to move. Fix what we can. A barrel of wine has leaked," Allarie shouted. "Pack everything up quickly."

The villagers picked up what things had been dispersed and unloaded the weapons they were holding, placing them back on the carts. They then began to move the carts towards the village again.

11

"The Hole in the Ground"

Karnaugh stepped out of the tree line. He could see his posse carrying another boar, and they were chanting together, "Whose house? Karnaugh's house!" The gaggle of soldiers held up the dead boar like a trophy. They were all excited to be a part of this group, so much so that they were chanting another man's name.

"Report!" Karnaugh shouted in the direction of the group.

The fair-skinned Crix stepped forward. He brushed some of his flowing, blond hair out of his face. "Our hunt was a success," he said smugly. "I know some of us would have wanted more, ha-ha." He exaggerated his words, spacing them out like cacti in the desert.

"Very good, very good. Let's get back to the village," Karnaugh said directly, nodding his head.

"Do you believe this to be enough, sir, ha-ha?" Crix asked.

"Absolutely! Forgar has headed back to the village before us. He has a task he said he had to do." Karnaugh gave an oily smile. "Let's head back, boys. We'll have to catch Forgar! Time to cook a pig!" His eyes bulged as he ran his hands over the jewels on his armor.

"Yes, sir. Nothing else to report, ha-ha," Crix stated unenthusiastically as Karnaugh had already whooped.

They climbed back onto their hyders. Forgar's small hyder was still there, and the others hadn't taken notice of it.

"Sir, there appears to be an extra hyder, ha-ha." Crix clapped his hands together after this announcement. He had been looking through the saddlebags in the back of the group, and he was the last one to mount a hyder.

"Well then, strap it to the others, and let's go, boys!" Karnaugh shouted. "We have a pig to roast, seriously this time. I am starved."

Karnaugh's group started to move, but Crix stayed back. "Out of curiosity, where did Forgar really go off to, ha-ha?" His verbal tic was spoken in a muted and restrained tone.

"I think he might have beaten us to the punch to get back!" Karnaugh said with enthusiasm.

"Sir, that just cannot be true. I saw you walk into the woods with him. The tracks in the sand…" Crix pointed at the ground and moved his arm towards the tree line, where visible tracks—indents in the ground from the big man— could still be seen.

"Must have lost him. Let's ride. No time to dally."

The other men circled on their hyders and began to ride back to Haneserrath.

"Sir, would you perhaps have some oil, then, ha-ha?"

Karnaugh rolled his eyes. "Of course, I have some oil for you! As a matter of fact, if we get back to the village, you can have a whole gourd!" He circled his hyder around Crix. "Come. We ride."

"Yes, sir, ha-ha." Crix rounded his hyder without hesitation.

<hr />

Reevus was stirring a kettle with his right hand while drawing with an elegant, long quill in his left. Beakers and wide gourds were lined along the walls of his lab, and various animal parts were strewn about and hanging on the walls.

A nude man stood in an empty space at the center of the room. He looked as if he was unfazed by his surroundings and almost unconscious. His face was blank; he was totally unresponsive. Reevus squinted his eyes as he drew pictures of the man. The model cast a giant shadow on the piece of parchment on which he was sketching.

Reevus took a beaker from his tabletop and gave it a shake. He lifted it up to eye level, and poured some liquid into a ladle, what looked like cactus water. He then circled around the table, with the ladle in hand, hovering his other hand below it, being careful not to spill. The nervous little man climbed up a step stool next to the naked hulk and then took the ladle to the figure's lips, gently lifting it up and pouring the liquid into the giant's mouth.

As the liquid emptied into his throat, the hulk's eyes turned inky black. The veins started to pulse in his neck. Blood rushed to his face, making it a violent red hue, and his overall size began to increase. The hulk screamed.

No one could hear the blood-curdling scream, as Reevus's lab was located in a cavernous hole underneath the back of Karnaugh's grand tent, for Karnaugh did not like the fumes that came from Reevus's experiments and oil preparation.

The scream startled little Reevus, who then scrambled away, trying to keep the table between himself and the towering brute. The hulk had not moved; he had only opened his mouth.

"Oh geez, next time we chain you from the start," Reevus muttered. He ran back around to his notes and scribbled down, "A vast redness, and size has doubled since the last dose."

"This bodes well for us!" Reevus exclaimed. He then started to skip excitedly around his lab, heading towards the hulk. With a wide smile on his face and still in midskip, he slapped the giant's muscular leg.

The hulk's reaction was immediate. As soon as he was touched, his arm whipped across his chest and hit Reevus. The impact of the blow dropped the little man, and he went shooting over his lab table and crashed into a bookcase. Reevus collapsed in a dazed heap on the floor, and the hulk did not move from where he stood.

• — • — •

Karnaugh's crew trotted back towards the village of Haneserrath, south of the tree line, deeper into the desert that surrounded the broken mountain. Crix's hyder gained ground, catching up to Karnaugh's.

"Sir, we are almost approaching the wall. Did you want me to go ahead and speak with the guard captain?" Crix asked.

"Please do. Tell them we have arrived and that we bring food from the hunt. Perhaps, it will distract." Karnaugh gave a cocksure smile. "Perhaps, they will be excited to share such a prize, to eat something other than that gruel. We are such philanthropic people." He shook his fist excitedly.

"Sir, in case anything else happens in there, I want you to be prepared," Crix cautioned. "They are stronger than they appear. I warned you of that, ha-ha."

Karnaugh was racking his brain for the memory. "I believe I do recall you saying we had lost less than anticipated. That is actually good; they will let our disappearance slide. Our priorities were different. We had no idea the trolls would come," he said through gritted teeth. "What do you think they will say of us?" Suddenly his confident tone had changed to one of concern.

"Sir, I believe that we will be fine. We will have Reevus cook the pig. It will be most glorious, ha-ha," Crix said confidently.

"Very well. Please approach first, and then come back to report to me." Karnaugh's golden armor was shining with an even greater intensity in the rays of the setting sun. He scoffed as he looked at his men. "We should just go right in. It is my village."

"Fear not, sir. We will approach the gates after I am sure it is safe." Crix held up a finger, his face stoic with oil-blacked eyes. They approached the wall, and Crix dismounted.

"Just make sure you look around, see what people are looking like." Karnaugh uncorked a vial.

Crix's head shifted from Karnaugh to the wall. His body then started to curl and widen as his tailbone extended. Once Crix had fully changed into a scorpion, he began to dig into the sand by the wall. On the opposite side of the wall, sand began to shift and crumble before Crix emerged from the ground. He changed back to his human form and made his way throughout the village, peering around at the villagers, who could be seen still picking up the mess, and the miners, who were heading back to the mines to work. He casually walked up to a villager.

The villager was startled by the tall, blond man with shining armor melded to a body that had shifted from the form of a scorpion. "Geez, man, where did you come from?" he asked.

"None of your business," Crix said curtly. "Where is Guard Killmead? I need him at once."

"Last I saw him, he was at the main gate, Mr. Shiny." The villager walked on.

Who are these people? Are they not the same ones we left?

Crix furrowed his sharp brows. "Excuse me? Do you know who I am?" Crix asked the villager, who kept walking. Crix widened his stride to catch up to the man. "Hold!"

The man stopped. He turned and looked at Crix. "I haven't the faintest clue. I have work to do; I am going to continue about my day. Or, do you need to feel more special?" He clicked his tongue.

Crix's furrowed brows sharpened, and his eyes turned to daggers. He raised his hand and struck the man across the face. "Disrespect me once more, and I will see you hanged."

The man took the hit and then spit a red loogie onto the ground. "Of course, more attention."

Villagers were peering from their tents to see what was going on. A few stepped over to where Crix and the defiant villager were standing.

Crix, on seeing more villagers approach, took a step back. He then shot an uncharacteristic glare at the villagers before changing back into his scorpion form and scurrying to the other side of the wall.

———————•———————

Karnaugh had been pacing as he waited for the return of Crix. His eyes were fixated on the hole in the ground, and he sighed heavily when he saw a claw rise from the sand. "Finally. What news of the village? Is everything back as it was?" Karnaugh's anxiousness was apparent.

"Sir, you might not—" Crix started while he was mid-morph.

"Hurry up, and spit it out. I want to know if we will get a rager going or not." Karnaugh was pumping his fist in the air while looking back at the rest of his crew.

The crew was whooping in response.

Karnaugh led his boys to the front gate, where he stepped up to the guard. "We are back from our hunt!" The golden shine of Karnaugh's armor reflected upon the sands before him.

"Welcome back, sir," the guard said deadpan. "Work is going on, as per usual; however, while you were gone, the village was attacked by trolls. The people are upset."

"Very good! We have with us a couple pigs!" Karnaugh smiled at the guard, who gave a dutiful nod of acknowedgment in return. "Would you be able to tell me where Sergeant Killmead is, Guard?"

The guard raised an eyebrow. "Sir, we thought he went after the trolls with you. They went outside the walls, riding the hyders."

"We must have just missed him. Please do tell him I am looking for him when he returns." Karnaugh strode past the guard.

Solemn people roamed the streets, some of them picking up the mess that the trolls had left. There were many broken casks, and the trolls appeared to have trampled most of the tent village. The wooden outhouses had been broken as well, and the villagers had hastily set up a tent in their stead.

At least they aren't crapping in the streets again. Karnaugh looked around the village and sneered in disgust. He gave himself a wide smile and shouted, "My people! I bring great news!" He chuckled to himself.

Most of the villagers ignored Karnaugh's shouts and continued about their day, but a few gathered in front of him. "What news, what news!?" they asked excitedly.

Karnaugh frowned, and his eyes glared at them. "Bring more, have to bring more."

The villagers were still standing nearby, looking at him pleadingly.

"Go!" he shouted at them.

Karnaugh turned back towards his entourage. "Forget it. Forget them. Let's get back to the tent with those pigs." He walked over to Forgar's hyder and opened a satchel. He stuffed his hand in it and withdrew a vial, popping the cork off the top and taking a chug. "Let's dunk them in some oil." His pupils grew black and larger in size. He waltzed down his line of men, stopping next to a hanging pig and slapping it a few times. "Do you think that'll taste good, boys?"

The crew grunted in agreement.

Crix approached Karnaugh. "We should go into the village. Our presence is sorely needed. These people have no respect, ha-ha."

"Have no fear, Crix," Karnaugh said confidently. "We roast them a pig, and they will come around. Nothing speaks to the people more than what they need. I can smell them now." Karnaugh walked his line of men after tossing Crix his vial of oil. "Are you boys ready for a party? Let's go!"

The crew started to jump, belting out a series of whoops into the air.

Karnaugh led his crew and marched forward into the village with them. The guards saluted them, and the villagers moved out of the way, a few gawking at them as they passed. They looked out of place, a large group of heavily armed soldiers in flashy gear.

A few crazed villagers ran up and threw themselves at the ground before them. Karnaugh waved at the ones who groveled and bowed subserviently. Several others marched beside the crew, waving their banners that bore the beer mug of Karnaugh.

"You get a piece of pig. You get a piece of pig." Karnaugh was pointing excitedly at his small crowd. "Let's go, people! Let's go!" He was attempting to hype them up, to draw more in.

People heard the excitement, and their faces started to appear around tents and over each other's shoulders. A boy appeared, laughing and shouting, "Guymuir! Guymuir!"

Karnaugh looked curiously at the boy. "Karnaugh! Karnaugh!" he said back to the kid. The kid looked at him incredulously. Karnaugh smiled and waved at the group of villagers, anyway.

Karnaugh and his crew marched up to his tent. Along the road was blood in the sand, and he could tell that people had been crying. As they hung their heads, Karnaugh continued to smile and wave.

Lit stakes led to the entrance of his enormous tent that was opulently decorated and lined with furs. Karnaugh unfurled the flap doorway. Inside, the floors were made of a rare wood that was dark brown, and the center had been cut into the sand to allow for the firepit, with a hole in the top of the tent to vent the smoke.

Makeshift walls had been made using more wood that was rare for the area. They were thick cuts of wood that were much deeper than what could be provided by the surrounding desert trees, and more expensive as well. There was a large dining table that was littered with golden goblets, silverware, and plates. The chairs that accompanied the large table were also made from the same wood as the floors, and the chair at the head of the table was lined with fur. There were cloth ports in the walls to simulate windows in the well-designed tent.

"I got this, boys. I'll be right back. Get these things ready for cooking!"

Karnaugh made a beeline for Reevus's room, which was under a floor port in the far back corner. He opened up the porthole and jumped down. "Reeeeeevus!"

Karnaugh looked around the lab. Liquid was boiling in several large pots. Vases, ceramic jugs, and various types of containers lined the walls of the cluttered room. Reevus, who was standing over one of the pots, grabbed a few crystals from a pouch and threw them into a beaker of boiling liquid. Heavy wafts of white smoke erupted from the beaker.

Reevus looked up to a smiling Karnaugh. "You are back, I see." He quickly picked up a beaker and stirred its contents around in a jittery motion. "We have made some progress. A crystal that was given to me by Crix a fortnight ago has done the trick on this batch." The little man placed the beaker down and clapped excitedly.

Karnaugh dipped a finger into one of the beakers and then put his finger into his mouth, withdrawing it with a popping noise. He gave an exaggerated laugh. "This is wonderful, Reevus!" He danced around in delight, knocking some of Reevus's glass containers over. "You have shit everywhere," he said as he wiggled a scarf off his leg.

"Try this one next, please. Have to wrap these up. Your trolls have destroyed many cactus-oil barrels." Reevus ran over to a drawered desk and grabbed a carafe. "Just hold steady for a moment." He dunked the carafe into his oil barrel. "Here now, here now, try this."

The oil in the glass carafe glowed. It was a subtle glow, nothing like the brilliant glow of the black crystal.

Karnaugh grabbed it and took a swig. He grinned while looking at Reevus, but then his face turned a sickly purple as his cheeks billowed and eyes bulged. Vomit spewed from his mouth, sudden and violent.

Reevus just barely ducked out of the way of the steady stream.

"Get rid of that, whatever that was." Karnaugh coughed.

"That was the same crystal that was found in the cave. Nothing is different, except this glow. I have no idea where it comes from."

Karnaugh looked at the glow with disgust. "Just throw it away." He turned to leave. "I need more of the good stuff."

"Yes, sir, at once." Reevus looked very confused as Karnaugh left him to his musings in the basement of the tent. He held up the glowing carafe. "Junk," he said to himself.

Reevus continued to hold the glowing glass in front of his face. He poured some oil into another beaker and then went over to his desk and sat down. He put the beaker back on an active flame for a few minutes before pouring a little of the liquid onto a silver tray that was on the desk. As the liquid fell onto the tray, he touched it with another small flame from a piece of cloth.

The flames should have been extinguished, but instead, the small drip created a large explosive energy, and Reevus was ejected with sudden force from his seat and tossed to the opposite side of the lab.

He rubbed his face. His confusion had only grown. "How is this possible? Cactus oil repels the flame."

He brushed himself off and picked up some of the beakers and papers that had fallen. He then returned to his desk and excitedly wrote, "Do not add fire to oil," on one of the papers that had fallen.

He looked back into the carafe, the glow reflecting off his charred face. "What are you?" Reevus spun the carafe, creating a small whorl at the bottom of the glass.

12

"And we're back"

Greyson and his group led the caravan of villagers. They had found several carts that needed repair, and a villager was able to fix a broken wheel to make one serviceable for hauling necessary supplies. Although the cart was lopsided, they still managed to push the supplies through the desert sand.

Allarie was moving up and down the lines, making sure the villagers were not about to pass out from the heat. An active rotation of villagers was required to move the cart, and they listened when Allarie shouted at them to take a break or to drink water.

"Miss Allarie, will you stay with us when we get back?" The little girl was walking next to the cart, trying her best to stay in its shade.

"More than likely stay with you! I don't have a place to go." Allarie smiled at her. "Wouldn't happen to have an extra tent, would ya? Should ask your ma."

The girl mimicked the smile. "I'll find something. We can be neighbors."

"We probably will have so much time to hang out. I'll tell you what—I can help you find something." Allarie held an arm out, her hand closed in a fist. "Tap it. It's a sign of agreement."

The little girl leaped out from the shadow of the cart, her fist extended to meet Allarie's. "I will find you later, then," Ally said with a knowing nod.

Allarie returned the nod before walking over to the girl's mother and whispering some words to her, both of them sharing a smile. She then spurred her hyder to catch up with Greyson, Martimil, and Ella, who were side-by-side.

"So, as I was saying, Marti over here's father was actually a famous, famous sailor." Ella reached out to Martimil, leaning over in her saddle to give him a nudge.

Martimil steered his hyder just out of reach, watching as Ella's body swung forward and sagged from its position atop her mount. He chuckled to himself as he lifted Ella back up onto her hyder. "Man was a toad. Again, however, he did have a nice compass—family heirloom now." He took the small compass from his pocket and gazed into the distance. "Knowing direction is priceless."

Ella looked at his compass. "The smell of sea, sea water is that way." She pointed at his compass, indicating east.

"Very good. Thank you, Ella." Martimil smiled as he closed his compass. "That would mean north is the way to go. At least, I hope so…" He shook his head and sighed, pausing for a moment, then shifted in his saddle before speaking again, "This desert is a wasteland, and we do not have the supplies."

"We will try to keep people in the shade. We have enough liquid to hold them over for another few days at least. Could we not boil some more of that wine, as well, just in case?" Allarie looked pensive. "I wish we were more positive on directions. Are you sure you do not remember anything? The question is for any of you." She shook her head. "Ella, do you mind going up above again? I feel as though we have made it a ways. I remember something of flowered cacti."

"Is she done rambling?" Martimil asked Ella. "I know the way to go."

"Don't be rude, rude. But, really, you should get some rest. I'll take, take a look." Ella changed her form and soared back into the sky as Martimil took the reins of her hyder.

Martimil looked at his compass and sighed.

———————•————————

"Stones might get thrown in your path, but can you guess what?" Greyson took a dramatic pause. "That's life, baby. And sometimes that baby grows to be a bird. Would ya look at that? She was correct again."

He was on hyderback, gliding through the desert. They had found the cacti with the flowered tops, thanks to Ella's eyes from the sky, and Martimil had guided them the rest of the way.

The village seemed peaceful, and they slowed as they approached. The fires were stoked, the farms were tended, and it looked as if people were entering and exiting the mines in the distance.

Martimil had been listening, riding next to Greyson. "Speaking of paths, I gotta tell you of the one we are about to take to talk to those druids, man," Martimil said.

"Save it for the boat ride. I am only going to be able to silently look at your mug for so long," Greyson said. "How long is that ride going to be? Now, that is an important inquiry."

"It can take ten moon turns. We should be able to get there in about that, barring any hiccups."

"Truthfully, the turns are going to be torture. The miners can't even stand being in the same tunnel as me for too long; I obsess about the rhythms. Maybe water slaps sound good?"

"Anything with water is better. Not having to keep riding these hyders sounds like an absolute plan." A slightly pained look formed on Martimil's face.

"They can hear you, you know." Greyson smirked at him.

"Last thing I need is a fight with one of these. Let's just get everyone back, okay?" Martimil chuckled.

"The village is right ahead. I would kiss the ground, but I really believe I have already swallowed enough sand."

Greyson's face lit up on approach. The rest of the people in the caravan also looked relieved, some running to the entrance to meet the guards standing at the gates.

"Ho!" a guard shouted, halting those who approached.

Greyson and the group he was leading approached the guard. "We come from the troll lair. We are with a caravan sent for by Karnaugh," Greyson said.

"Greyson, we know who you are. Where is Killmead?" the guard asked.

"He unfortunately was killed at the troll gate," Martimil answered.

People in the caravan were passing into the village, and those who had been taken from the village were returning to greet their families and friends.

The guard called over some of his peers. "I will have to ask you a few questions. Karnaugh is back from his hunt, and he will want an accounting from all of you."

"I am going to need you to take me to Karnaugh right away." Allarie stepped forward to meet the guard. "The villagers will get back to work and reaccustom themselves. The new caravan of people want to stay. Again, I need to speak with Karnaugh."

"And who are you?" the guard asked.

"I am the caravan leader. We were supposed to meet him for some sort of party?" Allarie responded.

"I believe he did address me about something like that; that seems about right. All right, follow me." The guard then guided them through the village.

Villagers were peering to see what was going on. Some miners were back in the mines, but others were still working on repairing the destruction to the village caused by the brutal troll attack. People were reuniting, happy to see one another, and the joy spread.

One of the villagers approached the mother and daughter from the caravan. "Just wait until Coal sees you again. He is going to be so happy; he has been absolutely distraught. In the mine, he's been dragging. Someone get Coal!"

The original caravan had apparently been a fairly large-sized group. The newcomers had unique feathered clothing, along with dyed hair and jewelry, all appearing to be affluent people who were in good health.

"All right, I took you as far as the tent," the guard said. "Time for my walk back now. Enjoy the day."

Allarie thanked the guard as he left, nodding her head.

"Okay, we need a plan," Martimil said.

Allarie spoke, "I will go inside and meet with Karnaugh. They know of me, and they will let me in to speak with him. The three of you—I need for his boys to be distracted. Maybe Ella can make them chase her as the seagull?"

"These are no trolls, trolls," Ella inserted.

"Their lack of intellect might surprise you," Allarie retorted. "Greyson, when they seem distracted, I need you to follow me into the tent. I think I can take him this time, but I will need some help. Wait for the distraction, though; we are severely outnumbered." She looked at the rest of the group.

"Do you know what is in those barrels by where they are standing?" Martimil asked.

Allarie took a glance. "Careful, it might be the cactus oil. Your flames would just die out," she said to Martimil. "I think I see Reevus, as well."

Karnaugh's boys were lined up along the side of the tent, an unwavering look in their eyes. Reevus moved to the front, facing them, his robes swishing in the breeze as he waved his arms at the stoic group. He addressed those who were there, as some of the group had gone to patrol the dirt path in the village. "We need to get these delivered to the shoreline. They are being shipped off our shores," he said excitedly.

"Quick, make your way in, then, if he knows of you, too," Greyson said. "Well, be careful, of course."

Allarie looked at him incredulously. "Okay, we can do this."

"You can do this," Greyson said.

"I believe in you, you, Allarie," Ella followed up.

Martimil nodded his head.

Allarie clutched the pommels of her daggers, straightened her back, and then walked out in front of Reevus and the group of boys.

"We need these shipped. Careful now," Reevus said to the boys, who were moving carts outside the tent.

Allarie walked up to one of the carts. "Reevus, where can I find Karnaugh?" she said smoothly to him.

The boys all drew their weapons and turned to confront the intruder, ready to fight.

"Can it be?" Reevus had a look of surprise on his face. "Allarie! How are you?" he shouted.

Allarie smiled at Reevus. "Long time, no see!" she shouted back at him.

The boys were still poised for combat.

"Oh, stand down, crazies." Reevus moaned in exasperation. He eyed Allarie again. "Did you come in with the caravan?"

"My goodness, I did! I wanted to go talk to Karnaugh to see what he wanted to do with the new villagers." She winked at him.

"Of course, Miss Allarie. I want to catch up later." Reevus waved his hand, each finger taking a bow at Allarie as she entered the magnificent tent.

She hid a mischievous smile. Perfect. Maybe this village will work out, after all. So smart, that one.

"The room at the end of the hallway," Reevus called out after she'd entered the tent.

The boys nodded their heads.

Reevus brought a hand across his face and laid a thumb and forefinger on his chin. The boys were marching with a new set of barrels, and there was a bright shine coming from the cracks in the lids. "The caravan is here, boys. Quick, I need more of you to go make sure they have been set up." He pointed at a few among the group, sending them off to the market part of the village.

"Not the glowing oil!" Reevus screeched.

The remaining boys had popped open a lid of a barrel. The men were sharing the oil, taking huge chugs of it, and now they were puking it all onto the ground in a luminous swamp.

Martimil watched as the boys fed on oil and then projectile-vomited a glowing puke at one another. Seizing the opportunity, he made no delay in launching flames from his fingertips at the vomit-ridden, glowing soldiers.

A scream came from inside.

As the boys were distracted by the flames and vomit, Greyson ran into the tent.

The flames exploded on hitting the iridescent sludge that covered the ground, immediately engulfing both those still trying to feed on the oil and the others vomiting it.

Reevus was standing there, watching Karnaugh's men as they screamed while futilely attempting to extinguish the blazing inferno. "No, no, no, no, no!" Reevus was scrambling to deal with the burning oil and Karnaugh's boys being consumed by the flames. He hopped from one foot to the other, a pained look upon his face. He was at a loss.

"You!" Martimil shouted at Reevus.

Reevus ran towards the village center, knowing that someone had thrown the fireballs. He immediately fished out a moss-colored vial from the many baubles in his pockets and tossed it on the ground. The vial burst, producing a dense and acrid greenish smoke that enveloped the area in a thick fog. He ran into the maze of tents.

Martimil and Ella ran into the cloud, searching for the small man. "Fuck. What was his name?" Martimil asked.

"You tell me, me. Reeves?" Ella replied.

Martimil squinted through the fog. "Unbelievable, the screen that made. Reeves? Where are you? We can talk."

"It is Reevus! And you just set my compatriots aflame!" the man said, clearly in a panic. "I do not wish to have the same fate. Be honorable in the talk," Reevus begged.

"I apologize, Reevus. We are really tired of fighting. I know this is sort of crazy," Martimil started.

There were a couple of boys crisping in the distance. "Yes, let's meet and speak away from here. No harm done. Either of us." His hands were outstretched.

"Agreed." Martimil shrugged at Ella, and she shrugged back. "Agreed!" he said again in a louder voice.

Reevus emerged from the fog. He walked up to Ella and Martimil and curtsied.

On seeing this greeting, the two responded with their own. "No oil, oil," Ella said.

"None," Reevus replied.

"What were your plans with the oil?" Martimil asked.

"We were to sell them to an island," Reevus replied. "We made an agreement with a druid there. That glowing oil would have been my first shipment."

"Who is this 'we'?"

"Karnaugh. Who else would there be? We are in the desert. Some druids sailed here from their island, and, well, I got to speak with them. Next thing I know, they order from me," Reevus stated calmly.

Martimil looked over at Ella.

"Did this druid, druid have a name?"

"If I recall, it was Varo. Usually, we have people stopping by the coastal towns. Luckily, Troutus doesn't say much about fishing boats." Reevus had a look of disgust on his face as he walked away from the smoldering corpses. "Who are you?" he asked.

"Well, this is Ella, and I am Martimil." Still at a face-off with Reevus, he waved his hands from Ella over to himself.

"I am Reevus. A pleasure to meet you. Please do not light me on fire. That is a horrendous death, and we definitely could have talked it out," the small man said.

"I think, think I have seen you once before. You do not come down to the miners' quarters often enough."

They walked down the dirt path into the village, where people were running around and moving things from the caravan that had just entered.

"Is this the caravan you came in with?" Reevus approached the carts.

Some of the boys had helped organize and set up the tents in the market. "Let's get this together!" screamed a sharp-nosed man who stood atop a chest. "Let's start this off swinging." The boys around him were all carrying what looked like fancy vases and bundles of worn spears and shields.

"Hey! I know where you got all of that, you slimy worm," Martimil shouted. "Those items are for the village."

The man looked over to Martimil and gave him a wide smile. "Oh, so nice of you to join us again."

Martimil looked over at Ella, who then nodded.

"Hold on, hold on." Reevus stood in front of them. "Before any insanity begins, we should ask our guests if they would like to turn themselves in, of course."

Reevus continued to walk over to the boys and the members of the caravan, who stopped what they were doing and stared at the two of them.

"Do you believe we are going to stop here, turn ourselves in? We just went through Amerthine's Grand Desert. I am not about to let some punks walk all over me now. Some even ventured with me. Why fight?" Martimil waved his fist.

"Why blow up half of our contingent?" Reevus retorted.

"You are acting as though I knew they would blow up like that." Martimil fumbled his words.

"It certainly seemed like that was your intention, and it came true," Reevus replied dully.

"Could we not talk about it now, or did you want to continue to test us?" Martimil gritted his teeth. Ella had transformed into her ram form.

Reevus looked around. "Be careful. He can start fires, boys."

Allarie passed through the imposing doorway to the giant tent. The wood-decorated hallways stretched extraordinarily far for a tent interior. There were several doorways in between statues of buff heroic men draped in jewels, and paintings that depicted heavily armored soldiers lined the walls.

"Gaudy," Allarie said to herself, rolling her eyes. She continued down the hallway, and voices could be heard as she passed by one of the rooms.

"All right. I'll head to the market, see who we can grab to go to the shore," a woman said. She was heavily armored in bright, shiny steel, with a blade at her belt.

"We need to be sure everything has been settled with the druids," Karnaugh said. "We have to get our boys down to the shore. There are people we are supposed to meet."

"They will still be there when we arrive. The hunt did not take long, and Crix will be able to speak with the village on your behalf as we head to the shore."

Karnaugh chuckled. "My boy Crix! Where has his scorpion ass been? We gotta oil soon. I feel like I just saw him." He breathed heavily.

"I haven't a clue, sir. He was last seen in the village; however, I have not seen Forgar, either, if you have an eye out for the officers." The woman started to nod her head.

"Meet with the others in the village, and make sure any accommodations for the guests are met. We need for them to stay," Karnaugh said slickly. "Dismissed," he ordered.

One of the two large double doors in the tent opened up, revealing the large room behind the woman as she walked out. Allarie watched as the woman walked past an armored statue that she was standing next to in the overly decorated hallway. She waited for the woman to leave the tent and then sneaked through the double doors. Karnaugh was hovering over a barrel, making what sounded like a cooing noise. She crept up on him, drawing her daggers silently.

"Ah, yes, this is one of them good ones." Karnaugh tapped the air as if it were an imaginary surface. He turned suddenly, and his oil-black eyes landed right on Allarie. "How did you get away?" He tilted his mouth into a grin.

Allarie bounced back a few steps.

"This is quite the surprise today! So many guests." Karnaugh smiled. He continued to stare at her. "Look at that familiar angry face. So cute," he mocked.

There was a bark in the corner of the lavishly decorated room. "What was that?" Allarie asked.

"The oil, of course, needed a protector. Take a look at this champ." Karnaugh gave a wide grin. "Lily, come here, girl."

A dog was on a chain near the barrels and looked emaciated; it recoiled on being called.

"Maybe later." He started walking to his bed, casually turning about, hands twirling in the air, aloof.

"You think you are so smart. That was very cowardly—using that stupid oil. Good thing I am still around," Allarie replied with a viscous sweetness, exaggerating her words. "I guess it just wasn't strong enough."

Karnaugh unbuckled his bright armor. "Well, you gonna join me?" he asked. "I could use some help on one of these buckles." He fidgeted his hands to grab at a buckle he could have clearly gotten.

"Fuck yourself," Allarie responded. "Get your sword, you coward. Poisons? Really? Pony up, now. Get your sword." She looked furious as she twirled her short dagger.

"You could have played this completely differently, by the way. Should have helped me with my buckles. But suit yourself." Karnaugh readjusted his buckles and stood up, still staring at her with his mouth agape.

His hands reached over to his sword and shield as she leaped at him. He barely had time to roll over the bed and prepare himself for the dagger strike. She came at him with another twirling strike. He held up his shield and, with a smile, blocked the dancing blade.

"I am not like you. I do not need to use tricks."

He rotated closer to her. "Okay, I get it. We were just having a playful spar, and you fell. It really isn't a big deal." He stretched out his last words.

"You lied!" She struck, the blow glancing off his armor. "You lied!" She spun and slapped his face with the butt of the other dagger. "You lied!" She then tried to follow up the dagger blows with a kick.

Karnaugh caught the kick. He brushed his face off with his other hand and then pushed Allarie forward, causing her to collapse onto the bed. "You see how emotional you have become." He quickly came up on the bed, pressing his immense weight on her, his breastplate flattening her cheek. "How much I missed you! I cannot believe I get to do this again. Fuck yeah!" he cheered.

"I will not let you win this time." Allarie wiggled with her short-dagger arm extended, cutting his cheek.

He slapped the blade away in a quick reaction to the cut. She rolled and shot her long dagger up towards the underside of his chin. Karnaugh took his shield and smashed Allarie's arm that was holding the dagger, pinning and crushing it. She kicked, and he took the blow, freeing her dagger for another slash. He raised his shield to block the counterattack and shadowed her with his size.

She turned the deflected blade with the sharp end facing down, sinking it into his leg with the sound of a rip and a crunch. She then proceeded to pull the dagger down and out, further opening the wound. Blood spurted out, and she twisted her dagger just right so as to hit an artery, forcing more blood from his body.

He grunted as soon as she withdrew the blade. "You bitch!" He took his blade and attempted to hit her with a downward arc, only to crash into the feather-filled bed. She was already up and going after him again with a series of quick blows. "You haven't slowed with time, either. Way to go!" he said through gritted teeth.

"Time has allowed me to figure out how to kill you!" She was attempting to get by his blocks, but he shielded himself well.

Blood was dripping on the floor. "Enough of you," Karnaugh grunted. He then rushed at Allarie with outstretched arms and the full weight of his body. She did not have a chance to dodge his grasp; he pinned her on the bed.

"Oooh, isn't this familiar?" He had her between his legs, sitting with his weight on her stomach, making it nearly impossible for her to breathe. Her face turned red. He looked down at her and started to laugh. She was squirming and trying to roll out from underneath him, and on every roll, he would shift his weight over with the roll and reposition himself so that it was as if she had done nothing.

He was still bleeding out, but it was ignored. He bent down and kissed her on the cheek; then, he uncorked another vial and drank some. He poured a little off the side of the bed. "And a little for the fallen boys."

"Get off of me!" Allarie shouted as she punched and kicked.

"Allarie, it is futile. Take a little edge off." Karnaugh then poured what he had in his vial on Allarie's face.

She immediately spit at him. "Just finish me, then. Save your precious oil, you pig."

Karnaugh then took Allarie's dagger and tossed it aside. "Much better. Much less threatening without the blades." He stood up, still looking at her. "Stay right there. I got something for you to try." He excitedly smacked her in the face as he leaped down from the bed and ran over to a barrel with glowing seals.

He took his vial out and plunged it into the barrel of glowing oil, withdrawing it when full. He then twirled with the vial and ran over to the bed and jumped up on top. Allarie was still dazed from the smack that Karnaugh had given her. He straddled her. He then raised up her chin and poured the glowing liquid into her mouth.

"Oh yeah, you remember that?" he asked her, smiling.

Allarie coughed and spit, her screaming face covered with glistening oil. Her eyes spun into the back of her head, and as they slipped back, she groaned in pleasure. Her eyes had turned pitch-black. She laughed, she screamed, she shouted, and she rolled under Karnaugh. She started to run, rubbing her nose and cheeks while searching the floor for something, smearing the oil and further worsening the condition of her face.

Karnaugh laughed. "What are you looking for? Your dagger is way far away. Enjoy the moment." He watched as Allarie stood back up and started to run again, this time towards a lit candle. "Whoa! You won't want to go that way!" Karnaugh said, leaping up from his position on the bed to grab her arm.

She tried to hit him with her other arm, but she just ended up being twirled and tossed back onto the bed by him. She screeched and slammed her fists into Karnaugh's chest, eyes still black.

Karnaugh clutched his bleeding leg. "I need to pay you back for this."

He drew his sword, lifted it, spun the blade so that it faced downward, and then crushed it into her knee. Bones snapping, Allarie screamed in pain. She reached for her knee, but he held her hand down with his foot. With a mischievous gleam in his eye, he then took the sword and punctured her other leg.

Allarie screamed until she passed out from the pain.

13

"Unforgivable"

"Would you look at that—makes you glow a bit." Karnaugh was holding a carafe over Allarie's mouth. She was unable to move her arms, unable to spit out the splattering oil. He gripped her hair, forcing her to stare straight up at his face as he continued to lift and pour.

In the hallway of the massive tent structure, Greyson saw beams of bright-blue light coming from a distant room. She has to be here somewhere. Where are they? He ran towards where he thought the scream had come from, running up to the double doors, slowing his pace as he placed an ear to listen in.

"Let me go ahead and put my finger right here." Karnaugh shoved his finger into Allarie's wound. She let out a gut-wrenching scream.

Greyson burst into the room and glared at Karnaugh, who was on the bed, straddling Allarie. One of Allarie's arms was pinned, the other pushing off Karnaugh's chest. Her legs appeared to be dead; they had not moved. Karnaugh had a sword in his hands and a wide smile on his face.

"You can go ahead and get right the fuck off her." Greyson looked at his surroundings. Barrels were haphazardly scattered around the giant bed; the room was large but dull.

"Allarie!" he yelled.

"She won't respond to you. She looks like she is happy to be here, actually. Why are you interrupting us?" Karnaugh jeered, swaying his shoulders and taunting.

"You picked your fight with an unbroken man. This is fucked, Karnaugh." Greyson circled the room. He sheathed his runed sword and took Killmead's sword from its scabbard.

Karnaugh gave an oily smile. His body shook a little in excitement.

"It is surreal to be here, and in front of you right now. Fuck, I hate you." Greyson started to swing the large sword left and right. "You know how often the miners and I have dreamed of this moment? You took my wife. She was everything to me. She doesn't just disappear to this fucking tent in the middle of the night." He held his sword forward from his body.

"Are you done?" Karnaugh picked junk from his teeth and flicked it at the motionless Allarie. "You are nothing, man. Absolutely nothing to me." He limped off Allarie. "I think I have seen you before. When was that?" He looked curiously at Greyson.

"That is right, bud. Stand the fuck up," Greyson said flatly. "We have names, you know. She had a name."

"Ah, yes, now I remember." Karnaugh giggled and clapped excitedly to himself. "Greyson, the guy who keeps trying to escape. I should have just killed you years ago. They like you down there, you know. Shame to waste your life here."

He continued to limp, blood leaking down the side of his armor, with a gash that stretched from his back to his chest and another in his leg. He had a black eye and a huge welt on his face. "Your wife was fun."

Greyson's eyes went blank. He charged ahead with the sergeant's blade. When he got close enough, he swung the large sword. But he was too close and unable to fully extend.

Karnaugh was able to block the swing. "Ooh, that tickled." Karnaugh circled his sword in his hands. "You are sorely outmatched, miner man. No picks here, but I do recognize that sword—you can't miss the little, pudgy man's sword." He was trying to hold back his laughter. "Just look at the length of that obnoxious bastard."

Greyson held the long blade steady with both hands, his right on the top and left on the bottom. The sword extended as high as one of Karnaugh's bedposts, which almost reached the ceiling of the tent. Greyson charged again, this time with the sword overhanded, and the blade tore into the tent, ripping the cloth. He ran to the back corner of the room, sword still extended, sunlight pouring in from the part of the tent's roof that had fallen.

Karnaugh laughed again. "This is the most entertaining thing I have seen today. If I do not kill you, you are gonna have to fix that." He shook a vial over his sword's surface, spreading the liquid along the blade with a piece of fallen tent cloth. "You won't be able to run…if you are looking to escape—I'll find you. Welcome to Haneserrath."

"You deserve nothing, Karnaugh."

Greyson charged again, this time with the sword lowered, hitting with a force hard enough to knock Karnaugh back, causing a slight stagger. He chopped with the sword, and Karnaugh blocked, spinning closer to Greyson's body and swinging his own sword. Greyson sucked in his gut, projecting his arms forward. It almost struck true, but the sword hit tent cloth instead of flesh, getting caught. Greyson had to drop the sergeant's sword and draw his other sword from its scabbard.

Karnaugh sliced through the rest of the tent roof so that a large part of it was dangling from above, splitting the room. The two men circled each other.

"You are just delaying the inevitable, and thank you for the new sunroof." Karnaugh smiled with a wink.

Greyson was on the opposite side of him, looking at the barrels around the room. A direct attack will not work. He is simply too skilled. So, besides the tent distraction, what now?

Karnaugh had gone over to a vase and uncorked the top of it, taking a scoop into his vial and chugging a little in the meanwhile. "Greyson...come out and play," he said, his voice an arcing singsong.

Greyson was on the other side of the tent cloth. He wanted to avoid eye contact, but it was important to see where his strikes were going. He peered around the side of the partition, and Karnaugh was still huddled over a vase.

"You won't go far." Karnaugh's eyes were ink black. "The death count reported wasn't high enough, so, actually, you being here will help those numbers." He started to beat his sword against his shield. "Come at me, Greyson. Charge again. I am ready this time," he taunted.

Greyson was musing over the fact that this man couldn't get past the oil. I'm standing right here, and the great

Karnaugh in his golden armor is still over his vase. Greyson turned to his left and saw a container similar to the one Karnaugh was huddled over. He proceeded to smash it.

"No!" Karnaugh looked up from the vase, gazing at the tent roof. The pools of black in his eyes looked lost. He scrambled to get to the other side of the tent cloth, stumbling away from the vase and then rushing headfirst at Greyson.

Greyson braced himself for Karnaugh's swing, but instead of a sword, a golden arm extended and swiped him out of the way. The crazed man was on the floor, trying to scoop up what precious oil he could cup into his hands.

A look of disbelief was on Greyson's face, but his expression shifted to anger when he heard a groan from the bed. Greyson picked his sword up and went rushing to swing at the intoxicated Karnaugh. He wound the swing up and shot his arms across his chest with the sword leading.

Karnaugh lifted his shield and blocked the swing with ease. He started to chew on his tongue, staring at Greyson with blank, oil-black eyes. His face was off, somehow. They looked at each other, sword and shield locked together. Greyson was heated, his face pained. A deep frown shaped his mouth. Karnaugh pushed off of him and returned to the oil.

"Are you fucking kidding me?" Greyson said in frustration. He walked over to another barrel and smashed it, rage showing on his face. "You want more? I'll keep going. I am so glad to be here to see this." He smashed another barrel.

Karnaugh's eyes looked barely human. "You should stop that now," he said calmly.

"Doesn't feel good, does it?" Greyson started to go down the line, heading towards Reevus's port, though he did not know it.

"No, no, no, no, no!" Karnaugh's face contorted. He ran over to where Greyson was standing amongst broken barrels, heavy amounts of blood escaping from Karnaugh's wounds. "What have you done?" His face turned to Greyson's. He was still trying to scoop up what little oil he could save. He grimaced as he stood up fully, wielding his sword and shield. "In the name of justice, I will stop you," he declared triumphantly. "Boys! Where are the boys?"

Karnaugh started to make his way towards Greyson. His movements had slowed considerably, and Greyson noticed that Karnaugh wasn't able to hold his sword the way he had before. His face was warped, and his eyes were inky wells, his movements slow and labored. This is no Karnaugh. This is a husk of a man, I know how those are, and this is absolutely not a fighter. Greyson looked at Karnaugh, who was still distraught over the spilled oil. Think. Think. What can I do to end this guy? I can keep coming at him in the state he is in, but he is still capable with that sword.

Greyson continued to smash the barrels until he saw Karnaugh get as far as he needed him to be. He leaped and grabbed hold of the ripped tent and pulled it hard, cutting it with the sergeant's sword long enough that he was able to run with it. And run with it Greyson did.

He sprinted past Karnaugh, who was huddled next to another barrel. Karnaugh looked up from his broken barrel, still trying to scoop up more and pour it into what was left of the bottom of the barrel. He was whispering, "Boys," feverishly to himself and was still openly bleeding out.

"Why!?" Karnaugh screamed as oil was pouring through his hands. "You and these other villagers ruined everything. This place would have been gold—we just needed less of you," he snarled at the tent wall from the back of his broken barrel.

Greyson smashed another barrel, adding to Karnaugh's agony. "You just needed to care about everyone, Karnaugh. You just needed to be a fucking good human." He tore the tent even more. "Fuck you." He ran across the tent again, the flap that he had cut in tow, bolting past Karnaugh, who looked up from the oil and realized what was happening.

"No!" Karnaugh shouted, raising his sword to cut the tent. His arm came down, but his strength was no longer there. "No!" he repeated and cupped his hands while taking another drink. He raised his arms again, this time hitting a separate section and not fully cutting the tent. He was getting desperate, and sweat was showing profusely on his brow as he dropped down to the floor, wanting to roll away.

As soon as Karnaugh dropped, Greyson saw his chance and jumped on top of him.

At first, Karnaugh was shoving and pushing his hands into Greyson's face. "No...no, no," he cried out. "What is a no one like you doing?" His speech was slurred.

"I am someone. I guarantee no one will remember you. No one remembers the selfish ones." Greyson grabbed ahold of Karnaugh's hands, which were slippery from the oil. "You are no one."

Karnaugh's fingers almost slipped out of Greyson's grasp as he tried to prevent the hand from escaping so that he could get an unblocked hit in. He smacked the oil-crazed man in the face with a headbutt. Karnaugh looked dazed by the blow, head shaking after it slapped against the wooden floor, his eyes still ink black.

"Gah." Karnaugh spit out blood and frowned. "Enough of this. It is really starting to hurt, and you are destroying all of the blasted oil." He started to whimper. "Reevus!" he yelled.

"It is too late for him, Karnaugh. It is too late for you and this oil business." Greyson wound up another headbutt and smashed right into Karnaugh's nose.

A sickening crunch echoed from Karnaugh's face. "Fuck, you have a hard head."

Greyson was still holding on to Karnaugh's hands. They had gone limp, and Greyson wiped his forehead. He smashed the fiendish shell of a man over and over. He didn't stop; Karnaugh's bones and teeth stuck in his fists. He punched Karnaugh's face repeatedly as the desert sun beat down through the sliced tent ceiling. Eventually, his swings started to grow weak; the face he was pummeling was a sloshy puddle.

"No more, no more, no more," Greyson repeated, tears in his eyes. "Not"—another smash in the face—"again." Punch. "Never again." Greyson's face had become crazed. "My fucking head!"

Allarie couldn't do anything. Her wide eyes had grown full of tears, as well. As relieved as she was at seeing Karnaugh gone, processing what she had seen was unfortunate. She finally managed to speak. "Stop, Greyson! I can't move, but stop," she whimpered. "Please, it is over," she continued. "He is dead. He is dead. He is dead." The last of her words were choked by her tears but getting clearer. She was still pulsing blue.

Allarie looked straight at Greyson, who had been sobbing, as well. Her tears immediately stopped, and her face straightened. A smile grew as her eyes turned to black. "What you did was fucked up, Greyson," she said, "fucked up, guy." She then kicked her feet into the air…and then her arms. She leaped up from the bed. "I can't get over feeling wonderful, however." She pulsed blue again as she fell back down. "Oh yeah, guy. You should have stayed home; would have totally done what you did right there." She pointed at the mess that was Karnaugh. "Too easy!" she screamed at the exposed sunlit roof.

Greyson was still clutching his head. "I know." He brought his hands down and stared at his bloodied fists. "It's going to be okay." His eyes were closed. "Going to be okay."

———————•———————

Martimil walked over the smoldering corpses of the boys, gritting his teeth a bit. He entered the tent and looked around. "Absolutely massive," he said in wonderment, and he continued on down the wood-walled hallway lined with paintings, swords, and shields. He took down one of the swords. He contemplated the shield, but weighed the sword in his hands and decided against it.

He was cautious, his head on a swivel as he wandered the hallway of the tent. He stopped when he heard crashing and the clanking of swords muffled by the sound of a heavy breeze whipping through the double doors ahead of him at the end of the hallway. The walls did nothing to dim the noise, and he heard people yelling at each other. Then, all of a sudden, the screaming stopped, and a completely incomprehensible sound could be heard. Laughter.

Martimil went up and peeked through the double doors. What he saw on the other side shocked him. Greyson started to slap the bed. Allarie's expression was whimsical and light, although she was unable to move much due to exhaustion. A corpse with a missing face lay near them.

"They did it," Martimil mumbled to himself. He burst the double doors open. "You both have done it! We are now free from that man!" Martimil said awkwardly with an arm outstretched and pointing at the bloody pulp that was once Karnaugh.

Greyson and Allarie both turned and looked at him. They were laughing as they stumbled off the bed.

"Okay, well, what now?" Allarie shouted in excitement. She went over to where the dog was tied up.

Greyson continued to chuckle as he walked away from Allarie. He grabbed Martimil and spun him on his feet, his celebratory smile becoming a frown of concern. "Allarie needs a little bit of time; she is inebriated and heavily in need of medical assistance." Greyson looked exhausted, but he turned his head and smiled again at Allarie. His hands were shaking and swollen to an unnatural size, and his legs wobbled as he struggled to stay upright. "I think I need to lie down." He shuffled over to the other side of the bed to collect Killmead's massive sword.

Martimil gripped Greyson, stopping him from completely falling down. "Allarie, can you come with me back down to the village?" He tossed aside the sword from the hallway wall and went ahead of Greyson to pick up Killmead's hefty blade.

Allarie looked spacey and was still staring at the hole in the ceiling.

Martimil ran over to the barking dog that was close to the broken barrels and looking very uncomfortable. He gave it a hearty pat to calm the clearly rattled canine. The dog licked his hand and then jumped onto the bed with Allarie.

"I think I am going to need Ella for this." Martimil frowned and shook his head as he looked at the worn-out Greyson. "Nope, whelp." He then looked over at Allarie, who was spazzing and stained with oil. "You are going to have to climb on." He backed up to her.

"Whoa there, buddy." She pointed at him. "Had a whole lot of…enough of that." She was waving her arm around, attracting the dog's attention.

"Oh, come now, Allarie. Quit screwing around. There are people waiting for us," he said adamantly.

Ella was peeking through the double doors just as Martimil had done. "You should only be back, backing it up over here," she said as she burst through.

"Too many emotions right now. But, thank Troutus, you are here." Martimil's shoulders slumped.

Ella popped into her bird form, flew over to where Allarie was standing, and transformed back. "Oh, she is a little drunk, drunk." She started to giggle. "Look at her swirling her arms…" She crept forward. "Seems fun, fun."

Greyson was still standing, clutching his head.

"Hey, Ella, take care of Allarie. I am going to take a walk with Greyson," Martimil said.

"Can you come here first, please, please?" Ella held her arms out while doing a dance. "Like, this is some, some good feeling stuff." She was reaching with outstretched arms. "Careful, careful now."

Martimil rushed over and squeezed her. "A job well done."

Greyson had already walked off.

"He's just jealous." Martimil sprang to follow. "Love you. Bye."

She watched him take off and turned to the spaced-out Allarie, who was now curled up and pushing at the unamused dog on the mattress.

———————•———————

"Hey, Greyson!" Martimil chased down the gloomy Greyson. The large sword was still in his hands. "Can you take this back?"

"Hey, Marti, I think it is time for me to go. I'll follow the trade trail, see where it takes me. There aren't any trolls anymore!" Greyson announced. "My fucking head!" He stomped his feet.

Martimil had a quizzical look on his face. "You all right, Greyson?"

"Yeah, I have actually never been better. I just never thought that I would ever actually walk away. Dreamed of it—sure. Tried it—sure. And the more I think about it, the more I almost want to stay to see what happens to the village." Greyson started to rub his face, his hands grinding on the eye sockets that were painted red with irritation. "I just need this pain to stop."

Martimil walked over to Greyson and laid a hand on his shoulder. "I have a suggestion for you. I asked you before. See the druids, man. I also do not believe clawing your eyes out will help."

"Please tell me we can check out your island, man," Greyson said as he looked at Martimil through a cage of fingers.

"Not a man on a solo mission, are you, now?"

"After these past days, I don't think I want to be without all of you," Greyson admitted.

Martimil looked Greyson in the eyes. "I don't think Allarie can come with us, though. This village needs someone like her. But I believe I have the place to take you for those headaches."

"She looks good, though, Marti. Let's be real." Greyson nudged him.

"Ella was completely right. I was so trying to back it up on her." Martimil made a motion to mimic piggybacking someone. "She is needed here, and you need to get those headaches worked out, friend."

"How quickly do you believe we can get the headaches settled?"

Martimil sighed. "I do not know, Greyson. I just know the damn druids."

Greyson sat down on a nearby bench. He took his runed sword from its scabbard, scratching what little rust was left on it. "Martimil, I think I have something more to give. I can't let this take forever. Again, the druids"—he paused—"your opinion of them isn't that high." He continued to scratch at the rust.

Martimil placed the giant sword down and took a seat on the bench next to Greyson. "It would be irrational to give you an answer to that. I am a fisherman, not a doctor." He tapped his knee. "Best chances are there. They have the best doctors in the land; that's why I'm bringing up those druids again."

"Listen, you don't need to go about convincing me anymore. I am on board. I need to figure this out next," Greyson said as he stretched his arms out, his tone becoming sharply optimistic.

"I have to amp myself up to go back and face those bastards myself, you understand," Martimil stated, putting his head in his hands. "They are really a miserable group."

Greyson peered at Martimil with a cocked grin. "Thank you for sticking me with such company."

"You want those issues to go away?" Martimil asked.

Greyson patted the sword and placed it back in its sheath. "You already know."

14

"This village needs you"

Ella dabbed ointment on Allarie's wounds, being careful around the severe cuts. She then placed her arm around Allarie, and they stumbled out of the tent with the dog yapping at their heels.

"Are you ready, ready to face the music of the village?" Ella patted Allarie's arm. "Of course, course, you aren't." She smiled at Allarie, cocking her head crazily.

"Where are we headed now?" Allarie slurred, bringing a hand up above her eyes. She struggled to look ahead as the sun's glare was stunting her sight.

Ella looked down at Allarie's bloodied knees. The dog had been trying to get at them. "How are you able, able to walk?" Ella shooed the dog, stepping in front.

Allarie was a sight to behold. She was a bloody mess, but all of her wounds seemed to have healed over. In spite of the gore, Allarie's glowing face made a halolike image around her.

"Come to think, think of it, this might be the perfect time." Ella was staring at Allarie's face with a hopeful expression.

"What's that supposed to mean?" Allarie was still slurring her words. "Look, the puppy wants to lick the blood."

"No, no!" Ella said sternly to the dog. "We need to find, find a home for you." The dog still looked pleasant, wagging its big tail. Ella gave it a pat.

"His home is right here," Allarie said.

"It is a her—no, no balls." She cupped her hands in an up-and-down motion.

"Oh! She is perfect!" Allarie was infatuated with her new furry companion. "It's not what you can do for your village, but what your village can do for you!" She giggled while talking to the dog.

"I wonder, wonder if she has a name?"

"Act as though I will not give her a beautiful name." Allarie continued to smile and pinched the dog's face.

"Well, well, what do you think it should be?" They went farther away from the tent, following the well-worn walking path.

"Lily. Beautiful flowers are not known to be found in the South."

"Yeah, sucks, sucks here. I think, think that will be a fitting name, then."

"Settled." Allarie was very pleased as she tapped her feet in quick succession, the dog mimicking her movements.

The two wandered farther down into the village. Voices could be heard, shouting close to the guardhouse near the front wall. One recognizable voice was from Pops, which had a sound of authority compared to the others.

"Shut it, Pops. We have to make the newcomers welcome," one of Karnaugh's boys said.

"Where is Karnaugh?" Pops yelled back at the towering man.

"Conducting his business," the man replied, hands on his hips.

Allarie and Ella were chatting with each other when Allarie saw that the armored man was about to strike Pops.

"Ho! Hody, hody, ho. Let's put the fist down." Allarie moseyed over.

"Shit, Lady Allarie. Surprised, I am," the large man said gruffly.

Past the guardhouse at the entryway, a hulking figure, which was making its way towards the village, could be seen in the distance. Allarie was squinting her eyes, trying to see what was moving. "Hey, Ella, would ya go check that out for me?"

"Right, right." Ella leaped into the air and changed into her seagull form. She flew out towards the distant figure.

"Pops, where is Haan? I would like to have a meeting," Allarie said. Her eyes moved on from Pops and settled on the others she could see.

"I am right here, Allarie. What is happening?" Haan came from the direction of the center market, slowly making her way towards the front gate. As she was approaching, Allarie was fervently waving her hand.

"Haan! We need to become closer." Allarie walked towards the older woman, smiling sweetly. "I have plans for this place."

Haan smiled back at her. Pops and the large soldier were still staring each other down. "Can we take a seat in the guard's shack?" Haan asked.

Allarie took Haan's arm and guided her towards the guardhouse.

"Allarie, are you feeling all right?" Haan looked at her curiously, her eyes shooting back and forth between Allarie and Pops.

"I have never felt better, Haan." Allarie's smile couldn't be removed from her face. They took a seat at a table in a rather dull and drab general-purpose room, a small candle being the only decor.

"You have returned! And in one piece," Haan cried. "Truthfully, a surreal moment for me." She was gazing into Allarie's eyes. "We were all cheering for you, and Karnaugh came back—disappeared as usual, however."

"I wouldn't worry too much about him, Haan," Allarie said sternly. "The next thing I am going to have to ask you is, where should we take this village?"

Haan looked at Allarie with emotion-filled eyes. "Allarie, we have so much help we could give these people. They deserve so much more." She gestured broadly towards the village.

"That is what I wanted to talk to you about." Allarie paused. "I need you on my side. I would like to be the replacement for Karnaugh."

"Well, Allarie, I would highly suggest you speak with him first. That seems a little presumptuous, do you not believe?"

"I wouldn't worry about him, moving forward; he found himself better suited to a big village."

"He has left?" Haan's shaky voice rose as she cocked an eyebrow.

"He has, indeed, left, leaving the village without a leader," Allarie spoke with confidence.

"He hadn't a care for the families in the village, and they did not like him, either. I will not ask further questions. I am glad he is gone, and you have my blessing." Haan added a nod.

Pops was still arguing with one of Karnaugh's old boys.

Allarie stepped out of the hut and, cupping her hands, called to Pops. "Pops, I need you, as well. I am going to need the elders to hear this if you would like to forward the word to them."

Pops was midglare when he realized he had been beckoned. "Allarie, what is it that you need?" His eyes peeled from the other man's eyes, and his heavily wrinkled face furrowed.

"Yes, there is a change." Allarie was sobering up. She shook her head to clear it further. "I am taking over for Karnaugh. I need support from you and the other elders."

Pops nodded his head. "No one liked Karnaugh. Best not to speak too loudly of him. He was very much unfit for this. I will support your claim, but you are not a known figure here. Lucky you are—you have Haan's blessing, too." He rubbed his chin. "You'll have to explain how you are the most qualified, however. I know of a few of the elders who would challenge you."

"Then, take up a sword and challenge me. I have thought this clearly through—how to dispatch that man and what to do to take over this village. I have the boys I need. I have those who will follow me to send an envoy to the South in order to hold them off from curiosity."

"Please continue," Pops said.

"The South is going to be an issue if you replace me with one of your elders. I come from the city, and I come from royalty. I know how we can make Haneserrath a prominent village." She looked hopeful. "I need you to believe in me."

"Well, like I said, I will support your claim. It isn't me that you will need to convince, but the rest of the village and the miners."

"About the miners, who would you suggest I speak with?"

"I mean, you walk with a very influential man; however, you'll want to speak to whomever he considers a replacement when he does walk out of here." Pops grinned.

"I am going to assume you mean Greyson. Yes, I will, of course, speak with him...also plead with him to stay."

"He wants to run from here."

"And I will not keep him here. He has helped us all out and deserves to go off."

Pops nodded his head. "Well, that is settled, then. I will speak with the others."

Allarie looked with a sense of finality at Pops. "This is wonderful."

The massive person in the distance finally came into view. Forgar was walking back to the village with Ella.

"Ho!" called a guard from the wall. He immediately looked flushed upon seeing Forgar.

A lumbering Forgar walked through the entrance, looking very groggy. His arms were hanging limply as he dragged himself slowly towards the guardhouse. "I need liquid!" he shouted.

"Do we have anything for him?" Allarie searched her person, but her canteen was dry, as well. One of the guards rushed over to give his canteen to her.

"This way, Forgar." Allarie walked towards the stumbling man.

"Do my eyes deceive me?" Forgar squinted. "Is that Lady Allarie?"

"Ah, yes, of course, Forgar. Welcome back, big guy."

"I thought you left us." He was visibly confused and looked positively parched, holding his hands out for Allarie's canteen.

Pops scoffed at the large man and turned away. "I am going into the village to visit Greyson and the miners."

Allarie nodded to Pops and shifted her gaze towards the large figure. "Now, just hold on." She withdrew the canteen. "Where is it you come from? Why were you not with the rest of them? Or was this another one of his games?"

"Thirst, Allarie," Forgar pleaded.

She gave the canteen a shake. It had more than she thought. Allarie finally handed him the canteen. "Forgar, he is gone." She watched as the hulk drank, life springing back into him with each gulp.

He wiped his mouth with one of his humongous paws. "Are you speaking of who I believe you are speaking of? If so, as glad as I am, I have a quarrel."

"I do not think you understand, Forgar. He is gone, gone."
She looked to see if Haan was out of earshot. "I will tell
them of his demise soon." She tapped on the pommel of her
dagger. "What happened?"

"He left me to die, but he overestimated his poisons."
Forgar unstrapped his hammer from his back, placing the
very large weapon so that it leaned on the outside wall of
the guard shack.

Villagers were looking on, and miners were starting to
pour out of the mountain. The villagers who had been
scrambling around with the new caravan were now cooking
the large amount of mush that would be given out for dinner.

"Strange. He did the same to me. Reevus makes his
poisons, that damned oil." Allarie pondered, furrowing
her brow. "You just came from the desert. Where did
Reevus go, then?"

"He often disappears. Have you checked his hatch in the
tent?" Forgar took another heavy swig.

"He can't have taken off far."

The miners were all dispersing to their tents before grabbing dinner. Loud chatter was breaking out among the group.
They all appeared tired but relieved the others had returned.

Allarie's serious tone did not waver as she sucked in her
gut and breathed in. "I will need your help, Forgar. I want
this village to work and to work well." Her posture was
upright, and she exuded confidence.

"I have no will to lead at this point. I am old and
tired." The hulking figure exhaled. "The boys might take
some convincing."

"They need someone they know. Now isn't the time to quit, Forgar. I have a request of you, when and if the village accepts me."

"They will." He handed the canteen back. "Nobody knows what they are doing. They are just following what is being told."

She nodded at him. "I feel like I almost have the people I need to support me in my claim. Thank you, Forgar. Also, a few boys might be looking for you still."

"They do not do much without direction."

"That is exactly what I need you for. They just need someone, and, basically, Karnaugh had them with that oil. If there is a way, let's get them off of that," she said insistently.

"The oil is speaking their language."

"I know there is still some left. Greyson did smash a good amount of barrels." Allarie was staring out of the guard-house and in the direction of the large village tent that had once been Karnaugh's abode. "If we can find Reevus, we might be able to improve the conditions in this desert village."

"Reevus can't be trusted. He is very close with Korgak," Forgar grunted.

"Reevus might be our solution to what we have left of the boys and for relations with neighbors and an island I heard about."

"You know we do not tread on water."

"You know we are in charge of this village, and I am going to do what I can to make this place work. My thought process has changed."

A seagull came flying down from the sky and shifted into a short woman.

"I did not have time to find something to eat, eat. Will it be gruel?" Ella sighed.

"That shit has to change, too." Allarie frowned at the mention of gruel.

"It is hard to feed a village. There isn't a lot in the desert, but if we can get regular hunting parties to the forest's edge, we will be able to hunt game," Forgar said, his old face brightening at the prospect of going back north to the tree line. "Just have to actually put forth the effort."

"Think on your next moves, Forgar. The boys have lost some numbers, and I will need you to resolve this by taking them away."

"What?"

"Not like that." Allarie looked at him incredulously. "I need you to go to the capital with them, clear up that our village is working. The miners will continue shipments."

"It is strange to hear from someone who knows what they are doing again, Allarie. He was an unfortunate man. Whatever fate befell him, it's better for humanity as a whole." Forgar nodded, then grunted, and sighed as he scratched his protruding belly.

"He lost his mind—the oil is dangerous. Why you also need to wean the boys off of the oil on your way to the capital, away from the other villagers. I know you want redemption, Forgar. This is it."

"This is, is it," Ella repeated.

"Who are you?" Forgar appeared confused as he examined Ella.

"She is another step of how this village will grow," Allarie explained.

"Where did she come from? I did not know we had another druid in the village."

"She comes from an island that has an abundance of them. We might be able to open another trade outlet," Allarie said excitedly.

"Her druids are there, yet she is here. How can this be?"

"They were fisherfolk. Their boat sank, so they found themselves here."

"It is still quite the distance to the shore from the desert. The village of Haneserrath isn't the most opportune of areas."

Allarie glanced over at Ella, who gave a shrug.

"This is the sand we decided to walk on. I found, found the village while flying around. I was lucky to notice the smoke. I didn't want to leave the water, but I figured civilization is better, better than wandering in the desert. Turns out I was correct." Ella sounded optimistic. "I made Marti go quite, quite a way."

"So, what would you need me to do first? To the shore or to the capital?" Forgar asked.

"I am sending Greyson to the island." Allarie paused. "He will speak on our behalf. They trust him in the village, and he also seeks the druids' help. I need you to head back to the capital."

"We do not have a boat. No one from the South has a boat."

"Ella, is there possibly a way to convert the caravan's wagon to a boat? I don't know what the fuck I am doing."

"We will need, need more wood."

"We will take from the large tent. This can work."

"I have zero knowledge on how to build a boat." Forgar grunted.

"Martimil can, can figure it out. He would like to leave as badly as I do. We will, will get it done."

"Forgar, will you help? I know we are basing this on word." Allarie looked up to the man and then out at the village. "Look around, Forgar. We are what we got. Karnaugh had you for dead, much like myself."

"Allarie, I remember your mother, and you are just like her. I know your heart will be in the correct place. And to be frank, after what I have been through, I am a bit tired." He let out a sigh. "Tired of disappointment."

"Forgar, I am just like you. Just a person. I make errors, but I know of the importance of others. And I need you to speak for me in the South."

"I am just a tired old man," he corrected her, holding up a finger. "So, unlike me, you have more of a voice. I will talk with who I know for you."

———————•———————

Three thin rocks with large bases were standing, one in front of the two others. A miner wound up his arm and tossed a smaller rock with all his might. The rock went shooting through the air and thumped harmlessly into a pile of sand, missing the thin rocks.

"Ooh, tough miss," Greyson shouted with a smile.

"Fuck," Garrett said.

Garrett dropped to the ground, did five push-ups, and then went to collect the rock. He picked the rock up and tossed it to Greyson, who caught it with casual ease in his cupped hands.

"Now, watch as the master of disaster does his thing." Greyson flicked the stone into the air, caught it, and then launched his own throw. Soaring through the air, the projectile hit the front pin just to the right, knocking it into the one in the back; meanwhile, the thrown rock deflected to the left, knocking the other rock over as well. All three of the stones dropped.

Greyson whooped. "Looks like it is twenty more for ya."

Garrett sighed. "You gotta be shitting me."

"So, just hear me out. Fuck Karnaugh, right?"

"Yeah," Garrett muttered as he started to push.

"What if I were to tell you he might be done."

"Done as in what?"

"Done as in done, done?" Greyson said awkwardly.

"I am not picking up what you are putting down," Garrett responded flatly.

"I killed him, Garrett."

"Fuck you."

"Where do you think I have been this whole time?"

"I just assumed the guards took you again to fuck you up."

"That is a hard no, Garrett. All that shit we talked, I finally lost it on seeing the guy. Like, actually in person. I couldn't stop myself. I was so angry." Greyson clenched his fist.

"It is all right, dude. We are out here now." Garrett patted his friend on the back. "It also appears like you are not being picked on, which...finally, Greyson."

"What is strange—I think everyone is just okay with it."

"So long as our day-to-day doesn't change. We still get gruel. For the most part, I do not think people really give a shit."

"True. That blasted gruel."

"What if I told you there're better things to eat than that shit," Martimil said matter-of-factly as he approached Greyson and Garrett.

"I would tell you bullshit," Garrett responded. "There is nothing out here. We get lucky on occasion. How could we do better than the gruel?"

"I am still so surprised that the South doesn't believe in seafood," Martimil mentioned.

"Fuck them. I believe in anything that sates my hunger," Garrett said.

"Then, Haneserrath should take advantage of being closer to the shore. I can teach you to fish," Martimil said. "Maybe you will help me make a boat in return?"

Garrett smiled. "Let's do it. Let's get away from this mountain."

"I believe we can use the wood from the large tent. We could expedite this and get Greyson and myself to the island to negotiate for the village," Martimil said.

"Garrett, this is a good opportunity for you, too. Get out of the mine, as well," Greyson said to the young man.

"Fuckin' duh. Think you are the only one who wants out? Who wants to be in a dark hole? Let's go to the water."

"Has a point." Martimil nodded his head.

"Someone has to, though," Greyson responded.

"Another point."

"Maybe, just maybe, we can get those caravan guys to go," Garret responded cheekily.

Greyson set up rocks again. He took a smaller rock and tossed it at Garrett. "Another quick game of pock?"

Garrett smiled. "I will not lose this time. You will be doing the pushing." He lined up his shot and sent the stone flying. His throw nabbed the pin in the front, knocking it over.

"Ahh there goes one. That's five for you."

Greyson dropped, pushed out his five, and leaped back up with the stone in his hand. "Okay, here we go again. You know how I do this." He wound up, then with a spin and full force of his arm strength, he let the stone soar. It hurtled through the air and smacked the taller rock, making it fall. Two rocks had been knocked over.

"Uh-oh, Greyson." Garrett dropped down and pushed his quick five. "If I get this last rock, that would mean I take the win."

"You won't. You choke—happens all the time." Greyson had a smug look on his face.

Garrett wound up, his eye on the last rock standing.

Greyson made a couple of whooping noises to distract Garrett. The stone was released, and it sailed through the air, slamming into the last standing rock and knocking it over.

Greyson let out a long groan to show his displeasure.

Martimil was standing nearby laughing. The sun was setting, and the villagers had started to get a fire going in a large pit in the center. In the distance, a large, hulking figure moved along with two smaller figures.

"Ah, that looks like it might be Ella," Martimil said.

The trio approached Greyson and his company.

"What news?" Greyson called to them while pushing.

"Come with us. We are headed to the fire. I figured you would be with the miners," Allarie said. "I am going to make the announcement. Do I have miner Garrett on my side?" She grinned at Garrett with hope in her eyes.

"As long as you send me and some of mine to the shore, as well, I am in," Garrett mused. "I'd like to see the water, too. I think most could do with an occasional change of scenery."

"Garrett, rationally thinking, I need you in that mine—they trust you in there. However, we can figure a way," Allarie stated.

"I hear sincerity in your words, and, frankly, I didn't have a say…ever. So, yeah, of course, makes sense."

"Allarie is addressing you because I am going to be leaving." Greyson looked Garrett's way. "You need to represent those in the mines."

"I never thought about it. Pops always did what he could for us," Garrett said.

"Time to give this part a shot until you can get to the shore," Greyson replied. "I might be back…eventually?"

"Was that a question, Greyson? You're not coming back. Why would you? Get away from this place. Go." Garrett smiled at him.

"Greyson will come back eventually," Allarie said. "That is a part of the agreement to send him to those druids for trade."

"Oh, I guess that is so," Greyson said. "I will be back for you, bud." He slapped Garrett on the back. "Let's get to the fire. We have an announcement to make."

The group headed to the center of the village, where people were gathered around a large fire. Tents had been set up for the new group of villagers who had accompanied the caravan.

"Keep them over there!" Pops called. More tents were being set up near the fire as the clamoring crowd searched for materials.

"Pops, you ready?" Greyson called. "Hey! I need every-one's attention up here really quickly. You all know me."

The crowd had been either helping with the setup of the tents or eating from the gruel plates in front of them. Their attention shifted, and their focus became the group that was forming in front of the feasting villagers. They took a pause to see what was happening.

"Karnaugh is not coming back to the village. He is gone." Greyson smirked. "We must have a replacement who speaks for us." He motioned for Allarie to step forward. "I say that Allarie takes the lead of the village!" he shouted to the villagers.

"Aye," said Pops.

"Aye," said Haan, her kids still close by.

"Aye," said Garrett with his troop of miners behind him.

"Aye," said Forgar, who had with him what was left of the boys and the guard.

One of the guards piped up. "Who the fuck is she? I don't need to follow a stranger. I could do just fine by myself, thanks."

"You are speaking to a princess of the South. It is in our best interest to follow her," Greyson retorted.

"I don't care if she came from the king's asshole. She ain't leadin' me." The man spit on the ground. "Also, fuck you, Greyson."

"I can attest that you do not want what the South will bring to us if you do not accept what has been given," Forgar stated. "He is right."

The man grimaced, but the rest of the townsfolk agreed on Allarie.

"Aye," said Allarie. She shook her head.

"No, honey, honey, they are choosing you." Ella gently nudged Allarie to make her stand up straighter. "Wave, wave." She smiled and nodded her head at Allarie.

"Speech!" someone in the crowd shouted.

Allarie had a look of confidence on her face. "Fine. I grew up in the capital, Odh Varol. I was set to be Karnaugh's wife. He poisoned me and came here, thinking I had passed. I had not. I followed him here. I have been watching you— watching you grow as a community and watching as my late husband neglected his people. I want to change that for you. I want to do better for you."

There was an audible cheer from the villagers, and some of the faces from the caravan lit up, as well.

"We need to figure out a way forward, and I have plans for us." Allarie started to pace in front of the crowd. "I need you all to not change how things have been going from a day-to-day perspective until we can achieve a balance." She had the crowd's ears. "We need to establish this village as a beacon on the map. We can do that with Haneserrath. We can make this a prosperous village!"

"What is she even saying?" a man in the crowd said.

"I do not know, but it is amping everyone up, and I feel it," another man in the crowd replied.

"That being said, we have to take to water."

The crowd grew silent once Allarie said that.

A man crept forward and spoke, "We, too, want to flow in the rivers with Troutus, but they say we are not allowed to swim until the afterlife."

"If that is your belief, then do not become a sailor. I am not holding you to it. I am, however, asking that you help, for this will benefit everyone. I still need people in the mines and on the cactus farms." Allarie lightened her facial expression and raised her tone, encouraging the man.

"That would mean you are allowing others to stray into the rivers. We have to keep up with the cactus milking, for water."

"No, I am telling you, Troutus will reward us for our resilience," she responded. "We know of an island that we could establish trade with. This village will thrive. There is a way forward."

"Yes, but the Great Lord Troutus demands us not go onto the water. He will not allow for any rainfall to happen." The man's face looked frightened.

"Troutus isn't your starving neighbor. But he would understand that we need a way forward, to work together and find a solution. There are those in this village that have already tried fish. Now is not the time for fear; now is the time to act." Allarie looked back at Greyson, who gave her a gleeful nod.

The man in the crowd seemed lost as he scratched his head, and others around him looked confused, as well.

Then, the young Ally cheered. As soon as the little girl's cheer erupted, the rest of the crowd joined in.

"Let us start by continuing to accommodate the new members, knowing that we are going to have to work together to develop. I am specifically talking to the guards and the miners. We have to work with one another... as equals." Allarie waved Garrett and Forgar forward. "I have two representatives, one from each group. If there is a problem, go to them first. This is what I suggest. We will continue to work together, and I will be around to help." She waved at the two of them. "Forgar and Garrett."

A wave of whispers went through the small crowd. "Who?" some of the people said out loud.

"Do these people know of you two?" Allarie asked in a much more hushed tone.

"I would gather not. However, now is clearly the time." Garret stepped forward rather brashly. "Hello! I am Garrett. I have been a miner all my life. Please come and say hello."

"The young guy," someone in the crowd said. "The young guy!"

Cheers ensued.

"See, that was easy." He walked back to Forgar. "Go ahead, big man. Introduce yourself."

Forgar walked forward.

On seeing his imposing figure, the crowd quieted and became pensive. Forgar cleared his throat. "Many have not seen me, as Karnaugh had hidden me away. I am Forgar, leader of the boys."

Booing and hissing of disdain shot from the impatient crowd. One of the boys held his arms out. "Moving forward, may we work together for a prosperous village."

"He is trying," Pops said. "Let us find the path."

"Thank you, Forgar." Allarie brushed his shoulder.

Then, she addressed the crowd again. "You need some sort of representation to speak with me. I am putting these two in charge of that."

The crowd cheered again at hearing Allarie speak.

Allarie nodded. "We can do this." She looked back at the crowd. "As we did in the desert, we will do again for this village. We need to rotate responsibility—the sun grows too hot; the mines grow too dark." She stared at the villagers who were in attendance. "Haan needs help."

Most of the crowd started to rush over to gather around Allarie as the rest of the group tried to calm the others down.

"Not the time. She has taken substantial damage from a fight. I am surprised she is even out here, but she did win," Greyson said.

He looked back to Allarie and the others. "Go back to the tent. We should clean it up, get what we can for the village." Greyson started to walk away, and Martimil followed.

"That was swift, swift thinking," Ella said. "I am not cleaning that shit, shit show up myself, Marti."

"I need to get me a seat somewhere to collect my thoughts. I need that bench again," Greyson remarked.

"Over here, over here." Martimil pointed to the bench that they had sat on previously and waved Greyson over.

Ella was standing with her hands on her hips. "Do what you gotta do, do, but I'll be inside cleaning up." She watched them walk away.

"Ella, I promise we will be back. Look at him—he is a mess. I am trying to get him to go with us." Martimil had a pleading look on his face, eyebrows in a wide arch.

"Sure, sure." Ella smiled, looking away.

15

"Hogfaw"

Greyson and Martimil walked towards the village center. Villagers were rushing around, figuring out what to do with the extra people. The people from the new caravan had been unloading and helping out in the village with the supplies taken from the troll keep.

"She rose to the occasion quickly. This is great PR." Martimil tapped his nose.

"What even is PR?" Greyson had a puzzled look on his face.

"Public relations," Martimil said knowingly.

"What in the world would a fisherman know about public relations?" Greyson asked, chuckling.

"You have other folks in the mines to chat and joke with. I have to see how to become agreeable to people while only talking to myself and, luckily, Ella on the high seas. You need to know a little about having a conversation."

"Dang, Marti. Well, now you can chat with me, too." Greyson sounded slightly perked up.

"Would be my honor, Greyson. I want you to eat from this tavern. You need to experience it once in your life. Also, maybe we can set up trade here…" Martimil's voice went high. "Goals, you know. Gotta have them," he said matter-of-factly.

"Like getting rid of these headaches is now a goal of mine, and, more importantly, closing those portals. I am excited for that." Greyson's mood was lightening. "Meet those druids you speak of—hopefully, they are nothing like Crix."

"Yes. No, nothing like Crix. Much bigger pussies, if I am being honest. They did a huge disservice to Ella, for which I have not forgiven them. What happened to Crix, anyway?"

"I really do not know. I think he disappeared. Did you ask Forgar about him?"

"To be honest, I forgot about the guy. Remind me to ask. He is slippery."

Greyson scratched his head. "He is a very strange individual I do not know much about."

"I don't trust him, Greyson. But I believe in you." Martimil grew more serious. "I'd like to help you with this portal business…and getting to our island, of course."

"Well, I'd like to let you know that you are well on your way now." Greyson flinched but sported a grin.

"Yo, follow." Martimil beckoned.

They walked towards the mines. Tired villagers with carts rolled by, filling stockpiles. Greyson waved at them.

Pops was standing with Garrett.

"Ho, guys. How have you been!?" Greyson walked up with a smile on his face.

"Greyson!" they said in unison.

"Did you get Allarie caught up?" Pops asked, his fingers curling his stringy hair.

Greyson gave a slight grimace. "Give her some time. She needs to nap off her wounds." He walked towards the mine entrance and grabbed a pickax.

"Ooh boy, do I want to make a move astern," Martimil piped up on seeing Greyson pick up the ax.

"Calm down and grab a lantern. I just want to make one more stop. Follow me, Garrett. We'll be back, Pops." Greyson gave a knowing nod.

Garrett, Martimil, and Greyson picked up a line and started to climb down the tunnel to where Greyson's usual working spot had been in the mine.

"Hey!" one of the miners shouted, his voice bouncing through the dark tunnel.

Soon after, an echoed response came from several other miners down the shaft. Slams of pickaxes could be heard throughout.

Greyson picked up his ax and struck rock, starting a rhythm. "I'm leaving!"

Other miners started to pick up on the rhythm. "Bullshit!"

More miners followed with "Shut up!"

"No, guys! I am walking out the gates," Greyson screamed. Too long. "Going out the gates!" He paused. "Good-bye!" The farewell boomed.

Greyson continued to swing his pickax in rhythm. He slammed three more times and then placed his ax down. "Time to go," he said to Martimil and Garrett.

"Why does he get to leave?" a miner asked. "Stop being a trog. Be happy for the guy," his neighbor responded.

Ella was with Allarie back in the giant tent of Haneserrath. Haan looked in at them scooping up the bed furs with Karnaugh's body still hanging limply in the center. Forgar and Garrett were lurking behind.

"Martimil would, would run from the cleaning." Ella rolled her eyes.

Allarie gently slapped her own face, snapping herself to attention. "To be honest, it is distracting me, sobering me. And Greyson needed Marti. Plus, there is no way we will finish cleaning up in here. Just look at all of these smashed barrels. They will get theirs."

Haan came bursting in. "Allarie, you are awake!"

"That was, was fast." Ella looked amused.

"Hello, Haan. Long time, no see." Allarie smiled as she wandered the tent, noticing everyone around her.

"Yes, yes, I saw you earlier. Karnaugh didn't listen to me at all, but I wish that he had. The man ignored the families," she said sullenly.

"I am no Karnaugh, and I know what I agreed to." Allarie's smile had gone straight, and she started to bark orders into the air. "Their mothers will come back. If we can get them off my walls, out of my mines...without hindering production...as much as we can."

"Yes, that is all a start, but the kids... I can help, of course, but they need their parents."

"Let's make a change, then, Haan. We can't cut production too much, but I guarantee the gold we do acquire from the mines will go to the families." Allarie started to pace. "We meet with the villagers and see if we can make shift changes, and also see what the new villagers could possibly do." She let out a slight sigh and then clenched her jaw. "They appear to only be spoiled brats so far, but everyone will have their use."

She tapped her chin. "I need to use Forgar. He needs to represent us in the capital. Korgak never liked me." She pivoted midpace and looked back at Haan. "Do you think I can trust him, however? I knew him before, and his character appeared to be different from the others."

"You never truly stop being young; you just cease to be able to do things after a time. So, I can't run as fast as I used to, but I just do not feel the need to run that quick anymore." Haan realized that she had started to fret and harp on elderly musings, so she took a pause before replying calmly to Allarie's question.

"I can't say. I have been too busy with families. Speak with him. I am glad you are going to take to this village. Like what Greyson said, I think we can all do better." She smirked. "I need to get back to the kids. Thank you for easing my thoughts, as well." She went back through the double doors. "I'll see you again soon. Please come by. The kids really look up to you."

Ella was still sitting nearby. "Well, dang, dang, lady." She threw a small piece of wood from a broken barrel at Allarie. "You are gonna, gonna have those hands full." She paused. "It is too cool, cool to have such a badass as a friend."

"Why, thank you," Allarie said.

Wood was being stretched and plied from the floors, leaving gaping holes in places.

"Do you think this will be enough?" Forgar asked.

"I have no idea how much wood is needed for a boat," Garrett responded. "Ella, have any idea how much we will be needing?"

"All of, of it," she replied with a smile. "This is so, so exciting!"

Both of the men groaned.

"I think it would be wise to get some of the villagers to assist us in tearing this place down. Troutus knows, they would be more than willing," Forgar grunted. He muttered to himself as he wandered off to the back of the tent.

"This will, in fact, take us forever," Garrett said loudly.

"Get some others. Find Greyson and Martimil. Let's get plans to build. We need this plan to work; the future of our village depends on it," Allarie said. As soon as she finished her sentence, a slap of the floorboards echoed from outside the tent.

"Would you be my representative at the island, Ella?" Allarie asked. "If you could get the ears of anyone there for us, I would be much appreciative."

"They do not, not much like me," Ella replied.

"I understand, but maybe if they heard of what you have done here…" Allarie gave Ella a warm smile. "Maybe if Greyson could spread the word, we could both benefit. That would be fitting." Her voice was uplifting. "The village would benefit immensely from that."

Ella frowned in contemplation. "The druids are a picky, picky lot. I will do, do what I can, but no promises."

Allarie nodded. "This is the best I can come up with for now. I am still figuring what to do about Odh Varol." She was picking up pieces of the smashed barrels.

Lily attempted to drink some of the spilled oil.

"No, no," Allarie said as she guided the dog away.

"What will we do, do with the rest?"

"It is dangerous stuff. Has no belonging in this world. As unfortunate as it is, if we can do a lesser production, we could sell this, as well." Allarie's face looked as if she were reading invisible text in front of her eyes, as if she were doing math.

"I cannot not tell you how to run this place," Ella said. "However, I wouldn't suggest encouraging possible addiction."

"I want to steer away from the mines, anyway."

"See how the boys, boys wean off of the oil," Ella interjected with a wink. "We can see, see what we can do with the rest of these barrels."

"It could be dangerous. They could come for the oil," Allarie said.

"Make them want it. This is for the village to grow, after all."

"We will try, then. See if we can establish something."

"We will, will establish something. The oil is good, good at building relations. The children will, will prosper." Ella shrugged her shoulders.

"I am going to need you to take the oil along with you. Is that something you could do if we build this ship?" Allarie suggested to her friend.

"You should bring, bring this up with Martimil."

"Can't you figure this out yourself, though?" Allarie asked.

"Marti is my captain, captain, my sweet captain," Ella replied. "But seriously, I do not wish this call, call to be on me."

They had been tossing scraps of wood into the corner of the tent. Allarie was looking around at the wooden walls, the furs, the suits of armor, and the weapons. She had a full armory inside of this tent—Karnaugh liked his shiny objects.

"Fair enough. Would you think an incentive would be, maybe, a shiny piece of armor?" Allarie's voice raised as she asked the question.

"The druids, druids will want none of this," Ella sighed. "I mean, you could make an attempt—you meaning 'we.'"

"What is it that they would want? I need to establish some sort of incentive."

"What healed you, you before? We nursed wounds before, but yours, yours just disappeared."

"I am not sure. It was some sort of glowing oil that Karnaugh used on me."

"Is that still, still around here?" Ella looked around. "They are healers, after, after all. The oil is everywhere in here."

The dog was barking over by a hatch covering in the ground.

Allarie looked over to see what the dog was barking at, shot a quizzical glance at Ella, and then ran over to inspect the hatch.

Allarie and Ella uncorked the top and looked down the ladder that led into the hole that was revealed. They were both hesitant since the hole was deep and stinky.

"Well, don't, don't look at me."

"Double negative. Must mean you would like to go first," Allarie said before giving a hesitant smirk.

Ella rolled her eyes and proceeded down. "Whoever is down, down here, you straight up stink," she called.

"I might be sick," Allarie said.

Allarie and Ella found themselves in the dimly lit laboratory and saw Reevus as he was scuttling around. They leaped down from the ladder. The ground was solid as stone, and they landed with hard slaps of their feet. Reevus seemed to be packing his belongings, frantically clinking liquid-filled vials and other lab materials.

"What's happen, happening down here?" Ella said quietly as she glanced around the cluttered room in awe.

"Reevus! You are not taking off on me, are you?" Allarie shouted. She shivered slightly at the smell, fixing herself and adjusting to the strange surroundings.

Reevus shuddered nervously. "No, why would I do such a thing?" he replied. He took a single beaker, gingerly placing it on the table in front of him. "Just repositioning, of course. Crazy things happened here." He slithered around the room.

"That you, Allarie?" Forgar revealed himself from the shadows.

"Oh geez, Forgar." Allarie looked at the large man briefly before turning her attention back to the smaller one. "I need to ask a favor of you, Reevus." Allarie brushed the tabletop with her finger, waiting for his response.

Ella followed closely as an acting bodyguard…until she spied an alluring book that called to her from a cluttered lab shelf.

"I am listening," Reevus said.

"We have always been on good terms, Reevus. Know that I will not do this village wrong."

"Yes, yes, a favor. Of course, I would do that for you."

"Reevus, we are so small, but I know we can thrive. I will sell your oils and continue to pay you as Karnaugh has," Allarie said with confidence.

Smoke was billowing from the various beakers, and noxious fumes filled the room. "Also, are you sure breathing that in all day is good for you?"

Reevus nodded in response to her question. "Nothing changes. Sounds fine to me. In turn, then, since your concerns are noted, get me out of this hole," he said quickly, snapping his fingers.

"We can do that. We can set up your new accommodations. While we do that for you, life will be good. I promise. I need for you to return to the capital, however."

Reevus's ears perked up.

Forgar noticed, and he spoke. "He will be fine with returning there. It is dragging him back that might be more difficult for you," Forgar stated.

Allarie glanced Forgar's way. "Would you be willing to go with him, then?" She tapped on the surface of the table.

"It is dangerous to trust one so." The old titan rubbed his chin and turned a suspicious eye towards Reevus.

"I don't have a choice. You want to take the task of going to the capital for me? I will disappear going back. Know my leaving here will cause suffering. I have a plan for this place, a future, so I will be back, anyway. I have found my purpose, and it is these people."

Ella shook her fist in the air and looked at Allarie with pride.

Reevus's eyebrow twitched. "Fine. Fine on all fronts. Send me to the capital."

"I need you to make a few more barrels before you go."

"I thought you would be done with the oils, that the cactus farms would be solely for their water."

"Yes, that is possible, eventually. I need more for the druids of the isle, however. I need them to open trade with us."

"Nothing changes."

"Reevus, this isn't forever."

Forgar and Reevus looked at one another, nodding their heads.

"We will do what we can; however, look at the boys, or what is left of them. Let that not happen to those druids," Reevus said.

"Relax, relax. It won't happen," Ella said from behind the pages of the hefty tome she was leafing through.

"They need to know of the danger," Forgar said. "I have had it, and I know how it changes one's behavior." He shook his head.

"The glowing liquid—how did you come about that?" Allarie asked.

"I do not quite know, but that was an interesting batch," Reevus said. "I can continue research at the capital. Just saying."

"Do what you will. What we have should suffice for the trade, hopefully." Allarie's eyes shifted from Forgar to Reevus.

"You will have enough. I have quite a bit stored away since the boys demanded a lot. As unfortunate as it was, half of them dying has allowed for a surplus in this tent," Reevus said.

"Yes, I held no love for them, as they had lost their humanity. But it is still a loss of life, and they will be remembered. Forgar, if you were close to them, I apologize sincerely. Reevus, I know you and the boys never got along; however, if they meant anything to you, as well, same. What has happened cannot be taken back."

"I don't give a shit," Forgar said.

"Allarie, honestly, honey, they didn't mean much to me, either."

Ella chuckled in the corner of the lab, her nose still in a book.

"Then, we are all in agreement. We make an effort to change things here. At least try," Allarie said with finality.

The group nodded in agreement.

The blood-curdling scream of an enraged man came from the back of the lab chamber.

"The hell was that?" Allarie said, staring at Reevus.

"I wouldn't worry about him. Last I checked, he was sedated." Reevus replied.

"Reevus, does he sound sedated to you?" Allarie drew her daggers. "The effectiveness of your potions is questionable."

A hulking man who was larger than Forgar presented himself in the darkly lit lab. He was a violent hue of red with pronounced veins in his neck. All he did was scream unintelligible shrieks and thump his chest aggressively.

"Ready yourselves," Allarie said.

Ella crouched down on all fours as her head grew great horns. Forgar did not have his hammer, so he cracked his knuckles and wound up his arm.

"Well, shit," Reevus said as he slunk back.

"It doesn't appear to be under control, Reevus," Allarie said. "What were you giving it?"

The hulk started to hiss and thump his chest before charging at them. In response, Ella charged right back. The hulk grabbed her horns, turning and throwing Ella. She went soaring through the air and slammed into a far wall.

In turn, Allarie went up and slashed at the hulk's face. He brushed off the cut as if the dagger had only grazed across his eyebrow. She turned her other hand to puncture the hulk's skin, but the blade glanced off awkwardly.

"Oh shit!" Allarie yelled.

Forgar lumbered over to the hulk. He was almost eye to eye, but the hulk was a head taller. Nonetheless, Forgar led with his fist to the hulk's face, sending blood soaring from the exposed wound.

The hulk looked furious after the hit and returned the throw. His fist met Forgar's face, sending him hurtling through the air.

"This is not good!" Reevus shouted, frantically skittering around his lab table. "You have made him angry."

"What do we do, Reevus?" Allarie was circling as Ella shook her horned head. "It doesn't speak!"

The hulk rotated its head, and its eyes snapped to Reevus. The man quivered and fled.

"Oh Troutus, run!" Reevus climbed the ladder of the porthole.

The hulk started to move towards the opening, but Forgar grabbed his shin and hindered his movement.

Ella rammed the hulk in the stomach, keeling him over.

The hulk grabbed at his waist as Allarie came flying in daggers first. One dagger plunged into his skull, and the other glanced off again.

The hulk screamed and slapped Allarie away. He was attempting to get the dagger out of his face as the ram circled.

Charging with horns leading, Ella leaped through the air and connected with the giant's head. After a swift crack, the hulk dropped, and the ram spun in its momentum. Ella reformed into a human.

"Reevus, you are going to need to get rid of him, one way or another. He is a threat to this village, and his presence cannot be tolerated." Allarie walked up to the hulk and yanked her dagger unceremoniously from its head.

"Of course, Miss Allarie," Reevus replied.

16
"Time to Sail"

Greyson gathered whoever he thought was competent enough to be a builder. Finding adequately skilled workers was a difficult task, and very few had tools that they could use outside the mines.

We'll think of something. Martimil was in tow, peering around the village. Greyson rubbed his head.

"We will need some extra cloth for a sail," Martimil said.

"Easy enough. Could just use my tent," Greyson responded quickly. "That way I can set up a spot to sleep when we get to the island, as well. Too easy."

"I have a place there; you don't need to sleep in a tent. I might have been stuck in the mines here with you, but I had plans to get back to my life, as well."

"Marti, over here, living like a king on that island?"

"I wouldn't say a king, at all, but Ella and I have a comfort going on." The old salt smiled to himself. "Things just happen, and look at us now."

"Yeah, look at us." Greyson nudged Martimil playfully, and they both laughed.

"I have a house there, a small place by the water. We have our own little dock, as well. Spiral staircase inside that goes into a loft looking over the water."

"I live in a cloth tent. That is some king bullshit right there. Did you have a moat, too? I have heard the stories from the North. More water than the bastards know what to do with, as we choke on sand here."

"There is an abundance of rivers and lakes, so I do not know why that happened to the South." Martimil pondered, knitting his brow. "My face exists, and I can feel it cracking down here."

"The South's whole concept on water is so flawed. We need it to thrive," Greyson said.

"The druids love the water. They say it is where they get their power from. I believe it. However, here in the desert…" Martimil clicked his fingers, generating fire. "I still have it."

"I have not a clue about magic. But I can swing a mean pick."

"Still trying to find someone who does know what they are doing." Martimil looked to the sky.

"We will find them," Greyson said with a smile on his face. "When free from this place, the world is ours to search."

"I will teach you to fish. I can go back to fishing, stay closer to the island. I wasn't smart the last time. We figure out the headache issue, and then you are on your own. I want to start a family."

They searched and called others over to help them out. They gathered a few miners, along with a couple of cactus farmers that the village could spare. Greyson and Martimil wanted to stop at the farms before heading to the big tent again.

"Suppose we should get the seamstress, as well. You know, kind of messed up the roof." Greyson chopped his hand in a downward motion.

Greyson and Martimil marched with their troop of followers over to the part of the village that had the specialty workers. The seamstress was located in this corner of the village, her tent being the closest to the cactus farms. Due to the lack of foliage in the desert, she had to use the thin cactus veins to sew clothing and tents together.

"Look who is back," the seamstress said. She was a small, older lady in plain clothing. Her cracked lips formed a cheerful smile on her kind face, but then she saw the rest of the crew that followed Greyson, and the smile quickly turned to a concerned frown. "There is no way I can clothe all of these people. It isn't cactus-stringing season."

"Have no concern, Tily, but I do need your assistance and your time for a bit." Greyson flashed a toothy grin.

Tily was still inspecting the group. "Okay, but why?"

"The big tent."

"What about the big tent? I don't want to see the place ever again, as wonderful work as that was. Karnaugh was such a miserable lout—absolutely drained the cactus crops."

"Wouldn't that work for you, since you need them dried?"

"You have clothing on your back. What we need is the liquid from their veins."

"They took that much for the oil?"

"They took that much for the oil."

"A heads-up—you will not have to worry about that any longer. But I need you to stitch up the large tent and for an extra favor, as well."

"What is in it for me?"

"Recognition."

"Get me food outside of the gruel, and you have a deal."

"You make this job tougher, but you have a deal. We will find something."

The two agreed, and the crew moved on to the large tent again. The village had been quiet.

The group reached the large tent, and the men brought their picks, hammers, and a variety of other tools so that they could begin to tear the place apart. Much quicker than what a few could do, the villagers banded together to strip the monument of excess Karnaugh had left behind.

Martimil guided the men in separating long pieces of wood that he could use to create a seaworthy ship. He pondered the work plan several times. How in the stars will I be able to create a boat in this sand village? Pray they do their best, and then we head for the shore.

"Hey, Greyson. What do you think of creating a camp down by the water for a bit?" Martimil asked. "Make sure this actually does work."

"That would make the most sense," Greyson replied. "Best bet we have is you, Marti. I should be in the dark mines right now, but, instead, we have these boys making you a boat. We will guide people to the shore, then!"

"Are they prepared to make such a trek? And can Allarie sacrifice the men during this strange time?"

"Not a clue. Call her."

"Allarie!" Martimil shouted into the large tent.

Allarie climbed from the hatch in the ground. Ella and a slow-to-show-himself Reevus came out, as well.

"I will be seeing you later," Haan said to Allarie. They both nodded at one another.

Haan peeked in, oblivious to any happenings. She had been clearing up the inside of the tent, as the contents were being organized and remnants were removed.

"Okay, and what is it, Martimil?" Allarie asked. "Thanks for your help, Haan." She waved at the departing woman.

"We need to create a port by the water. It is quite the ways away. We would need to establish a small gathering there as a way to deal with the new trade. Can we take some of these men?"

"We need their production in the mines and the fields."

"Can we make quick use of the caravan men?" Greyson asked Allarie. They all stood in a circle inside of the large tent.

"You know they are not suited for the job, nor would they be able to produce an equivalent to the amount you mine."

"We do not have a choice."

"We will have to make do with what we have. I agree that a port will be a necessity and also an adequate way to get to the shore for this village."

"You have a lot of work ahead of you, Allarie."

"I do, but I feel wonderful about it. So many faces have changed to hope."

Greyson smiled at her. "This village needed you."

"I can see you guys getting chummy, but we have a boat to build," Martimil said, tapping his foot for emphasis. "Need to be able to shape this adequately enough to make it to the island."

"Certainly enough wood, wood in here," Ella said.

"We still have that broken caravan wagon, as well. We should be able to use that as a baseline, and then we make it able to float," Martimil stated.

"Make it look like a boat, then." Allarie shrugged.

"A lot of people here have no idea what that even looks like," Greyson said.

"A wagon that needs to float; however, we must accommodate for waves. Follow this." Martimil drew shapes in the sand. "An extraordinarily bland drawing of the wagon without wheels, with a keel on the bottom and a large rudder."

Allarie crossed her arms as she studied the drawing. "You are going to need to instruct on all of this. Can you do that?"

"We are going to find out."

Greyson sighed. "There is no one else I would rather go to the ocean floor with."

"I forgot—you cannot swim, can you?" Martimil gave Greyson a curious look.

"How would you like me to learn to swim?" Greyson stretched his arms out wide.

"Weren't you all born of the fish or whatever?"

"Technically true, but according to scripture, we have lost the ability and must be good in order to properly swim again!"

"We need to make sure it floats," Martimil said as he looked back over to Allarie.

"I can give you a fortnight to get the ship built by the water. We are still behind on shipments, but, hopefully, some of Karnaugh's shit can suffice for now." Allarie looked more hopeful. "You guys got this. I do not have a choice. We have to get this established. Far South needs to know we will be fine with holding Haneserrath." Her voice did not falter as she said the statement adamantly.

"They need to know we will thrive here. I will take what I can from the mines to them, take whatever shiny piece of shit around here, too," Forgar grumbled.

"We will grab what we can from the tent and head out, then," Greyson said.

The crew that Greyson had brought with him were still ripping the floor up. The wood creaked as the boards held together by hardened mud were pried apart.

"As much as the floors need to be used for this boat, I think we could at some point create solid structures for homes, like the North does." Allarie began to pace as she pondered the future of the village.

"One thing at a time, Allarie," Tily said. "Your roof is coming down."

"Allarie, this is Tily," Greyson said. "She does the cloth work for the village. We are very fortunate to have her. As you see, we have shirts on our backs."

"A pleasure to meet you. I apologize for not introducing myself sooner."

"I need her to make the sail," Greyson said. "Only issue—we need to feed her something other than the gruel."

"Of course. I do not have a solution for that at the moment—we can ask around. But know this is an imperative mission for the village," Allarie said.

"We have pigs from the hunt. We will cook one of the smaller ones for you. This is a fair exchange for your help," Forgar said.

"Done. I will need materials for the sail. The roof appears to be very cleanly cut." Tily was measuring the cloth by a long strand, placing colored-glass beads down for length and width.

"Do we still have the leftover scrap tents from our excursion home?" Allarie asked.

"That we do. That would work," Martimil said. "Plenty of material in the cart."

"Let us get to work and get moving."

Allarie sent off Forgar and Reevus to collect what they needed to start their trek down south. They had their group of boys—and a few more of the caravan workers, as well—who would follow them on their journey and carry the supplies, including the oil they needed to sell for the village.

Haan had let Allarie know which villagers could be trusted and would be reliable. All Allarie could do was hope that the group would do what needed to be done for everyone in the village. It was not sustainable in its current state. The village should be able to do well and function in a manner that would sustain all of its inhabitants.

Opportunities for the island were Allarie's sole focus. Need to get that seaport open. Ella makes it sound so promising. Everything will work. If anyone can pull this off, it's Greyson.

Greyson was staring at Allarie, deep in contemplation. "You do know I will be there. I want to see this work, too. See what happens next."

"Again, I can't promise, promise a thing with the druids," Ella interjected.

"But we might be able to barter with the inn," Martimil said.

"Make your best efforts. I know this will work." Allarie's face lit up.

Martimil and Ella left the tent, carrying off a wooden board together. Greyson remained standing near Karnaugh's bed.

"I am less surprised by you and more overall happy for you. You bounce back so quickly. How...how do you do that?" Allarie asked.

"I know there is something better. All of this has to be worth it in some way," Greyson said. "I am here, when any other day... My usual days were spent in darkness. I've found the light. This is my 'some way.'"

Allarie flashed a smile, stepped over quickly, and laid a kiss on him.

"Will you help clean this place up? Help make this village whole again?" Greyson asked. "They respect you. They need someone who can lead."

"I believe I can make this a respectable village," Allarie said with a smile on her face. "I was meant to do this. Strangely, I will miss you, you know."

"Could always pack up and come along. It is a terrible place, here. I say that after asking you to help clean it up."

"You and I both know the Southern Empire would never allow that to happen. Diplomatically, they would slaughter everyone here. They would see to us not getting any assistance, and they would send soldiers—and not to help us. We have to make do with the stones we find. I will do my best for this place."

"I have no doubt in my mind you will."

"You will be back, correct?" she asked quietly.

"I'll be back. You know we have a mission!" he said excitedly, snapping his fingers.

"I know the mission. I know how important it is to you. I just wish you the best, and I do not want these to be the last days I see you." Allarie avoided eye contact.

"I will be back with news from the island. I will be back to stop more of those portals from existing. I can do this." He moved her face towards his.

"You can absolutely do it, Greyson." She smiled.

Greyson grabbed Allarie's waist and pulled her close as she kissed him. "It feels unbelievable to have someone believe in me," he said as he pulled back...and then swooped in again.

"I believe in you. I think you are something else. I knew it as soon as I saw you being dragged by that guard."

"That was embarrassing, but not the first time."

"I want you to experience what it's like to not be dragged."

"We seem to be getting there. Nothing comes easily, nor would I want it to. This will build me—already my story grows."

"I am so glad to be a part of it."

"Same with me."

Greyson and Allarie spent the rest of their time together plying the boards off the floor and moving armor from the walls in the tent. They broke down the large bed, as well, and took off the blood-soaked sheets, tossing them over by the crumpled body that had once been Karnaugh.

"We should probably get rid of that," Greyson said.

"I will get someone to do it for us." Allarie looked away from the corpse.

Greyson was already moving over to the large body on the ground. He looked at what was left of the unrecognizable face that protruded from recognizable armor. "We should at least remove the armor. That is going to be worth some coin," Greyson said.

"Sell it on the island if you can. The druids will not touch it, and I cannot sell it here. They will know where something like that came from."

"Let's give it a shot." Greyson unclamped the armor and took the massive chest piece from the corpse.

Allarie rolled her eyes. "Every part of that needs to go."

Greyson gave her a knowing look. "We are getting there. All this compensation armor. He still ain't a small guy."

Karnaugh's body was much smaller than anticipated, however. His legs had really kept the armor up. Puffed arms and legs, a long neck, and a scrawny midsection were revealed—a body that had not escaped the armor chamber enough.

"Whatever. I want people to get rid of it. Throw the blood-soaked sheets over him, please. Need to move him before he starts to decay."

Greyson wrapped the sheets around the body before dragging it from the tent and over to the wall.

Allarie watched as he dragged the body. She shook her head.

"You were the first man I ever killed." Greyson stopped to take a heavy breath. He bent over, clutching his head. "Fuck." He started to drag again. Over the hill to the hotbox, farther into the village, Greyson saw Martimil pointing at people and adding to the trade cart. The makeshift boat by no means looked well made; however, they were piecing it together. It was still on its wheels but looked like a water-ready cart as far as Greyson knew.

He dropped the body near the other burning corpses by the hotbox, snarled at the smell, and took off. He glanced up at the big tent, and then, with a shrug of his weary shoulders, he went back to help Martimil out.

"Ho!" Greyson called.

Martimil turned his head. "We put on another wheel, and it is looking more and more like a floatable object," Martimil mused. "We might die out there, you know."

"Oh, fully aware," Greyson replied. "We might die every day we live, so why not try?"

"Good point. However, I am not so keen on the ease of death, either." Martimil stood closer to the cart, slapping it.

"We might be by the water for a bit. Best go ahead and try to turn into a fish."

"I don't think that is how it works."

"We will have time to figure that out." Martimil looked over the cart again. "I have faith in this. It will work."

"We will make it work."

"Work, work." Ella was standing close by. "You are all so, so serious." She tried to adopt a relaxed posture.

"I get it. But you can fly away. I can swim, but not well enough for two." Martimil gave her a concerned look.

"Stop with the over, overthinking." Ella was painting with the dark cactus oil along the outside of the makeshift craft.

They had been loading the boat while building it so as to get it ready for the move.

"This looks solid!" said Allarie, who had walked over to observe the progress.

"You have no idea what you are talking about." Martimil grabbed a dropped gourd and loaded it onto the craft.

"Do you think you'll be ready to go?" Allarie asked.

"From all the looks of it, we should be good to go."

Everyone around looked excited and ready to take off. The crew had all joined around the boat. A number of guards, plus some extra people, were going to the shore to establish camp so that they could continue making the boat. The small girl Ally and her mother had shown up, both with their similar dirty-blonde heads.

"Can we help you?" the mother said, scooting her daughter forward. "Possibly a trip to the water?"

"You want to join us on another journey? Just to the shore, though?" Greyson said in disbelief.

"I would like to see the shore," the girl chimed in.

"Can the mother and girl come along with us, just to the shore, then?" Greyson looked over at Allarie.

"If they would like to go, I do not see why not. If they can find a way to make do by the shore, then more power to them. Haneserrath will always be their home, as is true for anyone by that shore."

"Overly optimistic about that. Not everyone is as nice as the little one there," Martimil said.

"Highly dependent on character, then," Allarie replied.

"Better."

The group had what supplies they needed, including the sail from Tily. She had done a quick triple stitch of the tent cloth they had available. Martimil said it would suffice for carrying his gusts of air long enough for them to get to the island.

The troop headed towards the gates.

Allarie stopped Greyson as the group continued their trek.

He gave her a serious look. "I just know that there will be a better tomorrow, especially if I just try, and I can't stop. Just look how far it has gotten me. I just hope I meet more people like you." Greyson gave her his usual follow-up grin. "I know they are out there."

"And you have a village of people who care about you. So, take care of yourself, Greyson. No, there is only one me out there; I promise you that. Come back."

He laughed. "Fair enough. Take care of those who stay behind. Take care of those who come this way. Take care of those guys in the mines. Tell the guards to fuck off some-times—it is fun."

"You think they will remember you, Greyson? The man who left the mines."

He wrapped his arms around her. "Yeah, they'll remember me. Soon, they will know me. I am already moving up from here, met a princess." He clicked his tongue. "Going around and closing portals. I didn't want life in the mines, and as much as I tried, it didn't matter. They always had the same reactions. They always had the same pity.

"No, I am saying now. No. This is my life, and I am taking charge, and I am forgoing the path of being a miner. I finally have the choice to walk away. I have to walk away. I know there is safety in monotony, safety within these walls. But, to me, this is misery, and no life that I want, nor should I be limited to it. After all, I have a world to save." He smiled, staring into her eyes.

"You had better be back."

"I will be back."

They soon separated, their hands the last thing touching.

———•———

"Do you have any miner games we can play?" Martimil asked as they were sailing.

Greyson looked over the bow, watching as the water was splashing against the side of the boat. "This is the exact opposite of a dark hole in the ground."

Ella had already been looking out over the water from above as the guys were riding the sea waves on the make-shift boat.

Martimil continued asking questions, "Just out of curiosity, do you have any coin?"

Greyson paused for a moment before flashing his friend a toothy grin.

"Why do you think I am still carrying this obnoxious sword around? Certainly do not assume the druids are going to be without compensation for a fix. And I am certainly not licking their boots for some help. I am really hoping that it just works."

Author's Corner

This is just a humanity thing. Learn to live with one another, care about one another, and never stop trying for better. You are cared about, and I want you to succeed.

Hope.

About the Author

My life has always been active. I even once won second place in a bass-fishing tournament. After a stint with the Connecticut National Guard, I found what was my ideal job, working in a basement. Then, tragedy struck in the form of a devastating car accident. I survived and found a new dream job writing. Currently, I reside in a small town in Connecticut with my dog Millie.